THE HUNT

THE WILDS BOOK TWO

DONNA AUGUSTINE

For Lisa

Edited by Devilinthedetailsediting.com
&
720 Editing

ISBN-13: 978-0692608319
ISBN-10: 0692608311

CHAPTER 1

If anybody walked onto this land right now, and saw me, a young woman with a head full of crazy red hair digging in the dirt of the garden, they probably wouldn't look twice. With a large yellow farmhouse at my back and little cottages nestled about the land surrounding it, I must have seemed like an average farm girl. They'd be mighty wrong.

I'm a Plaguer, one who's survived the Bloody Death, which, by the way, wiped out most of the human race. Yeah, it was quite an accomplishment by the ripe old age of four. After you do something big like that, a person might expect some major accomplishments by the time they hit eighteen. Who knew that not dying from the nastiest disease ever known to man would be the highlight of my life so far?

As far as highlights go, being a Plaguer sounded a lot more badass than it actually turned out to be. In fact, it was something best left hidden, like having a permanent case of the cooties. People tended to view me like I was still contagious and carried the disease around in my back pocket or something, ready to whip it out at any moment. Some thought merely laying eyes on me was going to strike them down dead. Others tried to avoid airspace—which always made me want to break out into a coughing fit for some crazy reason.

I wasn't sick, though. The only thing I'd been was a survivor, and if being a survivor was a bad thing, then I was the worst around. I'd scraped and clawed my way out of a lot of ugly situations and had no plans on quitting. Being able to read people's worst memories helped out a bit. That was one of the perks of being a Plaguer. Seeing the scars of someone's mind, what bothered them the most, really let me know what made them tick. Time and again, it had helped steer me toward people I could trust.

Most people had heard rumors of what Plaguers could do. The idea of someone seeing in your head, well, let's just say it doesn't encourage friendships. Between surviving the Bloody Death and the visions, I guess it's not a huge shock I ended up in the Cement Giant, the asylum that the country of Newco used to hide all its unwanted.

That day Dax showed up and offered me a way out, I'd grabbed it with both hands. I didn't know him but I took a gamble that anywhere else was going to be better than where I was.

That was how I ended up here, in the Wilds. The Wilds was exactly what I'd expected—absolute freedom if you were strong enough to take it. No government, no laws, no rules; it was a place custom-made for the strong and the brave—the survivors. It was perfect for me.

There was only one problem: people in the Wilds were just as scared of Plaguers as the people of Newco, and everyone around here already knew what I was. Hell, I'd worn a badge, a brand burned onto the top of my hand, compliments of the Cement Giant, broadcasting the fact that I was a Plaguer. I'd finally fixed that by skimming a couple layers of flesh off. My hand might have more scars, but it was still a big improvement.

As crazy and riveting as Plaguers and the Wilds might sound, I haven't even gotten to the juiciest part of the story so far. What was more interesting than surviving the plague that killed almost everyone and left you with some nifty visions? I'll tell you what. Being able to grow a couple of feet taller, sprout a scary set of fangs and a unknown amount of muscle covered in fur, and do it all on a moment's whim.

Yeah, that's right—for the first eighteen years of my life, I'd walked this Earth thinking *I* was keeping all the secrets and that *I* was the freak of nature. This misbelief of mine was fed by the fact that everyone else was under the same assumption, right along with me. Turned out we'd all been fooled. There was something a lot scarier than me, and he was hanging out right underneath our noses.

It's one of those discoveries that once you found

out, it gets stuck in your head. As far as the rest of the world knew, I was still the biggest freak. What they didn't know, and I didn't either until a month ago, was that Dax, the guy who'd rescued my ass from the Cement Giant not once but twice, turned out to be not so much a man as a whole lotta beast. Yeah, exactly like the beasts everybody was terrified by, the kind that roamed the forests at night and left an occasional carcass lying around as a reminder of what they could do. This was where the aforementioned fur and fangs came into play, and they're real doozies. Those fangs make the pictures of jaguars I'd seen in books look like cute little kittens. People hide behind their locked doors after sundown from these creatures.

Not that anyone would have a clue if you saw Dax now, in his dark pants and shirt, his sleeves rolled up, talking to the crew who patrolled the perimeter of the grounds. All you saw was a human male, tannish skin and dark hair. It wasn't like he had tufts of fur poking out here and there to hint at the truth. The huge fangs were straight white teeth and his eyes weren't glowing red like they had that day in the forest, but were somewhere in between the color of storm clouds and glacier blue.

Yeah, maybe he was tough. Surely the toughest man I'd ever met, and that made people tread carefully in his presence, but that was far from being a beast of the Wilds. Dax inspired respect from those around him, but it was because most people knew he was smarter than them. If they were too stupid to realize that, then they respected him because they knew he could kick their ass. Nobody knew the beast was lingering right there, under the surface, waiting to pick its teeth with their leg bone if they stepped out of line.

If they did step out of line, he'd know. I was convinced he had some superior awareness of everything around him, whether he admitted it or not. As if to prove my point, his gaze swung in my direction, as if he knew what I was thinking or had sensed me watching him. A slight charge shot through me, and I looked back down at the dirt and weeds, but the feeling didn't go away until he switched his attention back to his crew.

Couldn't help but want to giggle a bit at that too. The same crew that Dax was standing right beside at this very moment, the ones who were in charge of making sure nothing scary like a beast got in, had no clue that the scariest thing *out there* was already *in here.* If they had any idea, they'd surely pee their pants. I couldn't blame them for not knowing. I hadn't. But it was the truth. Dax was a beast, and maybe the only one alive that could shift back to human form. It still stunned me, even now.

I remembered the day I'd found out a month ago, as if it had just happened and I was back in the forest. I'd been standing there with Dax and then he'd become

9

the beast, and I'd become completely wordless. Even all fangs and claws as he'd been, I should've said or asked something. Instead, I'd stood mute and stared. I tried not to beat myself up too bad about that lapse. At least I hadn't run screaming from him. He'd been only a foot from me and I'd held my ground. Then he'd left.

Now, a logical person would think that this sort of man-turning-to-beast behavior would warrant some type of conversation between us. You know, a *Hey, what's with all the fur and you've got mighty big teeth* kind of chat, or something else equally informative. Nope. Not on this side of the illogical divide, it didn't. He'd been a man, then wham, he'd been a beast. Next time I saw him, he was a man again, and somehow I wasn't supposed to talk about it. I never imagined we'd not speak of it at some point or that it would have to go onto my ever-growing list of secrets I couldn't share with anyone.

Someone might assume from my past that I would be good at keeping secrets. They'd be correct on that score. I'm a superhero at it, and this situation was no different. I didn't dare say anything to anyone about Dax, but this secret was sorely testing my abilities. Maybe if he'd talk about it a bit, I could get past the whole amazement of the man/beast aspect, but he wasn't much for chatting—like, as in ever—and definitely not about this subject, as would soon be demonstrated by yet another attempt on my part.

I saw my opening as he walked away from the guards and made the mistake of getting too close to me. It was a mistake he'd been making less and less lately. Stabbing my shovel into the rich dirt, I abandoned the vegetables in the garden to fend for themselves against the weeds and fell into step beside him.

It was always a double-edged sword being near Dax. My pulse didn't just amp up from the exertion of keeping up with him as it did from just being near him. Close quarters with Dax made me feel more alive or something, as if his vitality infected my own. I'd wondered in the dark of night if it was the magic of the beast I sensed, but the air even seemed to smell different around him, like a storm was about to hit.

On the other hand, I wasn't sure he even noticed me sometimes. Like now, he walked without talking or even the slightest turn of the head in my direction to acknowledge my presence. It was crazy how a month ago the beast had been licking me—and not in the biting through bone and gristle type of way, but like I was a favorite chew toy—and then changed to this man who barely spoke to me.

He finally did something to mark my presence. He didn't look at me, but offered up a nice nonverbal message. The eyes rolling skyward were loud and clear, and made me wish for the moments he didn't communicate in any form, which was the other half of the time. That's what Dax was best at: letting you know exactly what he was thinking without expending the energy to bother speaking to you.

This brought us to what I considered my strongest trait, besides being a master of secrets. Tenacity. Did I mention yet that I was about as far from a quitter as you got? I hated everything that went along with that word. If it were up to me, the word "quit" would be struck completely from the human language. I'd had one personal lapse on the record about a month ago, and it had made me even firmer in my conviction that I would never slip again.

Dax's pace picked up, and I pumped my legs quicker to match his longer stride. "So, are we ever going to talk about…you know…the thing?" I didn't mention the word *beast*, ever. I thought it might make him more likely to talk about it if I didn't call him names.

He stopped suddenly, and my heartbeat grew a little quicker with hopes that this was the day he would divulge all his beastly secrets. Where did all the fur go? What happened to the fangs when he wasn't a beast? Did he eat—

No. I definitely shouldn't follow that train of thought. Some stuff is better off left unasked.

"You really can't take a hint," he said.

Thwarted again. Looked like I wasn't going to get any of *those* questions answered. He'd dashed my hopes to shreds with one imaginary swipe from his hidden claws. I did mention the claws, right? They were quite impressive. Almost as cool as the fangs.

"I just think we should have a chat about things. It would be good for you to talk. Get stuff off your chest." Especially the secret furry one. I still remembered reaching my fingers out and touching him there right before he'd left without a word.

I'd stood in the forest for hours afterward, waiting for him to come back. He hadn't. When I'd finally walked back to the house by myself, I'd felt the strangest disappointment, as if we'd shared something special and then he'd changed his mind about it and abandoned me.

That night, I'd sat there at dinner with a plate piled high with Fudge's meatloaf, a chair over from him. We'd eaten, surrounded by everyone else, and acted like nothing had happened. As if everything was the same and he didn't have the biggest secret known to mankind. I think we'd discussed the weather, if I remembered correctly.

I'd finished dinner and gone upstairs afterward and unpacked the bag I had ready, knowing I couldn't budge from this place now, not knowing what I knew. I had way too many questions. Plus there was his promise that he was going to help me become someone special. If there was one thing I wanted in the world, that was it. To be strong, special, be someone who didn't need anyone to protect them.

I'd gone to bed that night figuring we'd talk tomorrow. We hadn't. Then I'd assumed we would talk the day after. Hadn't happened. Somehow, a month slipped by quicker than I could polish off a plate of Fudge's brownies. Time was funny like that. If you didn't keep track of it, make the most of every moment, it could run away from you.

He leaned forward with that look on his face, and I should've known I wasn't going to like what was coming next. It was the *so, you think you want to play ball* look, and it never preceded anything good.

"You want to talk? Maybe we should have a sit-down. We can both lay all our secrets out on the table, make a whole day of it?" he asked, meeting my expectations.

Low blow, man. I held the words back, but they made my mouth twitch to the side for the effort. It was true; I didn't like to talk about certain things, and I'd thought he was cool with that. I didn't exactly have a past I liked to reminisce over. It wasn't filled with laughter and funny stories. Ninety percent of my life before now was stuff I'd rather forget and people I hoped were dead. Wow, even in my head that didn't sound so good.

Either way, he was missing the point. I didn't want to talk about my secrets. I wanted him to tell me all of his and call it a day. Why did people have to be so damn difficult all the time?

But yeah, I got the point. He wasn't going to talk about it. He'd shown me his secret. He'd let me as far into the loop as he was going to for now, and I could take it or leave it. No one forced me to stay if I didn't like the terms, as I'd been reminded of more than a few times. I couldn't leave here, though. He still had promises to live up to.

"Fine. I give up. I won't bug you anymore about—"

He started walking off as if we were finished.

I chased after him and then blocked his path, prepared to lurch to the left or right if he tried to escape. "*But* you did promise to train me. It's been a month." I had him now. Dax wasn't the type to renege on a promise. When I'd first met him, he'd acted like he didn't have a code he lived by, but everyone did. Some people didn't know they had one, but every action they took defined it.

He nodded, acknowledging his lapse and leaving me no clue to whether he might feel the tiniest bit bad about letting me down. "I've had some business, but we'll start soon."

Beast, human, whatever he was, I needed his help or I needed to make other plans. He needed to understand that an ambiguous "soon" wasn't cutting it anymore. "Do you realize I'm still hunted by the Dark Walkers? They aren't taking a holiday because you have business. I don't have soon. I have now."

It was true. The Cement Giant might have been blown to bits, but there were more of those Dark Walkers, monsters masquerading as humans, out there, and they wanted me for no fathomable reason I could think of. Of course, I wasn't intimately acquainted with the thoughts of creatures that looked like they were covered by a dark fog all the sunny day long.

"I'm fully aware." He nodded like he was really hearing what I was saying. Then he blew it by repeating, "We'll start soon."

He walked away, and I didn't lurch to the right like I'd thought I would. I remained standing exactly where I was, watching as he headed toward the gate.

"I don't have soon," I said, but he was already ten feet away and I was standing by myself. What I wanted to scream was *What business do you have that is so much more important than me?* But I didn't. He wouldn't have told me anyway. What I really wanted to know most, but would never ask, was *What changed in the forest that day you were the beast that now you avoid me?*

I'd expected camaraderie after sharing something like that. That his secret was going to give us some sort of connection, especially a secret of that magnitude. That me being one of the few people who knew he was a beast would make us closer. It didn't. Then I'd thought, at the least we'd be allies if nothing else. I wasn't so confident about that anymore either.

At this point, I didn't know what we were, but we certainly were not friends.

CHAPTER 2

My hands hit the dirt in the garden again, but I couldn't stop looking toward the gate he'd left out of a couple of hours ago. I knew Dax was avoiding me, but maybe he really did have things to handle. I had a funny feeling that being a beast was only the tip of his iceberg of secrets, the other eighty percent still hidden from view.

A little hand patted my shoulder and I looked up into Tiffy's cherubic face. She looked like the picture of innocence, as long as you didn't look too closely at her eyes, which held way too much wisdom for someone so young.

"He left again?"

I nodded. From my calculations, Tiffy was one of the three people who knew what Dax really was. I'd never asked her, but she'd referred to me meeting "Hairy" in the past. My hunch was that Hairy was the name she called Dax's beast form. Fudge was the other person, and she definitely knew. Dax had been one of the two beasts in Fudge's memories that had saved her when she was just a child.

The only thing that tripped me up with the Fudge

situation was that Fudge was nearly seventy from the looks of her. Dax appeared to be thirty—tops. If that had been him, shouldn't Dax be pushing sixty or seventy too? The math didn't add up, like it so often didn't of late, and tossed another question onto the pile of unanswered ones, as if *that* needed to get any higher.

I didn't ask Fudge about it. None of us talked about it: Tiffy, Fudge, or me. We were like the unholy trinity of secrets.

"He's handling a lot of stuff," Tiffy declared. Her fluffy red curls bobbed in the breeze.

I often wondered what went on in that head. Must be mighty interesting. "I'm sure," I said, not wanting to drag Tiffy into my crushed expectations.

"Yes. Completely," she said. She took my hand and then patted it, serenely calm. "I know there are things out there that really don't like you. Don't worry. I'll talk to my friends. I'll tell them to warn you if trouble's coming your way."

Inwardly I grimaced at her words, but tried to make sure the feeling didn't hit my face. It was bad enough that I was nervous. I didn't want to freak the kid out too. Sometimes I forgot how young she was, especially when she said things like this.

"Thanks." Her invisible friends had my back. Hoped that counted for something.

"I'm not sure they'll do it, though, since they're getting quite mad at you for not meeting with them."

"I told you to have them stop by my room anytime."

"I told you, Dal, that's not how it works. You have to go to them."

It was true. She'd been telling me for more than a month now on a weekly basis. I didn't know why her invisible friends had such an issue with coming in the house, though.

"Okay. I'll go meet them next week, maybe."

"I don't think you're going to do it," she said. Her hand dropped mine as she gave me a final smile before heading off toward the gate.

"Where are you going? Don't you want lunch?" I still couldn't get over how all these people took Fudge's food for granted. I hoped I didn't ever get like that. I wanted to appreciate every meal like it was my last. You never knew when it would be true. Most people didn't know when they were eating their final meal. How bad would it stink to have choked it down in a rush without any enjoyment?

Tiffy stopped and looked back toward me, her little brow furrowed in concentration. "I'm having tea and sandwiches with my friends today. They wanted to talk about you. I mustn't be late for it. They're deciding some important issues that I need to weigh in on."

"Important issues about me? Like what?" I swallowed past a lump in my throat and then reminded myself again that these friends were invisible. No one had seen them, not once. I'd asked around. They certainly weren't making any decisions about me.

"I'm not allowed to discuss that with you." She put her hands into the air, palms up, as if to say it was out of her control. "You could come and find out."

"No, I think I'll hang here for Fudge's food," I said as I watched her make her way to the gate, fully expecting sister-lover—

No, I said I wasn't going to call the guard who'd made out with his sister that ever again. The *guard* there would certainly stop her.

I was still scratching my head over the fact that not only did Tiffy have invisible friends, but they also hooked her up with tea, too. Everything about Tiffy was like trying to fit a square peg into a round slot. Tiffy was one of those people who you had to accept didn't fit into the game like the pieces that came in the box. She was her own custom piece with her own set of rules.

As if to prove the impossibility of everything that surrounded her, she neared the gate, and I expected the guard to jump to attention and turn her around. Instead he seemed to become mesmerized with something far off in the distance. Whatever it was, it was in the exact opposite direction Tiffy was approaching from. Tiffy walked right past him, lifted up the latch and let herself out, and closed it again without him ever turning around.

I got to my feet and brushed off the dirt as I stepped out of the garden, planning on getting her back here, or at the least following her, but Bookie bumped into my side and startled me.

"Let her go. She'll be okay. She won't go far."

Bookie, my bestie here, had earned his nickname because he was fascinated with books. Thanks to him, I now had a nice stack of reading material in my room from the old library he'd found when he'd gone exploring the ruins. He was pretty much the only one I trusted—as much as I was capable of trust, that is. Growing up in the Cement Giant didn't breed too much trust. Add the Dark Walkers trying to pry my secrets from me all those years, and it made me want to hold them closer.

I'd read somewhere that three weeks of doing something repeatedly made it a habit. I'd had fourteen years of keeping secrets. By my math, it wasn't just an ingrained personality trait after a length of time like that. It was an etching on the side of granite.

But Bookie was different. When I'd lost my friends, Bookie had helped fill the void. As much as I missed Margo, it was for the best we weren't together, and not just because the Dark Walkers were out there and surely still wanted me. I couldn't think of Margo and not think of Cindy and Patty, who had died, or the dream of us all living this grand, free life. Those thoughts death-spiraled into how I'd let them all down.

If I'd gotten to them sooner, maybe we'd all be standing here together about to go in and get some of Fudge's great cooking for lunch. That was now impossible. Death was one thing you couldn't quit.

"You're getting that look again." Bookie bumped into me with his shoulder and sent me off balance a bit.

He looked like he was growing at almost a daily rate lately. If he kept going, he'd be as big as Dax—in man form, anyway. I didn't think it was possible for a human to grow as big as a beast.

"What are you eating these days?" I asked as I looked over his frame that wasn't as lanky as it used to be. He looked more and more like a man by the day, but his eyes still had a boyish heart glowing out of them.

"Must be the spinach," he said, and I knew he was ribbing me about some old cartoons I'd found in the library. One had been about a character named Popeye who became super strong when he ate spinach. I'd made the mistake of eating quite a bit of spinach the next day. I mean, it had *mostly* been a coincidence. Can't blame a girl for turning over every stone in times like these.

"Good. It's gone," he said.

"What?" I asked.

"The *look*. I hate it. It's like the story didn't end the way you'd hoped."

I shrugged and shook my head. "Good thing the story isn't over yet," I said, and forced the corners of my mouth to go up even when they wanted to head down. Thinking about the Dark Walkers and what they'd cost me tended to do that. They were never far from my mind, especially when I was waiting for them to walk through those gates any day or thinking of what I'd do eventually to them.

"I must say, that's the lamest smile I've ever seen."

"That's because you don't look in a mirror enough." If I was the queen of keeping secrets, Bookie was the king of plastering on a smile, no matter how bad the storm.

I nodded toward the place I'd just seen Tiffy disappear into the woods. "I know you've never seen them, but have you ever heard of anyone who's seen these friends Tiffy talks about?" She just didn't seem that nuts. There had to be something to it. Or did that mean I was nuts to think that maybe they did exist?

He shoved his hands in his pockets. "Nope. Not one. Ever." His eyes shot to my arm, as if he'd just remembered something.

I tried to angle my body slightly away from him in the most nonchalant way I could, knowing exactly what it was that had just come to mind.

His brows dropped down and his mouth flatlined. "Why don't you have your sling on?"

The jig was up. I turned my arm toward him and made a show of flexing it. "Because I don't need it? My arm's good enough." I'd made the prognosis myself that very morning after a lengthy self-exam.

"Good enough isn't good."

He sounded just like Fudge right now. Sometimes I felt like everyone acted older than I did, so why did I feel so ancient most of the time?

I stretched out my arm in a continual show of strength even as I felt the lingering weakness wanting to set it to trembling. "No. But it's *enough.*"

He rolled his eyes but didn't say anything else, and I wasn't going to try and convert him to my way of thinking. The silence was enough for me. I didn't need too much of anything anymore, just enough. That was one of my new rules. I had a lot of new rules. In the past month, I'd realized I had some growing to do if I was going to become the person I wanted to be. Some things were going to have to go. Trying to make everyone think exactly as I did was one of them. I would do me and they could do them.

"Hey, can you sneak away for a run to the library tomorrow afternoon?" That was another thing I'd remedy at some point. I needed to learn to ride a bike. First I needed to get a bike, though, so that was on the back burner for now.

It wasn't like machines from the Glory Years were lying around for the taking. When you did find one, it was more likely to be a pile of rust than something that would run. A hundred and fifty years will do that to things.

He nodded. "Sure. Looking for anything special?"

"Everything." That was exactly what it felt like. The list of books I would need to help me accomplish what I wanted to do would never fit on the bike.

"Everything is going to be tough to lug back here."

"That's okay. We can do it in a couple trips." I used my bad arm to punch him in his. A little achy and not super steady, but it was enough.

CHAPTER 3

Dax hadn't come home last night, or not while I was awake. I would've heard him if he had. I hadn't heard him this morning either, so he must have left before I'd awoken. Maybe he hadn't come back at all.

It wasn't like I listened for him on purpose or anything. The guy's room was down the hall from mine. How could I not hear him coming and going when I was awake? Lying there in bed, it was tough not to hear everybody with the way the house creaked like an old man riddled with arthritis—an old man I dearly loved, I might add.

Dax was probably off doing who knew what again. Meanwhile, I was on borrowed time. Every day, I waited for a horde of Dark Walkers to show up here. Ms. Edith, the Dark Walker who had tormented me at the Cement Giant, might be dead, but I wasn't optimistic she would be the last of them. They wanted me. She'd said I was the key right before I'd killed her. I didn't know what exactly I was going to unlock, but if I was the key, they wanted in this particular door pretty darn bad with the way they had kept coming for me.

Here I was, a sitting duck, or a lying key, to be

exact. What was Dax doing? He was out gallivanting every damn day instead of training me to be the badass he'd told me I could be. The current situation was unacceptable.

Not that I'd been sitting idly by. I'd started working on myself nearly the next day, throwing knives with my good hand. But it wasn't enough, and my inner badass hadn't emerged yet. If Dax wasn't going to help me, I couldn't waste any more time just muddling through.

That was all ending. I'd made a decision yesterday. I'd thought fuck it. Or more accurately, fuck him—not in the literal sense, as that didn't work out so hot last time I'd attempted it. I tried not to have regrets in life, but when I thought back to how I'd laid myself out on his bed and told him to take me—still couldn't think of it without looking for the biggest rock around and wondering if I could fit underneath. No, this was more of a figurative fuck him.

Today was the first day of my quest. I got out of bed and dressed in my leathers, and one of the tank tops Fudge had made me, with a new determination. I headed downstairs and passed by the line for the breakfast buffet, where I caught a couple of dirty looks and a whispered "Plaguer" to start my day off right, and went straight to the source. I'd need some good sustenance for what I had planned.

"What did I tell you about waiting your turn?"

Fudge said as I entered the kitchen, waving her wooden spoon at me, the one that sometimes seemed to be permanently affixed to her hand. Her slightly robust figure animated its way through the kitchen, owning the space as surely as a bear in its den.

"Fudge, if you don't want me to be impatient to eat, then you need to stop cooking so well. I don't feel like I should be held responsible for reacting exactly as any sane person should. This could be my last meal, you know. You wouldn't want my last meal to be cold, would you?" I grabbed a plate from the cupboard and started piling bacon onto my plate from a tray that was destined for the breakfast masses who weren't brave enough to enter Fudge's den.

She looked upward and started moving her free hand in swipes across her chest before asking the ceiling to help her. Bookie had told me it wasn't really the ceiling she was speaking to. Fudge followed some religion called Catholic that was big in the Glory Years. Not many people had a religion now other than the Alter of Thyself. It was probably too hard with the way people lived these days. From what I'd heard of her religion, most people in the Wilds would be damned to hell after a day of what most considered normal living.

She was still shaking her head in disapproval as she started piling eggs onto my plate, in direct contrast to her fake disapproval.

"You can't exist solely on bacon," she said, and I

knew she was rationalizing her favoritism toward me. I dug being among the favorites. I returned the favor by rationalizing why it would be bad to point out how she fed my bad behavior, because it would hurt her feelings. We both came out winners this way. Rationalizing was a beautiful thing when it worked right.

"I'm trying to disprove the theory that one cannot survive on bacon alone. Plus, it's only primarily bacon in the mornings. I've got plenty of variety left for lunch, dinner, and multiple snack times." I shoved a full piece of bacon in my mouth and asked, "Have you seen Dax?" before I bothered finishing it.

"He left yesterday afternoon and—" She stopped speaking mid-egg scoop. "Don't you get that look. It's not like he's out having a grand time."

When had I become so transparent? And how much did she know? "You know what he's doing?"

"No. But I trust him." She piled a couple more pieces of bacon on my plate, trying to buy my silence on the subject, which, of course, worked. The things I'd do for bacon even scared me.

No one won an argument with Fudge anyway. It was impossible. She nailed you with these stares that sent the toughest into silence. I took my plate of bacon off toward my spot before I got nailed with another stare just for good measure.

No matter what happened from here on out, at least

I'd started the day off well. I left the kitchen and walked close by the breakfast line, where I made sure to flash my ill-gotten goods. I took a nice deep breath and said, "Mmmm, fresh from the griddle." Then continued on my way.

The back porch was wonderfully empty as I found my spot on the bench with my big plate of bacon and other sides, thanks to Fudge's contribution. I was going to eat like a pig today—maybe not exactly like a pig, as that would be cannibalism, but that was a whole other topic. Later on today, I'd be going on a run with Bookie to find some good books. I'd read up on everything from shooting guns to jujitsu, and maybe some interrogation techniques while I was at it. If Dax wasn't going to train me to be a badass then I didn't need him. I'd train myself and I needed to get serious about it. No more fumbling around in the dark.

Moobie had been self-trained. Yeah, yeah, he might be an imaginary character from books, but so what? That almost made more sense in my opinion. If an imaginary character could do it, then I certainly could. But first I was going to enjoy some of Fudge's cooking and fortify myself for the upcoming adventure of learning how to become a badass through self-help books. That was how I would look at it, too: a grand journey of self-discovery.

I took another nice big bite of salty bacon, trying to forget about the pig, the one I'd named Wilbur that I'd noticed missing in the pen yesterday.

I was chewing on the tasty meat that I refused to believe was once Wilbur when the screen door squealed open. It sounded worse than Wilbur probably had when he'd gotten stuck with the butcher's knife, if indeed he was truly gone. I wasn't prepared to accept that yet, or at least not until after breakfast.

Boots hit the wooden floor of the porch in a stride I'd recognize anywhere and sent little chills that echoed through me. So Dax had finally come back from wherever he'd disappeared to yesterday, and it sounded like he wanted me to know.

When he decided to be heard, he sure did it well. It was sort of strange how much noise he made when he wanted to, or how heavy his steps sounded on the wood, like maybe he still weighed as much as the beast, even in the form of a man. Maybe that extra size when he was the beast shrank down and he was packed in more densely when he was a human? I needed to find out how much he weighed. This was definitely one of those questions that had to be answered, if only in the name of science. Maybe he'd actually answer if I explained it that way? Could any upright person refuse science? Dax wasn't exactly upright, though. He was slanted at best.

The heavy steps came closer until he was blocking my view of the lawn and the view of people starting their morning chores.

"Meet me in the small barn in five minutes." Even without looking up at him, Dax's voice got to me. Like the deep, raspy quality of it scratched an itch somewhere deep inside. It was kind of like a mosquito bite. That first scratch was heaven, but damn if it didn't drive you crazy soon after. That was what it was like with Dax. I couldn't wait to be near him, until I was for a while and he did something that drove me crazy. Sometimes I thought he did it on purpose, but why would he want to piss me off?

Order given, he turned and headed back inside.

I went to speak before he was out of sight, but the bacon I was trying to swallow grabbed on to a tonsil for dear life and launched me into a fit of coughing. It was just long enough to give Dax time to clear the porch and set the door to squealing again. It was Wilbur's revenge, for sure.

The bacon finally gave up the struggle, but I'd lost my chance to show my full indignation. I'd been waiting weeks for him to start training me, and now it was drop everything and come right away? I'd just written him off and taken matters into my own hands. I'd realigned my plans, and they were damn good...

A noise seeped out of me, a cross between a disgusted sigh meets a groan of irritation. Who was I kidding? My plans sucked. They included a whole lot of reading and even more guesswork so that I could model myself after someone who was a fictional character from books most people hadn't heard of. It was so bad I almost felt I needed to mock myself, because I certainly deserved it, and a good opportunity to mock should never pass without a word, even if it was directed at me.

So here I was, plateful of Wilbur and the dictator calling. I could pretend that I could learn everything I needed from books, but reading wasn't exactly the same as doing. I'd learned that lesson well. Then there was the fact that Dax certainly knew things that weren't written down—anywhere. As far as information went, I had more than a suspicion that Dax's down cards were a royal flush compared to mine. Oh yeah, that's right. I hadn't even been dealt into the hand yet. I hadn't so much been playing as getting played so far.

I did the only thing someone who held absolutely no cards did. I carried my plate of leftover Wilbur into the kitchen and headed out to the small barn, the one that served as a gymnasium—or in my case, a *place to beat up newbies.*

It sucked to have no cards. Once I became a badass, things would change. I'd be the one kicking ass and I'd do anything to become that person. By my count, I'd already spent too many years getting my ass kicked. It was definitely time for a change.

* * *

As I crossed the field toward the small barn, the

place was coming alive like it always did in the mornings. Everyone had a job. Well, almost everyone. I didn't. Or not one assigned to me, anyway, even though I'd asked. Neither Fudge nor Dax seemed to want to give me anything on a regular basis. Fudge had told me to ask Dax. Dax had told me he was too busy to talk every time I'd managed to corner him.

After four or five mornings of watching everyone do their thing, I knew I had to have a thing, too. Everyone here had a thing. If I didn't have a thing, I didn't feel like I was really here somehow. So I'd handled it myself. Like today, if I hadn't had plans on meeting Bookie later or been heading to the barn to meet Dax, I'd be in the garden again, to the main gardener's chagrin. It wasn't my fault he wasn't a good weeder and I'd discovered gardens needed constant tending.

I pushed open the wooden door to the small barn. The place looked just like it had the last time I'd been here: mats on the floor, a bag hanging in the corner, the smell of hay clinging to the air that was stacked along the wall, and rays of sunshine streaming in through the window, set high above the door. The only thing different this time was me.

The last time I'd come here and sparred with Dax, I hadn't really believed that it was going to be a fair fight, or as fair as it could be fighting with someone who had an unknown but significant amount of weight on me. Back then, deep down, I still hadn't thought someone who could really hurt you would hold back from doing so. Yeah, I'd left with some bruises, but nowhere near the beatings I'd taken at the Cement Giant.

Turned out that I loved sparring. It had been one of my first moments of really feeling alive. No, better than just alive—alive and empowered.

I'd like to think that the feeling had come solely from the fighting, but truth was that part of it had come from who I'd been sparring with.

When I stepped into that building and saw Dax there, fur or no fur, fangs or not, some of the yearning I'd felt that day still tugged at me a little, but we weren't meant to be, even if the blossoming woman inside me wanted to carry on and scream *no, it had to be him.*

But whoever I was meant to learn about that part of life from, it wasn't going to be him. I'd moved on from that place. All he was now was my teacher, if indeed he was finally stepping up to the plate. That was okay. It was all I needed from him.

CHAPTER 4

My eyes adjusted to the light, as he remained leaning against the back wall. I walked farther into the barn and stopped in the center without saying anything. He'd called the meeting, so I stood and waited to see what he had planned. I was done asking for anything.

I pointed one leg out and raised my hand to cover a strategic yawn, but inside I nearly tingled with excitement. Would he finally start training me? Was this what I'd been waiting for? Was I on the precipice of greatness? Most importantly, would I be able to kick his ass by the time I was done? Now that was a goal worthy of striving for.

He pushed off the wall and then walked past me to the door. Instead of leaving it open like he had last time we'd practiced in here, he pulled it closed. The bar landed across it with a thump. Whatever the day's agenda was, clearly it was not open to spectators. Good to know.

He crossed the barn until he stopped in front of me. His eyes ran down my length, like he'd never seen me before. There was a slight shift of his head a fraction of an inch down, and then back up. The movement could've been interpreted as a nod of approval, if one was so inclined to optimism. I wasn't sure if my glass was half full or half empty these days, and I didn't know if I cared to be labeled either way. I *used* to be an optimist. I definitely refused to believe I was a pessimist.

Whoever came up with that stupid glass should've been shot. Why couldn't you just say it had half its contents and leave the labels to the judgers? Why must a glass cast me one way or another? Or better yet, tell the label makers to go screw altogether, pour a shot of whiskey in it, and put the glass to good use?

I had enough issues to worry about besides people calling me names and glasses giving me labels. For instance, what my hair looked like right now, and jutting my hip out in just the right angle to show off my new curves. *Oh yeah, I'm a woman now, Dax, so take that!*

"You've put on a couple pounds. That's good."

I smiled. I'd definitely put on a couple of pounds, and in all the right places—according to Tiffy's estimations, anyway. She might have been six, but that kid knew some shit. "Thanks. I've been trying—"

"But you're still scrawny as hell."

My fingers stopped preening my hair and my hip lost some of its jauntiness. Well, that wasn't very nice. And I thought I was the socially awkward one raised in a sanitarium. He must have been running around those woods all beastlike a few years too many.

Although the beast actually seemed nicer than the man. The beast liked me. At least it seemed like that. It had licked me. Dax's real fangs didn't seem to come out until after he was back in his human form.

He crossed his arms in front of his chest. "You need to eat more."

"Did you not notice the heaping plate of Wil— bacon? I'm eating. I can't fit more food in than I already shovel in on a daily basis." I knew because I'd tried. Food was one of the highlights of my new existence outside the Cement Giant. I ate every moment I could, and in a pretty wide variety. No one could say I was slacking in that area.

He nodded as if he didn't like the answer, but not enough to bother arguing.

Feet braced apart and face set in stone, it was times like this he appeared so closed off that it seemed like I'd never known him at all. Like he was someone I'd just met and not the man who'd saved me, told me he'd help me and that I didn't need to leave. It was as if the man who'd revealed his deepest secret in the woods a month ago didn't exist.

He dropped his arms and took a step to the side, taking me in from different angles. "Here's the deal: right now you are an unshaped pile of sludge."

Sludge? I had to remember what I read in that meditation book and stay calm. I needed a teacher. I had to pick my battles. I should let this go and rise above. Whatever didn't improve me wasn't worth the energy to fight. "Sludge? That's a little harsh, no? I mean, you couldn't have said clay? Isn't that the term? Unshaped clay?" Okay, so I was still working on my temper. People didn't change overnight.

Not to mention he could use a little work himself. What was his problem? I crossed my arms and mimicked one of his standby stances. It looked like the biggest bruise today was going to be to my ego. It was as if ever since he'd turned into the beast in front of me, his personality had tanked.

He was lucky he'd saved my ass a few times or we'd be through. Fortunately for him, I was the loyal type. Even better for him was that I needed a teacher and he was the only one with the right credentials, a BA, as in Bad Ass.

"No. I'm in charge. I choose the terms." He took a few steps and began a circle around me.

The muscles on my face started to tense up, wanting to shift into something that might resemble lemon face, but I held it back until he stepped behind me. I wasn't going to argue any further. I mean, it wasn't like I wanted to keep being *sludge*, after all, and he did have the royal flush. It stank to have no cards.

As irritating as he was being, my body reacted by standing a little taller and sucking in a stomach I didn't even have. Why should I care what he thought?

He circled back around to my front as he continued speaking. "There's physical strength, of which you are almost completely devoid."

I looked down at my arms. They were thin, but I had a little bump growing on the good one. I'd been lifting books with my good arm every night now that I could exercise without consequences. In the Cement Giant, if you got caught exercising, they made sure you couldn't do it again for a long time.

"Then there's mental."

I wasn't a slouch in that department, at least.

"You're passing decent in that area," he said.

Passing decent? I'd thought I was better than that. I might not be the smartest person in the room, but I wasn't usually too far down the line either. But I was going to suck these comments up and say nothing.

That lasted less than a second. "Wow, decent? Really? Don't pump me up *too* much. My ego might run out of control, and next thing you know I'll insist on being called something other than sludge or another equally crazy notion."

He ignored my comment as he stood in front of me. We were face to face, only a foot or so apart, and that energy he exuded was starting to satiate the air around me.

"There's one area left. Most people don't even realize it exists, and yet it counts for more than anything else combined. By a landslide."

"And that is?" I asked, expecting to hear how bad I sucked in that area, too.

His eyes stared into mine and everything else around me disappeared into a void. His mouth softened into what might have been the beginnings of a smile, but not quite, before he said, "Magic. That's where you're strong."

Magic. The word alone made me want to mimic his almost-smile. I didn't, not wanting to look all goofy and newbie-like over the praise.

We'd never talked about magic but I'd known it existed in some form for most of my life. I relived people's memories. That had been proof enough for me. Then there was Dax. He turned into a beast. Now if that wasn't proof magic existed, there was no proof that would make you believe. Now someone who had a clue was about to let me in on all the secrets. I hoped.

But that didn't mean there weren't some issues with what he'd just said. "If I'm strong in the magic category, how come I can't do anything other than see memories?" I didn't say, *Where's my version of fur and extra hundred pounds of muscle*, but I was thinking it. This was the stuff I'd been waiting for. I wasn't going to say or do anything to risk getting him angry now, like bringing up a topic he didn't want to discuss.

"How do you think you can throw those knives you wear so well with impossible targets when you've never been trained?"

My eyes shot to the one at my ankle. I left the one I holstered at my hip, only using that one for special occasions. "Maybe I'm a natural?"

He made a derisive noise that was much sexier than a snort but way more insulting at the same time. "Not even close."

"If it's magic, how come I can't throw straight all the time?"

"You forget, you're still—"

I held up my hand, motioning for him to stop. "Wait. I remember. Sludge, yeah, not forgetting that one anytime soon." I pushed the sludge insult and everything else he was dishing out today aside. I didn't know where the bad attitude was coming from, but this was the exact reason I needed him. He had knowledge. I needed knowledge. If he wanted to call me sludge as my new nickname? He was welcome to do it, as long as he helped me become a badass. "How does this magic work? How come I've never had it until recently?"

"Why do you think they kept you so weak? Limited your food and sleep and—"

"I know what they did." I hadn't meant to cut him off, but everyone had their soft spots. Talking about the Cement Giant was my vulnerable underbelly that I preferred not to show.

His expression was blank as he said, "You can't be sensitive about it."

"I'm not." It would've helped if I hadn't snapped

43

that last statement. It was hard when he was staring at me, assessing me like he was reading some instruction manual that was telling him what made me tick inside.

"Or get defensive."

"What I am is impatient to hear why it made a difference," I said, faking a sweet and calm tone of voice that hopefully hid the barbed wire fence erected around my past.

There was a slight narrowing of the eyes, a low exhaled breath, but he continued on like he hadn't just called out my fraud.

"Magic takes strength. You were too weak to use it. You've spent the majority of your life in a state of mere existence. The energy you had was going into keeping you alive. The healthier you are, the more it flows."

I kicked at a stray piece of hay by my boot as I replayed his words. Years of barely existing, never enough food, constantly being woken for midnight interrogation sessions and then forced awake an hour or two later. And that hadn't even been the worst of it. My life had been hell in the Cement Giant. I hadn't even realized how bad it had been myself until I got out and had a comparison. Finally, part of what they'd done made sense to me. It shouldn't have made me feel any differently about it, but it did anyway. At least there had been a reason and it hadn't come solely from hatred.

"You need to understand, magic doesn't just reside

within you, but is everywhere. Part of your strength is your ability to channel it, being able to use it. Think of it in terms of a bike sitting and waiting in the barn. If you don't know it's there, you aren't going to take it out for a ride.

"Some people can't touch the bike. They know it's there but can't open the barn door. It might as well not exist for them. Other people can only partially access it. They can get the door open, get the bike out of the barn, but can't get it to go past a crawl.

"And for some people, the engine purrs like a tiger once they figure out how to stroke it right."

I stuck my hands in my pockets to stop from fidgeting as I bit my lower lip. He wasn't talking about sex, so why was I imagining my hands stroking him? His hands all over me? This was what I got for getting the book with the topless guy and girl with all the hair flying on the cover last time I went to the library. It was bad enough I'd had to deal with Bookie looking at me funny. Now I had all sorts of sexy-time images dancing in my head.

I did a mental shake. He was my teacher. That was it. I had to keep my head in the game, even if he was throwing out that strange energy that made my body tingle like the scene in chapter four.

Magic. He was finally spilling all the secrets. No more sexy books if it was going to mess with my head.

Or maybe only one sexy book a week? A girl

needed her vices.

"So I'm probably a 'roll the bike out of the garage' type? I can get it out of the barn but not drive it very well?"

He walked over to a beam and rested a shoulder against it. While I waited to hear the outcome, it was hard not to notice he looked a little like the guy on the sexy cover.

His face could've been carved from stone, but then I saw a small smile curve his lips. This was a real one, and the sparring partner I'd had in this barn weeks ago, the one who relished in having a playmate, peeked through. "No, you'll do a lot better than that."

I was afraid to ask, but some of the optimism I used to have poked through anyway. "What exactly are you saying? Do you mean that now that I'm healthier, I'll have more magic?"

"What I'm saying is, now that you're healthy, you're not only going to be able to take the bike out of the barn, you'll be kicking up dirt and stones in your wake."

I felt my own expression mimicking his. But try as I might to honor my new set of parameters, and just be happy he was finally helping me, I couldn't leave it alone completely. "Why are you helping me now?"

"I told you I'd help. I'm helping."

"But why?" As much as I would've liked to imagine this was out of the goodness of his heart, I had a feeling there was more to it than that.

"Are we being honest here, or are you still living in Moobieland where everyone does things because it's the right thing and for some ridiculous code?"

I kept my chin up and my face stoic even as his words were chipping away at me again. The smile was a lost cause, though. I didn't know what was wrong with him, but I was all for honesty. My code might have been made up, but weren't all codes? Some person looked around and decided they wanted to be better? Have a higher standard? He could say whatever he wanted about my code; that wasn't something that was going away. Wasn't even up for debate. But again, I didn't argue. I wanted answers, not arguments. I needed to finally know where I stood with Dax. Where I stood in his world.

"Lay your truths on me," I said, and I meant it.

"You can see Dark Walkers. I can't. I need that asset enough to help."

"But why did you take so long?"

"I was weighing the costs."

"What costs?"

He straightened up from the beam. "I'm here. You don't need to see my tally sheet."

I guessed that was the end of that, but I could live with it. Yeah, according to my new self, it was enough.

"So you still want to hunt Dark Walkers?"

He strode across the barn, and there was something

in his movement that was pure beast. A lesser person would've stepped back, but I held my ground.

"You know what I am. Don't ever forget it. It will never change."

I might not always know his thoughts, but he was right. I knew what he was, a hunter, and like no other I'd ever seen. That was one thing that hadn't needed to be said. Instinct told me that there was a bigger reason, beyond being born from a Plaguer, that he was a beast, and the only one that could master every aspect of it.

He was warning me off. I didn't know why or if I was even interpreting his words correctly, but he didn't get it? There was no warning me off. I needed his help, and at any cost. I'd been past the point of being warned off by four years old. Warnings didn't even slow my stride. I wanted to be like him and would pay any cost.

"Where do we start?" I crossed my arms over my chest as I waited to find out what came next.

"We figure out how you tap into the magic."

"If you change into the beast with magic, then don't you know how to do it already?" How could someone who turned into a beast not know how to tap into magic?

He was shaking his head before he said a word. "I know what you're thinking, and you're wrong."

"How do you know what I'm thinking?" I asked, wondering if this were some sort of magic too.

"The same way I know what you just thought now.

Your distrust in people is painfully obvious at times."

"So then you'll tell me how this works?"

"Everyone has their own connection and way they channel it. You need to learn to connect to it. The more you do it, the easier it gets. Think of it as creating a well-worn path."

"So how do I go about that?" I asked. I did want to know, but I wanted to move the conversation on even more than wanting the knowledge.

"Close your eyes."

"Why?"

"Just do it."

I had to force myself not to argue and do as he said, even though it completely went against the grain of who I was.

"Empty your mind."

"Completely empty? That's a tough one. You know—"

"Empty," he barked.

"Okay, okay." It was going to be tough. I didn't like an empty mind, and I wasn't very good at the emptying part.

I felt him lay his fingers on the flesh above my neckline, and it felt like it was burning my skin. That wasn't helping the emptying, for sure.

"Visualize a light deep inside of you. Feel it burning within your chest."

"Okay."

"Don't talk."

Really? This was the teacher I picked?

"Slowly, let that glow fill you, your arms, legs, fingers, until it consumes you.

"Know that your skin is nothing. It's an illusion. You don't stop there. The glow extends past you and into the ground you are standing on, the air around you—it's all connected to you. With every breath, you take from it. With every exhale, you reach out to it."

I stood there, eyes closed, with no idea what he was talking about, but trying to play along. That was when I felt a warmth growing, like someone had placed a hot compress against my chest. It was quite nice, to be honest, as if I was snuggled up around a hot cup of cocoa or something, or maybe like I'd taken a big shot of whiskey.

"That's it," he said, as if he knew something was happening. How could he know my chest felt warm? Did it reach his fingers? His hand left my flesh and I heard him as he stepped back.

My body was moving before I gave thought to what I was doing. I ducked low as I felt a draft of air coming from right where my body had been a split second before. I dropped to a roll and jumped to my feet halfway across the barn, eyes wide open now.

"Wow, how did I know to do that? I can't even do that when I'm trying to." Now this was the badass stuff I'd been hoping for.

"Because your instincts are good when you don't overthink them," he said from a good ten feet away now.

"But how did I know you were going to try and hit me?"

"You used magic, the magic within and all around you."

I did? This was even cooler than what Moobie could do. "What else can I do?"

"Whatever it is you planned for the day, gardening, helping Bookie with the animals...I've got other plans."

I watched as he left the barn. It was a start. It was enough.

CHAPTER 5

The door to the big barn, where the horses were kept, creaked as I pushed it open. Bookie's head popped above one of the stall doors where he'd been checking on a foal.

"How's she doing?" I knew this one had gotten colicky on and off since birth, and he'd been keeping an eye on her.

"She's looking good," he said. "You ready? When I saw you go into the small barn with Dax, I thought maybe you were canceling this afternoon."

"No way. I have to be ready." Until I was where I needed to be, I wanted to get the books. I'd never depended on anyone completely before and I couldn't start now. This past month had taught me that. What if Dax flaked out on me again? No. All avenues forward were being left open. I didn't only want a plan A—I wanted a B, C, and D, too. Sooner or later the Dark Walkers would show back up here and I had to be as prepared as I could when the time came.

"No one would let you get hurt. It's different here. I would do anything to keep you safe," he said, his stare faltering slightly before he went back to running his hands over the foal's sides, checking for bloat even though he'd already said the foal was doing okay.

I rested my hands on the stall door as I watched him work. "Bookie, that's the problem. I don't want to need protection. It's always different until it isn't. I don't want to depend on anyone else. I can't. You don't understand the things that are coming for me."

"How do you know they'll keep coming?"

"I just do." *Because I'm the key to something.*

I didn't know how else to reply to that, so when the conversation sputtered out, I let it. I backed up and watched as he exited the stall and moved to another horse.

Bookie was a natural at healing. He wouldn't hurt a fly, and yet he'd taken part in blowing up the Cement Giant to help save me. People had their limits of what they could do, especially the good ones like him. There was only so much of a load their minds could bear before they broke or became someone they couldn't live with.

He'd make some girl really happy one day. I wouldn't be that girl, even if I thought his feelings might run a little softer toward me. He deserved a house and a family, and that wasn't where my life was headed. He should be with someone as kind and soft in the center as he was, and that wasn't me either. He might not know it yet, but I did. If I ended up with anyone, and that had a really large question mark by it, they'd have their hands full.

"Is Dax helping you now?" Bookie said after a good five minutes of silence had elapsed.

I nodded as we entered into uncharted waters. We'd never had this talk, about me or what I was, and I didn't know what he knew about Dax. I was sure he didn't know about the beast.

"Bookie, you know I'm…" There was a reason we hadn't talked about it. I tried to think of the correct approach. "I'm different. You know that."

He nodded.

"Turns out, it runs a little deeper than just seeing memories."

He nodded as I waited for questions I didn't have answers for.

"Is there something I can help you with, besides getting books and stuff?"

This was worse than the questions I was dreading. He was looking at me, huge hazel eyes practically pleading to be of some help. How could I tell him that he didn't have what it took without crushing him? I knew what it felt like to have to sit on your hands and feel useless when your friends needed you.

"The books are a huge help."

"There's nothing else?"

I wished I could think of something, but he'd know it for a lie. I shrugged.

He looked back at the horse before he said softly,

"But Dax can."

"Sort of, yeah." Why was this conversation feeling so horribly awkward? And why did I feel like I was getting sucked even deeper into a vacuum of emotional muck?

I snapped my fingers and then clapped my hands together to keep them from doing their telltale fidgeting. "You almost ready to get going?" *And get on the bike, where it's hard to speak?*

"I think maybe there's something else we should start doing now that your arm is 'enough.' Something I can help with." His smile, the one that had looked forced before, got a little warmer. "If you're game and feeling up to it?"

"Lay it on me." I would've tried to become a fire-eater if it meant we could stop talking.

He wiped his hands off on a rag as he stepped out of the stall. "Come on," he said, waving me toward the smaller door out the back of the barn. I followed him, looking for clues to what he had in mind.

The bike he always used was sitting there, waiting.

"I thought you didn't want to go to the library?"

"I don't." He walked over to the bike but stopped by the handlebars. "Don't you want to learn to ride?"

He didn't have to ask me twice. I nearly skipped the last steps over to it and climbed on. I leaned forward, imaging the wind hitting me as I rode this bad boy through the Wilds.

He started pointing to different handles and levers. "This is the clutch, the brake, the gas—"

"What do I do with all of it?"

He smiled, realizing I had very limited exposure to mechanical things, and ran through a more in-depth explanation. If I did this and twisted the handle, it would go. Do this and it would stop. After a few repeats, I thought I had the basics. Was even feeling a little cocky when I managed to start it on my own.

"See that tree?" He pointed to one about fifty feet away. "There shouldn't be any grooves or ruts that'll mess you up between here and there."

I grabbed the handle that controlled the fuel and rotated it forward. The bike reacted like I'd cranked it full blast, and then the top wheel was kicking up before landing again and taking off at a crazy speed toward the tree.

Three seconds later, the bike was on its side and sliding forward as I landed on my ass, which was definitely going to be bruised tomorrow. After a split-second evaluation, I surmised that nothing hurt enough to probably be permanent damage. I'd had enough experience doing self-triage to know.

Bookie was running over to me, but I was more concerned about the bike. Bikes were nearly irreplaceable, practically priceless out here. Even replacement parts were rare. Bookie was always on the lookout for spare parts when he went "digging," as he called it.

He squatted down beside me. "You okay?"

"I'm fine," I said, already sitting up. "I'm afraid to look at the bike."

"It's been through worse than that."

I wasn't so sure. He was saying the right words, but I saw his gaze trying to size up the damage.

"Go check, please?" I said. I didn't need to ask him twice, as he headed over toward where it had slid quite a ways farther.

I was sick with the idea I might have ruined his bike. Worse, there were people watching now, and I needed to stand up before they felt like they had no choice but to check on me. Nobody wanted to avoid that more than I.

Some of the people, the ones who didn't openly hate me, had gotten it into their heads that I was favored by Dax for no fathomable reason. They did this forced tiptoe thing around me that I despised. I could deal with hate and fear, but for the love of all that's right in the world, don't fake like me. Life was too short to waste energy faking anything.

I bent forward and a hand on my arm gave me a boost up, and I realized my Dax radar had fritzed out with my bruised bum.

"What are you doing?" Dax asked.

I'd thought it was pretty obvious, but okay, I'd play along. "Trying to learn to ride a bike."

His voice was low and irritated as he said, "You can't."

"Why not?"

"Your magic screws with the mechanics."

"That doesn't make any sense."

"Did the bike just take off like it had its own mind?"

I thought I'd messed up, but that sounded pretty accurate. "You ride."

"Because I have control of my magic. I need you alive right now. You can learn to ride after I don't."

"You could've warned me."

"I didn't think I had to." Dax dropped my arm and walked away before Bookie finished rolling the bike back to me.

He looked in Dax's direction and then at me. "What's wrong?"

"He's such a dick sometimes. He'll do one nice thing and then turn into a total dick the next minute, like he can't figure out whether he wants to be a nice guy or a dick."

"Do you think you used the word *dick* enough? Didn't you pick up a thesaurus last trip, against my better judgment, by the way?"

"It was more worthy of taking space on the bike than your dungeon book. Who are you even going to play those games with? Don't we have enough real stuff to worry about without your fantasy dragons?"

"It looked interesting. And the thesaurus was because you didn't want to be redundant in your speech. Considering how much good it's done, the dungeon book was more worthy of the trip, not to mention the other book."

My face felt a little warm at the mention of the other book, and I evaded that subject altogether. "Tirades are exempt from the redundancy rule. And stop cutting off my tirade about Dax."

"Sorry, screech away."

"I wish he could just figure out whether he was a dick or not so I could decide how I should treat him, is all."

Bookie was back to staring after him. "I think he's got one thing figured out."

"What's he got figured out? That he needs me alive so he can use me?"

"He wants to do something with you," Bookie said as he watched Dax crossing the field.

"What does that mean?"

He kept watching Dax as he was walking away, and shook his head. "Nothing. You're right, is all. He wants to use you." He finally turned away from Dax.

"The bike is fine other than another ding or two to blend in with the rest. You ready to give it another go?"

"I think we should call it a day."

"You don't usually give up this easy," he said. "You okay?"

"Yeah, just a little bruised." Mostly my pride, though, at having to pretend such a little bruise would take me out of commission, but I didn't feel like opening up the whole magic can of worms with Bookie.

CHAPTER 6

I'd thought I couldn't have an unpleasant meal. Sitting there with a tableful of Fudge's food, how could I not be in a good mood? I was right. Even with the tension that seemed to be brewing under the surface tonight, it wasn't anything a little red meat couldn't handle. I couldn't wait to take that first bite, as everyone knows the first few are the best.

For some reason the tension seemed to grow even thicker as Dax joined the table. Tank, the basement dweller and Dax's go-to enforcer, seemed preoccupied. Lucy was looking really smug for some unknown reason, while Tank was shooting daggers her way with his eyes.

Bookie was sitting on the opposite side of the table, diagonal from me, not looking overjoyed but not upset either. He'd seemed off ever since Dax had come over during the bike lesson this afternoon. Tiffy was doing her own thing as usual, but this time it was making shapes in her mashed potatoes, which was something very like a six-year-old for a change. Fudge was Fudge, as always. Nothing budged her mood much.

I used my time productively by heaping a massive

amount of potatoes on my plate before anyone noticed that perhaps I'd gotten a little greedy. If they kept slacking, the pile of corn I was about to dump next to the potatoes would put the other pile to shame.

I'd almost made it to the carrots before anyone noticed, but it happened to be Dax, who only nodded in encouragement. It kind of annoyed me. I didn't want an okay. I liked the idea that I'd won the extra food by stealth. I plopped the bowl of corn down with disappointment and moved on to some stuffing, but it just wasn't the same now.

Then again, it was hard to be disappointed with anything at the moment. Fudge had really outdone herself today. Not only would I be happy, I was going to be nearly ecstatic after this meal.

"I've been getting word of strangers in the area," Dax said, dropping the news like a bomb on the table, saying the only thing that could possibly take the glow out of my soon-to-be-full belly and the lure of red meat in front of a carnivore.

Strangers could be people from Newco, Dark Walkers, bounty hunters. There were so many undesirables that fell under the "stranger" label that it almost ruined the sampler bite I'd just taken. The potatoes didn't taste quite so creamy anymore, the corn not so sweet, the gravy a little bland. Not bad enough that I stopped eating, but it certainly slowed my chewing down a fraction of a second.

I looked about the table, measuring the general mood. Tank seemed even more annoyed with Lucy for some reason, which seemed to please her. Bookie looked concerned. Fudge was looking at her plate like she knew something, and Tiffy was now looking closer to forty than six.

Tiffy was the first to speak. She calmly laid her fork down on her plate and asked, "And what exactly does this mean for me?"

"You don't leave the gates alone. No more sneaking out."

That was the end of any possible discussion on who these strangers might be, or any other rational discussions. Tiffy broke out into the loudest wail I'd ever heard coming from someone her size. The only thing that I could discern from her noise was something about not abandoning her friends. It was hard to be sure, though. To say her fit put a damper on the evening would be like saying a tornado was a little breezy.

"Can't they visit you here?" I offered up when she took a break to get a new lungful of air. I mean, they were invisible. No one was going to be able to stop them from coming.

The only thing this did was set her off into a louder wail. There might have been a "no" in the middle of the screaming, but again it was hard to decipher. When it looked like she was settling in for the long haul, no matter what anyone said, the place evacuated quicker

63

than if a skunk had just wandered into the room with its tail raised.

Dax was among the evacuees, and only stopped long enough to stop by me and yell over Tiffy's screaming, "Inventory tomorrow."

Ugh. I hated inventory. I didn't pitch a bloody fit like Tiffy was doing, even though I was sorely tempted to get in on the action.

But why was Dax telling me about inventory? This was normally a job I did with Tank, or occasionally Lucy. "What time does Tank want to leave?" I yelled back before he walked away.

"In front at six."

I nodded, finding it easier on the ears than to join the noise. Dax had probably only given me the message because Tank had already run off to hide underground, where it was quieter. Bookie was rolling his eyes and stuffing a napkin with food as he ran out the backdoor, probably figuring the barn would be quieter than remaining anywhere in the house. Lucy had disappeared while I'd been taking a bite of potatoes.

Unlike the rest of them, I valued a good meal too much to abandon it for some screaming. Tiffy took a momentary break, the room going silent and luring me into a false security before she let out the worst of it. The kid was really going to make me earn this one.

Just when I thought the night was going to be unsalvageable, Tiffy stood and ran up the stairs, Fudge following her, alternating between trying to calm her down and yelling at her to stop. Tiffy's screams started to die down, and I realized I was sitting here in front of a huge meal, just me and all this food. It was a sin to waste it and the ice was getting low in the cooler box, so I should just eat it to save Fudge from worrying about it going to waste. It was the right thing to do.

CHAPTER 7

I was chewing on jerky instead of eating bacon and sitting in the bushes instead of waking up slowly on a nice, comfy bed. I liked sleep. I liked it almost as much as I liked food. People who've had all the food and sleep they want don't appreciate those things as much as they should. Gluttony and sloth needed to be embraced every so often.

Why didn't I have bacon? Why had I dragged my body out of bed at an hour that should be illegal? So that I could sit on a bunch of weeds and stare at a hole, a "trader's hole," to be specific. It wasn't much more than a small wooden shack, but these places hadn't gotten the name "hole" for nothing.

It wasn't like there were proper places to meet in the Wilds. Places like these were where everyone came to do their business, their trading, or make their—more often than not—underhanded deals. I knew Dax had some of his people trade his oil and gas from his mysterious rig here.

I'd learned a lot of things this last month, like that oil was one of the reasons why we had sugar when so many in the Wilds didn't. Why we always had fresh meat and produce, too, even when a crop failed and none of the animals went missing. I'd heard that oil had been big during the Glory Years, and even now, after the mechanical world had died, it was still holding its own.

Before I set foot out of Newco, I'd had a romantic notion of everything having to do with the Wilds, but I'd learned quickly it was just as tough as the rumors had made it sound. After I'd sat in a few of these real-life, honest-to-goodness Wilds establishments, I'd realized I loathed these places. Most of them were filthy. The only thing worse than going inside one of them was being forced to sit in the bushes watching other people go inside them, while I was getting eaten alive by bugs, the variety that felt like they were pulling my hair. Everyone told me I was crazy, but damn if those critters weren't stealing strands. Even still, with all of the downsides, I wouldn't trade the Wilds for a million Newcos, no matter how many inventory sessions I had to do.

I'd been doing this watching business at least once a week, ever since I'd decided to stay at the farm. When I worked with Tank, it was pretty easy. Lucy never shut the hell up. I'd never done it with Dax, even though he was the one that ordered them.

Inventory, Dax called this. I called it bullshit. Dax wanted to chart how many Dark Walkers were coming and going in the area. He wanted to count them.

I wanted to kill them.

But instead of spilling blood, I wasted pencils as I jotted down their most distinctive features and general descriptions in the notebooks he gave me.

This was the gig, whether I liked it or not. For the record, I didn't. I'd voiced my complaints pretty loudly from the get-go. I'd been informed via message that I could leave at any time. I'd countered that Dax was rigid. I'd received more messages that I could leave at any time. I'd tried several more times to let him know I didn't like this plan—no one could call me a quitter, even if it was in the area of complaining. I'd received the same answer each time via surrogate: I could leave.

Thing was, at the time I couldn't leave, not after he'd dangled the carrot of being able to help me. I definitely wasn't leaving now that he'd finally started offering me answers and telling me how things worked. He had me by the short hairs. Actually, I had really long hair. I wasn't sure that statement was accurate, but a lot of other people with long hair used it when they were screwed, and "screwed" pretty much summed up my situation.

I heard Dax coming back from wherever he'd disappeared to a couple of hours ago, and my patience was about as nice and fluffy as the dirt I was sitting on. I still had no idea why he was here today.

He sat on his haunches beside me. I heard the sigh and then the headshake came. Another problem with him being here? He could complain directly to me while I was still in a spot to correct what he didn't like.

His finger tapped my sheet. "Not enough detail."

Tank and Lucy never complained when I gave them my list for the day, and all it had on it was tall, short, blond, or brunette. They just took it.

Sometimes I'd hear a complaint passed through the grapevine from Dax about the lack of description a day later. I'd say sure, and then continue to do it my way. If he couldn't take the time to complain to me directly, I hadn't found any overwhelming reason to worry about it.

Maybe that was why he came? To complain I wasn't doing it right? Now that he was starting to hold up his end of the bargain, I might try and comply with his need for more details, but I still didn't see the point.

"Why do we need so much detail? Why are we watching them at all? If we were killing them, then I could understand the purpose of these little trips. I don't see what good *counting* them does."

He took my notes, his shoulder brushing mine and his thigh getting very close to my arm; not that he seemed to notice. I wouldn't have either if he didn't throw off energy like the sky was about to open up and a bolt of lightning was going to strike. Had he always been like this or was it getting worse?

"The more information, the better. It's about the bigger picture."

"I don't care about the bigger picture. I'll take a little one with a dead Dark Walker in it."

"Sometimes you have to wait for the things you want." He looked at me with a blank expression for a moment, his eyes flitting to my lips and then back again, and I felt myself flush slightly. It was like he was running on full blast today. "You're young but you'll learn."

He was in la la land. I hated when people commented on how young I was, as if my age made me stupid or weak. I'd already shed Dark Walker blood and been through hell. I might be young in years, but I felt like I'd live an eternity, and my soul felt ancient. "I'm not that young, and what does that have to do with killing these suckers? Have you forgotten that I killed my first Dark Walker at the age of four and another one about a month ago? I'm plenty old enough."

His lips didn't move, and his stare got kind of far off, even though he was right beside me. He broke eye contact and handed me back my list before looking to the hole. "They weren't expecting it. It's different now."

"Fine. Maybe it is, but I think we should see how different. Let's get in there and fight the good fight."

"Not yet. I want to get an idea of their numbers. I help you; you do what I want. That's how this works."

Get their numbers now that he had me, that is. I was the only one around that could identify them. How come I didn't have more leverage in these negotiations? There was something seriously wrong with the way this kept working out. I wished I could pick up a book at the library specifically on how to deal with Dax.

"You're a beast. Not a scientist," I said, the B-word slipping out along with my patience.

A single brow arched. "And you look like a gatherer."

Ooh, that one hurt. "I'm a hunter and you know it."

"You might be eventually, but you don't look like it now." He grabbed my wrist and held it high, looking at my bicep. "You'd barely be an appetizer for the beast."

"So you do eat people!" Details like this were almost worth being called a gatherer.

"No. But keep annoying me and I'll make an exception." He dropped my arm.

I fell back onto my heels in the dirt and bushes. "Why don't we follow them, at least?"

"Not yet."

"Why?"

"I want numbers first before we chance spooking them. Bigger. Picture."

"Well, this picture looks like a messed-up Picasso to me."

"How do you know about Picasso? Didn't think that would be in any of your Moobie books."

I knew what he thought about Moobie, my spy

reads. "No, he isn't, but I have read other things in my life."

When he didn't shoot a comment back at me, I turned to look at him, figuring I was missing the sarcastic reply that was probably displayed on his face.

He didn't look sarcastic, though. He looked like he was recalling something.

"That's right. They had classes there."

There was the Cement Giant. He was right, in a way. Once a week we'd had "class" where most of the girls in there pretended to pay attention, and you were guaranteed a passing grade no matter what you did, even taking a nap. It had been a farce for the public. *See how good we are? We're helping these poor souls so that you won't have to think about them. Let us care for these sad, pathetic creatures.*

The classes hadn't been pretend to me, though. I'd learned everything I could. They'd been the highlight of my week for too many years to count. The bitterness swelled, and that was when I thought of the fact that the place was rubble now. It helped; a little, anyway.

I liked to pretend I'd never been *there*. And even if I was forced to remember, I certainly wasn't looking to talk about it. I hated talking about that place. There was no reason to. It was over, and I'd eventually figure out a way to torch the memory from my brain.

He turned toward me. I don't know what he saw in my face, but there was a single nod and I knew the subject was dropped. It was about as close to an apology as I'd ever gotten from Dax on anything, but the nod and following silence sufficed.

I'd decided apologies were like Kryptonite to him. I didn't need the word to know the feeling. He didn't throw heaps of salt into my wounds, and I returned the favor by not twisting the knife in his with any mention of his brother. We both had experienced enough festering wounds to understand pain.

He knew loss. Even before his brother passed, he'd been scarred. I'd sensed the history in him because I'd walked the same path of loss, and once you'd walked that dark road, you spotted it pretty easily, knew the twists and turns like you were right at home.

Damn it. There I went, getting all soft and stupid when there were monsters to kill—or watch, in this case. Which brought me back to a much more pressing matter that had everything to do with now, and that was all that mattered. In my opinion, yesterday could go fuck itself. I didn't need it anymore. Today and tomorrow were much more interesting.

I got my psyche all nice and neatly packed up again. The packing took a little longer than it used to, with a couple more ghosts to cram into the box I kept under lock and key in my mind, but I managed. "Talking about the bigger picture, mind explaining what this picture actually is for me, since I'm not great in the abstract?"

"This is the way it's going to go. We get a count. Then we find their base. Then we strike. In that order and on our schedule, methodical and concise. Is that something you can live with?"

And cold. He'd left that word out, but it hadn't really needed to be said when it came to Dax. He was either glacier cold or burning you with his fire. There was no middle, but it worked for me.

"Killing Dark Walkers? Oh yeah, I can definitely live with that."

CHAPTER 8

Up too early again, but this time I didn't mind. The sun had gotten up before me and I had time to grab breakfast in my spot before I met Dax by the old tree.

It was going to be a good day from the looks of it, as Lucy wasn't in her spot, which was irritatingly within earshot of mine on the back porch. I was halfway through my eggs when Tiffy came and sat beside me, her head shaking slightly, a sad little half sigh escaping her lips.

"It didn't go well the other day," she said as she settled next to me on the edge of the bench.

"What didn't go well?"

The question set off another round of head shakes. "The meeting with my friends, and now I can't even talk to them and try and fix it."

Ahhh, the invisible friends and her had a falling out. The kid had almost gotten me nervous for a second there, making me think something was really wrong.

"Oh. I'm sorry about that." I leaned back and shoveled some more eggs in my mouth as I took in the morning sunshine and watched the people milling about. There was something very pleasant about watching people go about their day, getting up with the sun and working outside in the fresh air, no worries about monsters coming to get them. Made a calm, nice life almost seem possible.

"No. I'm sorry. I don't think it's going to be good. I did try." Tiffy patted me like she did when she was trying to console me. Where had she picked that up? Must've been something from Fudge, although I'd never noticed Fudge patting anyone.

"I'm sure you did your best," I said around a mouthful of bacon, having no idea what she'd tried. Her hand repeating the patting motion, like maybe if she patted me enough, it would be okay.

"Oh, Dal, if you only knew. I think I managed to salvage some things, but I'm not sure. Time will tell." Every other word was long and drawn out. If we were back in Newco, the kid would've been destined for the stage with her dramatics.

"I'm sure it'll be okay, Tiffy." I gave her a couple pats back with my free hand, figuring maybe it worked for her.

Dax stepped out onto the porch, looked at me, and said, "Let's go." I nodded and he walked back in the house. Time for some more practice, and I was raring to go.

I gave Tiffy a final pat on the shoulder. "It'll be okay, Tiffy. Why don't you go see if Fudge has some chocolate stashed away for you?"

She put her arm to her forehead, shielding her eyes. "No. I just need to be alone for a while."

"Okay, then," I said, and left her on the porch. I dropped off my plate in the kitchen and gave Fudge a warning that Tiffy was having one of her spells before heading out to meet Dax.

* * *

I was in the middle of the woods looking at my old friend, Mr. Assassin Tree. *So we meet again, my admirable foe.* Of course I said this in my head and not aloud, not wanting to open myself up to Dax's mockery and scorn of the facial variety. Also, technically, it really hadn't been very long. My foe and I met quite often, at least a few times a week, and always on Sundays. It wasn't like I had been sitting on my hands completely while Dax saw to his more important matters.

"Stand here. You're going to throw this knife at that target until you hit it." He pointed at the left eye of the assassin. Of course he did. He'd noticed that the left eye was less damaged then the rest of the face. I could nail the nose and the right eye, even the mouth. For some reason the left eye was always a pain in the ass. Of course, I could still do it, or had been able to since last week.

I let the knife fly from my fingers and it landed

exactly where I wanted.

"No good."

"Are you on drugs? Of course that's good. I did exactly what you wanted."

He walked over with none of the happiness in his step that was bursting out of me, and grabbed the knife.

"Did you go eat some cranky human today? Is that what's wrong with you?"

"I told you. I don't eat people."

"Or at least not the happy ones. Were their muscles too tough? Maybe you should try some babies," I said, trying to wring a little bit of the business from him.

He stopped in front, grabbed my hand, and placed the knife in my palm. "You have some funny moments. That wasn't one of them." He stepped aside, allowing me a full view of my assassin.

"Fine. Eating babies, not so funny." I lifted the knife and pointed toward the target. "Care to tell me why that wasn't good enough?"

"Because you hit that based on practice. Based on physical ability alone. I need you to hit your mark with magic. You have got to be able to control it, or one day you're going to get into a fight with your pants down. Don't you understand that? What if I sprang into the beast all the time? You need control."

The words sounded like a painful screeching to my ears, but I knew he was right. Lack of control was definitely on the list of personality traits that I needed shed.

"Even without control, you'd be a good adversary; maybe you'd even be great in time. But you have to be better than that with what's coming for you. For what comes next, you have to be invincible."

"No one's invincible."

"You have to be."

"How do I manage that?"

He reached to his hip where a gun was strapped and handed it to me. "For now, practice."

I turned the gun over in my hands, a bit in awe of such a small thing that could do so much damage.

"Close your eyes—"

"You told me not to do that anymore when I'm aiming."

"Listen to me. Close your eyes and feel for the magic. Then open them. Once you do, I want you to use the gun to shoot that." He pointed to the tip of a piece of dead bark that was sticking out of the tree.

"That's like…" I squinted. Apparently my eyes weren't so magical, because I felt like I could use a pair of glasses right then. "A centimeter big?"

"Yes. Now do it."

I shoved the hair out of my eyes, knowing when I tried this I was going to need to be on the tippy top of my game. My lids fluttered shut and I tried to sense the warmth, the burning energy that felt like it was growing in my chest. The more I concentrated, the more it felt like there was something actually in there.

"Is this burning psychosomatic or is there really something going on in here?" I asked, tapping my chest but not opening my eyes.

"Stop talking and concentrate."

Uh oh. Someone's patience was running thin again. I went back to concentrating on the burn, figuring if it was really there and going to cause any damage, it would've done so the first time I'd tried it out.

I shed all my other thoughts and focused on the feeling. The more I concentrated, the more it seemed like I could see it in my mind, a small flame within me. I imagined myself stoking it until it was piping hot, but strangely not uncomfortable as it grew, like it was last time. Then the air around me seemed to become hot as I mentally reached outward like he'd said.

"That's good. Open your eyes and try it now," I heard Dax say. I opened my eyes and lifted the gun. Power exploded from my hands, and I wasn't altogether certain it was just from the gun. The tip of the bark disappeared.

"Good," Dax said, king of the understatement.

That had been freaking awesome. I wanted to hop around the clearing, because that was a shot only a badass could make, but played it cool instead.

"You still feel it?"

I nodded. It felt like I was cocooned by the sun on a perfect summer day.

"Hold it. I want to try something different."

"Okay," I said, committing before I knew what he wanted. It didn't matter. If it was using my newfound magic, I was down for it. I was going to be the sickest thing that hit the Wilds in a generation, maybe two, maybe even the last century. *Try and screw with me now, bounty hunters and Dark Walkers.*

"Put the gun down and pick a part of my body to hit."

"Really? Anywhere?"

"Yes."

"What if I hurt you?"

"You won't."

I scratched my head. "I don't know if I'd be so sure of that." I buffed my nails on my shirt as I said it and gave him the look, the one that said he might be biting off more than he could chew. It was mostly a joke, but in another month it might not be.

"I think I've got this."

"I mean, if you insist." It wasn't like it was a sucker punch. He was asking me to do it and all, even if I didn't mind taking a swing at him. Wasn't like he didn't have one coming.

"Make sure you concentrate, because you aren't getting a free shot. You're going to have to earn it."

I tightened my ponytail, trying to force some escaped hair back into it as I looked him over. Face? Nah. I liked his face, even when he was using it to mock me. Plus, I was the one who had to look at him. A gut shot would be good enough, maybe hear a little *umph* as I knocked the wind out of him. That could be pleasant.

"Concentrate," he said as he moved into a fighting stance and turned his body slightly to the side, making the target smaller.

I felt for the warm glow inside and gave it a mental stir, realizing it was easier this time than even the last two times, and focused on my target. I launched into action. He was a blur as he dodged out of the way. My knuckles hit something way too hard to be flesh before my legs came out from under me as my momentum threw me off balance and I was the one gasping for air.

He walked over and leaned down, looking at me and smiling.

"Not funny to mock me because I missed. I could be critically injured right now." My palm found his and he pulled me to my feet, and I stood there demonstrating I was fine. It would take a lot more than that to keep me down.

"You didn't miss," he said.

"Hitting the tree doesn't count."

"You hit me."

"I hit you?"

"Yes."

What the hell was he made of? I knew I'd hit hard. I'd felt the blow vibrate all the way up to my shoulder and nothing? Not even a little pain on his face? What fun was that?

His head tilted to the side as if he saw something going on with me that I couldn't see myself. "People have certain aptitudes. Mine is strength. I think yours is aim."

"Aim? Can you elaborate on that?"

"It means when you aim, you don't miss. That's why you almost drove into the tree yesterday."

"So if I pick a target..." My words trailed off as I thought through what he meant.

"You hit it." He took a few steps back. "Get the gun. The more you practice building the magic up inside, the less you'll have to try. It'll happen almost without effort."

He picked out another target, this time one I couldn't see clearly at all. It was a blur in the far distance. I didn't close my eyes but managed to stoke the fire within me anyway. I pulled the trigger.

"Did I get it?"

Dax was smiling this time, as in a full smile with teeth and everything. "Yeah, you got it."

CHAPTER 9

My entire body felt stiff this morning, but I didn't care.
Dax had warned me after practice yesterday that I
would be. He'd said using magic was like working all
the muscles in your body at once, and it took some time
to get used to it. I think the only reason he said anything
was he figured I might mistake the soreness for a
symptom of the Bloody Death returning, and I'd
disappear in the middle of the night.

He was right. It was hard not to think the disease
might return one day and I'd be responsible for taking
out all of the people around me. But knowing what
caused this soreness made me want it to hurt more. I
was on the brink of greatness, and this pain was paving
the way.

There was a knock on my door before I heard Dax
say, "Be ready in ten. We're making a run. Pack a bag,
too."

"Got it," I yelled back. Did he actually ever sleep?
I sure hadn't last night. I'd barely been able to call it
quits as the sun was setting, and then after I'd come up
to bed last night, I'd concentrated on the burning magic
I could call forth.

Even spending another day in the bushes, like it seemed I'd be doing, didn't dent my good mood. I was like happiness forged in steel. You just couldn't bang this good mood out of shape.

I threw on my work clothes, basically the only thing I wore anymore, so it was a good thing Fudge had wrangled me up a couple spares. I didn't consider myself a dress type of girl, not anymore, and especially not white ones. The leather pants and tank tops were much more fitting to who I was now and who I was becoming. I tucked my knives into place, one that I hung off my hip and another tucked into my boot, and got ready to go count Dark Walkers.

By the time I got ready and had my bag, Dax was waiting outside for me. He reached for my stuff, strapping it onto the bike, and I climbed on. Even his lack of details wasn't bugging me today. Nothing and no one was budging this mood.

We'd barely made it out of the gate when he stopped the bike.

"You can't do that while we're driving," he said as soon as the engine quieted.

I cleared my throat and said, "Stop what?" No way he knew.

"I get that you want to practice, but you can't do it while you're sitting right behind me."

Damn, he did know. "Sorry. Just thought it was a good use of time to practice, and all."

"That's fine, but turn it off."

I cleared my throat. He hadn't told me how to do that. Maybe if I didn't think of it?

He shook his head a few minutes later. We were still sitting in the same place. "If you can't squash it, blow it out."

"Blow it out?"

"Take a deep breath and then blow it out as quick and strong as you can."

I nodded, not that he could see me where I sat behind him. I did as he asked, filling my lungs beyond capacity, and then blew out harshly. When I did, the branches on some nearby trees rustled.

"Did I do that?"

"Yes," he said, seeming a little more agitated than he was a minute ago.

Still didn't bother me. Nothing could. I was walking on clouds today.

* * *

We stopped a few times for a couple meals of jerky before we settled down for the night in the middle of nowhere. Dax started a fire and I bundled up my bag to use as a pillow. A huge tree not far from us caught my attention, and I stared at it, trying to figure out what was drawn on its trunk.

"There's an R carved into that tree," I said. Who

would come here and carve random letters into trees?

"It marks the territory we're in as owned," Dax said from where he was settled down not far from me.

"Should we be on it, then?"

"It's fine. I know the owner."

Not surprising. Dax seemed to know a lot of people, good, bad, and shady.

"When are we going to get to this place?" I asked, wondering how many of Fudge's meals I'd miss. If I was this happy on jerky, imagine life like this with her cooking? Plus, I couldn't remember the last time we'd traveled this far for a hole.

"Tomorrow morning." He lay down, his eyes shutting for the night.

"You're not going to scout the area?"

"No."

I guessed he felt safe enough. I laid my head down and dreamt I heard wind chimes as I drifted off to sleep.

* * *

I shot awake feeling like I couldn't breathe, even as my chest expanded. My eyes sought out Dax, lying a few feet away. He already was giving me his full attention, probably because I'd sprung up like I'd been attacked.

"What's wrong?" he asked as he leaned closer.

"Just a dream," I said. I didn't know if I'd woken

him or he'd already been awake. I felt better knowing he was there, even if I didn't share what woke me.

It had been the strangest dream I'd ever had. I'd awoken to the feeling that I was encased in cement. It felt as if someone had taken as much rock and sand as the Cement Giant's wall had contained and smothered me underneath it, burying me alive. My skin felt damp, like I was feverish, even in the morning chill.

He nodded and settled back down where he was, a few inches closer to me now.

I settled my head on the makeshift pillow as I tried to get my heartbeat to stop thudding like a spooked horse, thundering away from a perceived threat.

An hour later, the sky only showing the first signs of dawn, I heard Dax get up. "If you aren't going to sleep, let's get going."

I grabbed my bag and headed toward a stream we weren't far from. No matter how much water I splashed on my face, I couldn't lose the feeling that something was off, like the dream was clinging to me even now.

I could see Dax watching me, knowing something was off, but he didn't say anything, and I was climbing on the back of the bike soon after.

We pulled up in front of a large metal door, a monstrosity of a thing that stood about twenty feet high by fifteen feet wide, less than an hour later. The only place that I didn't see dents were the spots covered with too much rust to show. Still, even for its dilapidated state, it looked solid. It was as if the rust were merely a facade hiding the strength below. Like an old bruiser who might have been past his prime but could still throw a serious beat-down. The brick wall that framed it added to the overwhelming feel that if you wanted in this place, it was going to be by invitation only.

This was definitely *not* a hole.

"Why are we here?" I asked, wondering if we were looking for an invite ourselves after what he'd said at dinner the other night. I didn't want an invite. I wasn't looking to leave the farmhouse, at least not yet. We'd killed all the threats that had come by the farm. Didn't that buy us a little more time? Hopefully? Couldn't we kill a few more if necessary?

"This place is called the Rock. It's one of the communities I trade with."

I should've realized we weren't going to a hole hours ago. No one traveled at night, and it wasn't something he'd had us do to watch a hole in a while. People were afraid to travel after the sun went down, and if you weren't scared, it marked you as something different, something other than what everyone else was. That wasn't the type of sticking out you wanted to do in the Wilds. If you didn't blend, you were a target. Not that Dax had to worry about defending himself, but it could lead to other unwanted questions.

"I'm glad they like to trade, but why are *we* here? Like *me,* specifically?" Dax disappeared all the time, maybe to places like this. I wouldn't know, though, since not once had he invited me along for the ride, or anywhere for that matter, unless it was something to do with Dark Walkers.

Ahhh, now it made sense. This did have something to do with Dark Walkers. I was here to vet this place, label it as being clean of the monsters or point the suckers out. That led me to my next conclusion. Would he care unless we might come and stay here? Was the person in charge of this place going to vet me and decide if I got an invitation?

I realized Dax hadn't bothered to answer my question, but I didn't really need him to anymore.

"You could've at least warned me. I would've brushed my hair." I ran a couple fingers through the knots, not sure if I was improving it or making it crazier.

He tilted his head, giving me a shot of his profile where he sat in front of me. "I thought you only did that on Sundays?" A dimple poked through, melting a little bit of the glacier.

What he said wasn't true. I actually brushed it every day, not that anyone could tell. It had a mind of its own. "I would've done it a day early," I said, joking back.

A loud grinding sound filled the air as the old fighter let down his guard and the metal door creaked open a crack. We watched as the door continued to open, moving slower than a slug crawling along a riverbank. I hoped it was safe inside, because this would be one lousy emergency exit.

"I thought maybe it would be nice to show you around," he said, finally answering my question with a load of bull before he gave the bike a little gas. We moved forward slowly, which was too fast for my taste, as I didn't care to be behind any wall ever again. I rested my gloved hands on Dax's waist as we entered the Rock.

The place was a lot more inviting on the inside than the exterior had led me to believe, but not enough to make me forget about the walls. There were rows of moderate-sized houses and a lake in the distance. It reminded me a bit of some of the pictures I'd seen in books of the Glory Years, before the Bloody Death had left its scars.

In those pictures, people would be out on boats and fishing, and it wasn't even for dinner. I'd read that they did it recreationally back then. Unbelievably, they would throw their dinner back in the water and try and catch it again. I guess it shouldn't be a shock that most of that DNA had died off. Who threw away their own dinner? Sometimes I really didn't understand those people.

Dax stopped the bike in front of one of the larger buildings in the center of the houses. I got off and spun around, taking it all in. The only word I could come up with was *charming* as I looked around at the houses and benches with flowerpots beside them. There were kids playing in the street, and I thought about how it must have been back then, when places like this supposedly existed everywhere. Even the people walking around, a lot of them looking like Dax and I but not quite as scary, didn't ruin the utopia-like picture painted.

Dax kicked out the stand on his bike and walked over to me where I was standing in the middle of the street. "It was a gated vacation community during the Glory Years."

They'd had everything back then and hadn't even appreciated it. Now it was gone. Only pockets of places like this left to remind people. Even here it wasn't really the same. I'd seen the watch posted just inside the gate, the guy with a gun in the tower. I was damned sure that any fish caught in this lake wouldn't be tossed back in. "Friggin' Glory Years."

"Bitter much?" Dax asked me.

Thinking about how it used to be, I nodded. "Yes. I am, thank you."

"At least you're not in denial."

"You say that like it's a good thing. Denial's got some serious positives. I've seen it in action. I'd love to jump on that happy train. Looks like bliss to me."

He shot me a look that said *but then you'd probably be dead*. He was right. You couldn't make it in the Wilds if you weren't one hundred percent aware one hundred percent of the time, but it was nice to dream.

His eyebrow popped up and I couldn't let the unwarranted look go. "Stop with the face. You know I was mostly kidding."

The corner of his lip ticked up. It made me want to smile in return. I liked when I busted through his wall a little, and not just when I was making him go nuts and his temper finally got the best of him. There was a sense of humor under there, buried deep beneath the frost.

"Come on," he said, leaving the bike in front of the building and walking down toward the lake.

It was obvious by the stares we got from the locals that they didn't see many outsiders. It was the same back at Dax's. If you wanted to survive in this world, you kept it close and tight, only people you trusted around. I respected it.

We stopped on the rocky bank of the lake and he gave me the look, like the ones he'd given me in hole after hole when I'd first started IDing Dark Walkers for him.

I looked about the place some more, making sure I didn't miss anyone milling about. At its heart, the place wasn't that much different than our own, a farm area, some animals grazing a bit farther off on cleared land, people going about their day. Nothing shocking.

I knew he was waiting for an answer, and the idea

of lying crossed my mind. What if I said the place was crawling with Dark Walkers? But then I'd have to ID some people, and I knew what would happen then. Plus, the bigger problem with that was I wasn't a good liar— not good enough to get past Dax, anyway. But I could withhold information with the best of them.

Lying was a whole other ball of wax. The only time I used to be able to lie was to Ms. Edith, and that was only because I gave her exactly what she wanted to hear. People like that are easy to lie to. That lunatic only wanted bullshit most of the time. That would never fly with Dax.

"From what I can see, the place is clean."

A group of young girls I'd checked out walked closer, eyeing up Dax and giggling. Dumb idiots. They were too young and innocent to handle what he had going on.

Dax shot me a look.

I shook my head, letting him know they were human.

"Then what?" he asked.

Sometimes it was aggravating how much he noticed. What did I do? Squint a fraction of an inch too much? "They're fine, besides being young and stupid."

He full-on laughed at that.

"What's so funny?"

"They're your age."

I watched the group of them head down the street,

seeming so impossibly young even though they probably were around eighteen, give or take a couple of years. They walked as if they were oblivious to their surroundings and nothing could touch them. They'd probably lived their whole lives in this place, behind these walls, protected, ignorant of what it was like in the real world, what people were capable of doing to each other.

"You're wrong. I was never that young."

"Be glad of it."

"Trust me, I am."

He took a step forward and said, "Come on. There's someone we need to see."

I followed him back toward the brick building and the heart of the community. When I stepped in the place, it felt like I was walking into a different era. There were all these pieces of furniture, tables and bookcases, that looked like they had a wood pattern but weren't really wood. We passed into an area that looked like some kind of waiting room, with a couple of people sitting on benches across from a door to the interior.

Dax's knuckles hit the door and then immediately proceeded to the knob instead of waiting for a reply.

A man with dark auburn hair and broad shoulders looked up from where he sat behind a real wooden desk. I caught a glimpse of annoyance before recognition lit his face and his expression turned warmer.

"Rocky," Dax said.

Rock? Rocky? Looked like we'd found the owner of this place. Rocky was handsome and appeared a few years older than Dax was, or the age Dax looked—his true age was still up for debate, or would be once I found someone to debate it with. Rocky's appearance wasn't what struck me most about this man, or not his attractiveness, anyway. He looked as tough as the walls that surrounded this place, like he had been born weathering the storm.

"Becca, we'll continue this talk later," Rocky said.

I belatedly tore my eyes from the man behind the desk to see Becca sitting there on the other side. Her skin had a nice flush and her hair a healthy sheen—not that she hadn't been pretty before, but this new home was definitely agreeing with her.

She stood abruptly and nearly knocked over her chair. It might have helped if she was paying attention to what she was doing as opposed to staring at Dax.

Was he shooting her the same intense look? Next they'd be asking me and Rocky to step out and give them some privacy. Not that I'd care. They could do whatever they wanted. I wasn't jealous—but this was a work trip, and he shouldn't be making eyes at some woman while we were on business, or he should've come alone.

I turned to shoot him a look that told him he better cut it out, but I found an impartial expression there. His heart might have been pitter-pattering, or he might not have cared an ounce. There was no real way to tell.

"Dax," she finally said.

He nodded.

"Hi, Becca," I offered.

"Hi, Dal," she replied, and finally pulled her eyes away from Dax, the longing turning into something…"less excited" would be the kindest term. That was when I realized her expression changed because it was me and Dax here, together—alone. I knew what she was thinking, could feel the hurt. That was when my emotions shifted from annoyance with Dax to pity for her.

I hated pity. I didn't like the word or the condescending nature of the emotion. There was nothing redeeming about it at all. None of that changed what I was feeling for her, and pity was the most accurate label.

I wanted to tell her that Dax wasn't with me, not like that, but I couldn't. That would've turned a dollop of awkwardness into a pile of dung's worth of the stuff.

I watched as her shoulders stiffened into an upright position, even as her eyes grew slightly watery. She moved past us, nearly tripping on a coat stand by the door this time, as her eyes kept shooting to him. The minute Becca cleared the door, Dax shut it behind her in a firm-ish manner that had me staring at it and then him. Had that been a *goodbye, good riddance* door shut or a *hurts to look at you* type?

"Dax," Rocky greeted him with his hand outstretched, and Dax gripped it firmly, drawing me back to the matter at hand and away from my internal debate of *who cares, how much do they care, and why do I give a shit*?

Dax and Rocky weren't tripping over themselves to hug each other, but I could tell they definitely liked one another in a *you're a guy like me and I get what makes you tick, so we can hang* manly kind of way. I wondered, did this man really know what Dax was? Probably not, but you never knew.

Rocky held out his hand to me, and I didn't immediately pull mine out of my back pocket where I sometimes buried it. By the time I did, the moment had already turned awkward, or more awkward than shaking with a Plaguer was to begin with.

"It's nice to meet you, Dal," he said.

He knew my name. The hint was obvious. He knew who I was. Or more importantly, what I was, a Plaguer, and he was okay with it.

I whipped my hand out, trying to cover the lapse, and banged my knuckles into his accidentally.

He grasped my palm like I was just some regular person. He acted like I hadn't just looked like an idiot and shook my hand.

"Quite a grip you've got," he said, and I realized I'd overcompensated, and immediately loosened my grip.

"Thanks."

"I've heard a lot about you."

I squinted but resisted looking to my left.

"Not from him, that's for sure. Bookie stopped by here not long ago and couldn't shut up about you."

I nodded, remembering Bookie had mentioned that he'd gone on an errand for Dax.

Rocky motioned to the chairs behind us. Dax righted the one Becca had turned over and I grabbed the chair beside it and settled in. I took a moment to decide what I thought of Rocky. He seemed nice enough, but was he really?

It suddenly hit me. Holy shit, I'd just shaken hands with the guy and hadn't gotten a vision, not a whiff of a memory. How long had it been since I'd had one? I'd been around the same people at the farm for too long to judge. I'd gotten all of their bad memories out of the way, so there was no way to tell from them. Maybe it was a fluke? Perhaps it was just Rocky? I did get a blank sometimes. It wasn't like it never happened.

No, I hadn't picked up anything from the guy opening the gate, even though we'd gotten pretty close to him. Nothing from the people we'd passed on our way in here either, even when the young girls had beelined it closer to Dax and come well within range. That was too many people coming up blank. Something was wrong. I forced my hands to relax on the arms of the chair once I noticed I was clenching and unclenching them into fists.

I looked at Rocky while Dax and him talked, and realized with terror that I had no measure of this man. For the first time since I'd been four, I was left with nothing but my human senses to determine if he should be trusted. If Dax hadn't vouched for him in his own way, I'd have no idea if he was the worst human being to walk this Earth or a saint. I gave up on trying to relax, gripped the wooden arms of the chair, and tried to squeeze every ounce of concentration I possessed to focus on him. Even as I could feel my skin grow moist from sweat, most likely from panic, I got nothing.

Focus on the glow, the warmth. That was what I needed to do. Stir up the magic, the burning in my chest that would grow outward. Was it there? Barely. I could feel it warm slightly, but then it sputtered out.

Dax nudged my foot with his, and I belatedly realized that Rocky was talking to me. I nodded and smiled, having no idea what he had said, hoping I'd given an appropriate reply.

The confusion that flashed across Rocky's face told me I hadn't. Dax started speaking, drawing Rocky's gaze, if not his full attention, back to himself.

I tried to stay focused, to hear what they were saying, but my mind couldn't stay put on them or even in this office. I needed to get to more people. I needed to know if everything had changed.

A pit that had been growing in my stomach bloomed as I realized that whatever had woken me from sleep might not have been a bad dream. Something was wrong with me, and my body and mind had tried to warn me. If I'd lost my visions, maybe I'd lost everything? This place might be crawling with Dark Walkers and I wouldn't know. I could be sitting across from one and trapped by walls.

Dax stood, and I realized we were done here. He leaned over the desk to shake with Rocky. I stood too and made my goodbyes in a blur before I took the first chance I got to get out of there.

I heard the door to Rocky's office shut, knowing that he'd been watching me like I was some sort of absurdity, but I was unconcerned about anything other than whether I'd lost my abilities. Who cared about an invite to somewhere I didn't want to be when my apple cart might have just been dumped over and my life turned upside down?

I knew Dax was on my heels, but I didn't stop and tell him what was happening. I didn't care. All I cared about was getting a vision off somebody and proving I was okay.

"What are you doing?" Dax asked as I veered off and stepped unnaturally close to the people sitting in the waiting room.

They both leaned back, more shocked than aggressive, and I was moving on before it became an issue. I'd seen nothing from them.

I ran outside, Dax on my heels as I found another woman and moved close enough that I should've picked up something. Again. Nothing. The woman walked quickly away from me and I remained still. That was five nothings in a row. One nothing wasn't alarming. Two might have been a fluke. That was five. Five was a disaster.

"What are you doing?" he repeated as he came to stand beside me. He had lost all patience by now, and I didn't care. I had bigger problems. Technically, *we* had bigger problems.

I turned and gripped his wrist. I never touched him willingly when not absolutely necessary, not since that disastrous night when I'd offered myself. He looked down at my hand and then back at my face, and I guessed he was aware of it too.

I didn't let go, gripping him tighter. "There's something wrong with me."

"What?"

"They're gone. I'm not…"

"What's gone?" he asked.

"My visions." I grabbed his other wrist. "Maybe everything."

He grabbed my arm once he realized the scope of the problem and urged me toward the bike. We were in front of the large metal door a minute later, and it seemed even slower now.

Finally, we weaved out the entrance and he pulled to a stop once we were a few miles away. I got off the bike as soon as he stopped, and circled around the area, trying to sort things out in my mind. First I couldn't feel the magic in the office, or barely, and now the visions. This had to be connected somehow. What was wrong with me?

He got off the bike and stood still, staring at my moving figure. "When was the last time you saw something?" he asked.

"I don't know. I've been with the same people for a while. There hasn't been anyone new to judge by." When I'd first gotten these unique insights into people's minds, I'd hated them. Ninety percent of the time they were traumatic, and I was thrust into the heart of a person's worst fear, trauma, and/or humiliation that they'd ever experienced.

I'd learned to live with them, though. Then I'd realized they were a gift. I'd relied on them so heavily for so long, and now they were gone. I could barely think past the possibility of it.

"Get back on the bike," he said.

"Where are we going?"

"To find out how deep this problem runs."

"Dark Walkers." Of course that would be his first concern. I didn't complain, as it was running in front of the pack of worries for me, too. It was going to be really hard to fight an enemy I couldn't see coming.

I didn't ask any more questions as I hopped on the bike after him. We took off again and didn't stop until we were parked outside a familiar hole. I remembered seeing this one on one of our longer trips. I couldn't decide whether to run inside or refuse to go in. Did I want it confirmed, or was this the time to jump on the denial ride? I got off the bike. I couldn't afford the luxury of denial.

I looked at the building, which was little more than a shack, and hesitated for a second before walking toward it. Dax, with a rare show of patience, waited while I took my time.

I felt his fingers wrap around mine and squeeze, then let go. Instead of it calming me, all I could think was Dax was trying to be reassuring. Had he ever done that before? I might really be fucked.

"You can do this," he said.

I was pretty sure he didn't have any such faith. He was probably just trying to pump up my courage. I knew he needed this almost as much as I did.

"Please stop being nice. You're freaking me out."

"Good. It's not my style anyway."

If I hadn't been so nervous, I would've laughed.

I took a deep breath and nodded, mostly to myself. I wasn't a wimp, and wouldn't become one now. I took the first step forward and marched into the hole, knowing Dax had my back.

I pushed the door open and scanned the few

patrons in the room, a couple of guys sitting at a table by the bar and a single man behind it. Clear so far, or so it appeared. Either there were no Dark Walkers or I was screwed.

I found a table in the corner, which would give me the best vantage point of the place, and settled in to wait. When the barkeep raised his head and looked over at us, I didn't wait for him to come to the table and called out an order for a double whiskey.

Dax cleared his throat, and I didn't need to see his expression. "I'm not a wimp. I just need whiskey today, so deal with it. It won't change anything."

He didn't say anything, and I pretended that there wouldn't be an expression on his face if I looked, which I wouldn't do. He was a glacier, and that was fine. Other people had things called nerves.

Every time the door pushed open, I hoped to see a Dark Walker. It was the first time in my life I'd wanted one of those around. As each person came and went, I almost thought I'd hug one if it would just show up.

I downed the whiskey when it came and resisted the urge to order another, for the first hour or so.

Four hours later, I turned to Dax and nodded toward the door. He stood without saying a word. He didn't look disappointed, but I couldn't help but feel he must be. I was, to the very core of my being. I'd lost my ability to spot my enemy. This was a disaster. How could I avoid them if I didn't even know who they were anymore? For the first time I understood why Dax valued this ability so much.

We made our way to the door. I gripped the handle and swung it open. That was when I saw him. The dark mist hovering all around his body as he walked toward the place. I looked away quickly, not wanting to show my hand, and I didn't actually have any real desire to hug him either, but I was still relieved.

I looked at Dax. "We're good. At least with this."

I saw understanding there. I also saw the tension that he'd hidden from me under his ice ease from his frame. He was as relieved as I was as we left the place.

CHAPTER 10

We didn't go straight to the farm after the hole, and pulled up to the dead tree after it was already dark. I got off the bike without asking what we'd stopped for. My hand went to the knife at my boot, my fingers feeling the well-worn wooden handle that felt so right in my palm.

"No. You need something harder." He reached to his hip and handed me his gun.

There would be no lucky shots with a gun. I wasn't good enough with it to leave any room to pretend that the magic had helped. I scanned the area for an impossible target and found it on a twig hanging low, about fifty feet away.

I closed my eyes, concentrating on the glow, the burn I needed to build in my chest. Try as I might to build it, the tinder would barely light. I felt like my magic was a match in a strong gust, doomed to extinguish before it could really take hold and burst into a flame. No matter how hard I concentrated, it snuffed out, like it couldn't get enough air or something was suffocating it. I opened my eyes and aimed, already knowing the outcome before I pulled the trigger.

The twig was still there.

I could feel Dax staring at me from where he'd moved back, ten or so feet away to give me space. I knew what he was thinking. I was thinking it too. My so-called magic seemed to be stalling. This was the time I should be stepping up, not falling down.

I closed my eyes again, trying to draw forth the burning glow. I didn't open them back up, and aimed without looking, anything to trick the magic into kicking back in and hoping it would force whatever was in me to wake up. I pulled the trigger again.

I opened my eyes to see that stupid twig still there.

"Fuck!" I screamed at the trees and into the air, to no one and everything. I couldn't seem to get the magic to take hold, no matter what I did. It was getting smothered.

A shudder ran through me, as I thought of the dream I'd had and the eerie coincidence of the timing. Could it have been something else that did this to me? What about what Tiffy had said about her friends? No, that was crazy. We'd been alone in the middle of the forest. No one had been there. It had been a dream.

Dax walked over and took the gun from my hand and holstered it before he said, "Let's go back. It's been a long day."

"That's it? You don't want to keep trying?" I asked, wondering if he'd feel the same if we'd still been waiting to see if I could spot Dark Walkers. We'd sat there for a lot longer and he hadn't suggested we leave once.

"I've been gone for more than a day. I want to check in."

"I guess it's okay because I can still do what you need."

He shrugged. "Yes, that's part of it. This isn't the end of the world. You have magic. It'll come back. Stay close to the house and don't leave the gates," he said, as if that fixed everything.

I shook my head. "You don't get it."

He rolled his eyes, and I could tell he thought I was kicking into dramatics and showing my age. How did you explain to someone who could become a beast what it felt like to be vulnerable? I'd been so close to being able to defend myself, not need anyone to back me up, and it was gone. There was nothing okay about that.

"You aren't any worse off now than you were last month. I'll keep you safe until we get it worked out."

"You are the one that doesn't get it. I can't be weak. I'm tired of being weak. So tired you can't possibly understand. How could you? You're"—I waved my hands at him in frustration—"you." We stood a few feet apart, but the differences, especially now if I'd lost my magic, were more like miles. "You're strong. You've been strong almost your whole life. You don't get it. I don't want to need anyone."

"Fine, but I'm heading to the house because there are people there who do need me," he said.

I watched him walk off and realized he couldn't understand this. I didn't care if he left me here alone. I didn't want someone to protect me. Needing someone to protect him was utterly alien to him. He thought I was being ridiculous, maybe even selfish, but he'd never been weak. He couldn't understand what that was like.

I turned back and stared at the tree, but knowing there was something else I needed to do. There was someone I had to talk to. It was a crazy long shot, but I had to find Tiffy. Even if there was the slightest chance "her friends" had something to do with this, I had to explore it.

I was almost to the gate when I heard a tinkling melody, like wind chimes hanging from a porch on a day with a gentle breeze.

I was surprised that there were people living over here. I'd thought that everyone that didn't live on the farm itself was to the south. I changed directions and took a couple of steps north, trying to pin down the location so I could hear them more clearly. The chiming picked up slightly, now sounding almost like a chorus, but it was still a strain to hear. I walked farther north, but as soon as I walked a step too many, it seemed like they were coming from the west. I circled the area, trying to find the source of the noise that sounded so similar to the noise I'd heard that night I'd awoken before we went to the Rock.

The chiming sound died. Maybe it was the wind passing an odd branch and causing the noise, or perhaps I was too tired and starting to lose my mind. I hadn't felt right all day.

I finished my walk to the house and was glad Dax wasn't there. I heard a humming Fudge, who I'd greet afterward, in the kitchen. I didn't want witnesses to the coming conversation, and I was hoping to find Tiffy alone. I did. Tiffy was curled up on Fudge's bed with a picture book in her lap.

"Tiffy, I need to talk with you." I sat down on the edge of the bed.

She smiled and placed the book beside her, giving me her full attention. "Yes?"

"Did your friends do something to me?"

"I don't know. Might have. I haven't spoken to them since the other day, so I don't know."

"Do you know what they might have done?"

"I'm not sure I'm allowed to tell you."

On to the next awkward question. "Tiffy, are your friends human?"

Her mouth scrunched to the side. "I don't think so, but I'm not sure. We don't discuss that either."

This wasn't going as well as I'd hoped. "If you see them, can you tell them I'd really appreciate a chance to speak to them?"

"Sure. I'll pass the message along." She picked her book back up, clearly finding that much more interesting than I was at the moment.

I got up but stopped at the door, "Tiffy, one last thing. Does anyone live over in that direction?" I asked, pointing north.

"Nope."

"Thanks."

I walked from the room realizing that I was so desperate to figure out what was wrong with me that I'd just asked a six-year-old to put in a good word with her invisible friends. I nearly reeked of my own desperation.

CHAPTER 11

I got up at the crack of dawn, without anyone making me, and ate jerky for breakfast, by choice, rather than waiting for Fudge's breakfast. I was in a hurry to get to the tree. I knew what the stakes were, that Dark Walkers would be coming for me. I refused to take a baby step back, let alone a giant leap into a pile of dung.

I'd stay out here all day if I had to. I'd brought enough jerky to get me through until dinner if needed, and would do this every single day until I forced the magic to come back.

My target before me, I didn't waste time greeting my assassin, and got right down to business. I closed my eyes and concentrated. I had to feel it, the burning. If I could feel it burn, I was getting it back.

Raising my arm, I visualized the knife flying from an impossible distance as I tried to stir the inner flame within me. I could feel it start, but it sputtered out quickly. I'd never noticed it in the beginning either. Maybe it didn't have to be there every time? I let the knife rip from my hand and did a small prayer like Fudge did, even looked upward while doing it. Just because the burn hadn't come when I'd thrown didn't mean the knife hadn't hit its target.

I opened my eyes and looked in between the assassin's carved ones, hoping to find my blade sticking out. It wasn't there. My eyes dropped lower to the forest floor and then higher on the bark. What the hell? Not even close?

Dax walked into the clearing, knelt down, and picked up my knife. "Looking for this?"

It had fallen wide—like eight feet wide. I wrung my hands together before I caught myself. What had just happened? I'd made that throw over and over again without thinking and I'd never missed. I'd always nailed it. It must have been a fluke. I couldn't be hitting the skids that bad.

"What are you doing?" Dax asked as he stood, tossing my knife and catching it.

"Were you following me?"

"No. Did I see you head this way and decide to come here? Yes."

I marched over to where Dax was standing and grabbed my knife from him before he could throw it again. I marched back to the spot I'd been and then went a few feet farther.

He moved clear of the tree without me asking, not that I would've. I was going to make this shot without a doubt. He wasn't in any jeopardy.

I lifted my hand with the knife in my grip and let it

fly.

It landed ten feet wide this time.

"So how's this working out for you?" Dax asked, in perfect deadpan. Sure, now he decided to get a sense of humor.

I ran two hands through my thick hair, pulling it back from my face as I tried to understand myself. "I don't know."

He grabbed the knife from the pile of leaves it lay upon and brought it back to me. "Decide you are going to do it and then do it."

I nodded, taking the knife again.

"Concentrate this time."

"Why are you here trying to help now?"

"Do you want my help or not?"

I couldn't answer because I didn't know myself. If he could help, yes. If he was going to end up being a bystander as I failed repeatedly, no. Too bad I didn't know which way it was going to go so I could answer him.

I closed my eyes, threw, and missed.

I did it again.

And again. Each throw, I became a little more desperate, and he got a little quieter until neither of us were speaking. I wasn't looking over at Dax, having my answer on whether I wanted him there as he watched my utter deterioration.

By my tenth miss, the silence was killing me, and I

glanced over to where he was, not knowing what I'd see there. Frustration? Anger that I couldn't seem to get my act together?

What I saw was so much worse than that. He looked like he… It was hard to even come to terms with the way he was looking at me, but it was suspiciously similar to the look I'd given Becca the last time I'd seen her.

"I don't need your pity. I'll get this."

"I know you will," he said. "But maybe you should take a break. You're tired and your arm isn't good enough to go this long."

Who was this man? Dax never wanted to give it a rest. He pushed. That's who he was. It meant one thing. He didn't think I could.

"I will get this, and I'm not tired." It was a lie. I'd woken up feeling exhausted, but I wasn't quitting. I wasn't a quitter.

He did the opposite of what I asked and leaned against the dead tree.

"Move!"

He did, but instead of moving away from the tree and out of my line of fire, he headed toward me. "Come back to the house. Give it a rest."

"I have to get this."

"You're not getting it today. There's something wrong and it's not getting fixed this way. You haven't even come close. We need to try something different. "

"I can't give up. I didn't get this far to just give up now."

"For tonight you can. I don't know what's wrong, but we'll figure it out."

I brought my closed fist to my mouth as I stared off at the trees. Dax was right. Whatever was off, it didn't seem to be righting itself.

"It'll kick back in. Magic doesn't go away. You have it or you don't. If you have it, you always have it."

"Do you know that for a fact? How do you know there isn't someone out there that lost it for good?" I asked, poking holes into his statement and hoping he'd be able to close them back up.

"I don't know, but it's what I believe."

I nodded, realizing the holes were still gaping.

Maybe everything he'd said was wrong. When he'd told me that day that I could be something special, I'd wanted to believe him. I'd stayed because of that.

The special wasn't shining through anymore, and I was starting to have some doubts about how much special I had in me. What if I was only ten percent special and he'd just noticed it on a good day? What if I didn't even have a whopping five percent? I didn't think that would make me almost invincible. By my guess, based on absolutely nothing but pure speculation, which of course made it accurate, almost invincible had to be closer to ninety percent special, at least. After all, we *were* talking invincible. People weren't walking around like that all willy-nilly.

I was so lost in my pity party, attended by just me in my morass of unspecialness, that I didn't see the threat coming. I didn't sense the attack until I heard a growl and a clawed hand was shoving me out of the way and into the bushes.

It was too late, though, as the group of Dark Walkers descended on us. Dax was human one second and then full beast, slashing through our attackers like they were papier-mâché as they swarmed. Blood was spraying as bodies fell—but there were a lot of them, and they kept coming. There had to be at least ten of them to our two—or our one, if you counted able bodies capable of defending themselves.

Hell if I wouldn't try, though. I couldn't let him fight this out alone. I climbed back to my feet and out of the bushes he'd shoved me into with a knife in my hand. I'd die beside him before I hid like a weakling.

I saw a Dark Walker coming at Dax's back and threw my knife. It landed right in his throat, like I'd aimed. Even with all the chaos going on, I couldn't help but realize I was throwing better then I should be. I'd used magic. I wouldn't have been able to make the shot otherwise.

That moment of shock cost me, though.

Hands wrapped around me, one across my midsection and the other around my neck. I kicked backward hard enough that I threw my attacker off balance. We went down together. I heard a nice *ummph* as I landed on top of a male, if size was any indication.

I wrenched free of his grasp while he was stunned, and turned on him. I didn't have a weapon in my hand, and the guy outweighed me by a lot—like, a tree trunk lot. I heard chaos behind me and knew I couldn't count on Dax, who had his hands full. I was going to have to fight this mammoth alone. This was not the day to come to terms with the fact you definitely weren't invincible.

I reached for the spare knife at my ankle, and it cost me leverage as he flipped me, gaining the top position. But I had a weapon in my hand again. I focused on his face. My chest felt like it was on fire as I eyed my target, and no matter how he tried to grab me, his hands couldn't seem to stop the knife in mine from reaching its target.

It was a beautiful shot, right through his eye socket. It would've been perfect if I hadn't gotten a little squeamish. Stupid me turned my head at the last second, as I tried to spit out the black shit that got in my mouth as the weight of his dead body drove the hilt of my knife into my temple.

* * *

"Come on, Dal, wake up."

I'd barely opened my eyes, and the first thing I

thought of was my knife repeatedly hitting its mark. "Dax, the magic came back when I was fighting." Then I realized I was pressed against his naked chest, practically on his lap.

"How do you feel?" he asked, his voice sounding rougher than normal. Red still glowed behind his irises.

"I'm fine. The guy fell on me after I killed him, is all." The splitting headache wasn't anything compared to the painful awkwardness I was feeling. I started to squirm off his lap before I gave him the impression I wanted to be there. I looked around and asked, "What happened to the rest of them?"

His arm behind my back still, he carried me over to a tree and rested my back against it. There were dead bodies everywhere.

"Oh. You happened to them."

"I'll be right back."

I nodded, forcing my eyes to not look down there as he stood. Then I looked anyway. I was a human after all.

Wow, okay then. That's what that looks like completely naked.

I pushed myself upward into a standing position, using the tree for leverage. It triggered a little fuzziness in my head, and I hoped some of the blood would drain from my face before he came back.

I should've been scared. More Dark Walkers knew where I was, but there was a silver lining. I could still see them, and I'd used my magic. I was at a disadvantage, but I wasn't totally helpless, either.

Dax came back, his clothes tattered and barely holding together.

"Come on, let's get back to the house. Can you walk?"

I pushed off the tree. I was a little wobbly, but stayed upright.

"I can do it," I said, while I calculated the distance.

He urged me forward but didn't touch me again until I almost tripped. His hand gripped my elbow but then let go of me right away, like he was trying to avoid touching me. It was for the best. I'd rather struggle along on my own, since he was throwing off that weird energy in droves, maybe the worst I'd ever felt from him.

When we got to the gate of the compound, Bookie happened to be nearby, and came over right away when he saw us approaching.

"What the hell happened?"

"Group of bandits," Dax said. "Take her into the house. I'm going to go find the doc."

* * *

"Doc say she's fine?" I heard Dax ask outside my door about an hour later.

"Yes. He checked her over after I did. A couple

bumps, that's it. Go see for yourself," Bookie told him.

"I've got other things to tend to. You stay with her."

I heard Dax's footsteps leave as Bookie walked in my room and shut the door behind him.

"You know he's telling everyone that same bandit story, but I'm not buying it."

I nodded. Bookie wouldn't.

He grabbed a wooden chair from the corner, dragged it over to the bed, and took a seat. "So what really happened?"

Dax had polished it into something completely different, and I should probably follow suit. But this was Bookie, and I hated lying to him.

"Was it those Dark Walkers?"

"Yeah, a bunch of them. He probably doesn't want to scare anyone, but there were—two of them," I said, catching myself at the last second. There would be no way to explain how we would've been able to fight off ten without outing Dax. Just because I trusted Bookie, it didn't mean I could make Dax.

"That's not good."

"I know."

"What does this mean?"

"I don't know."

CHAPTER 12

It was later than I normally got up, and I heard the knock at my door a minute before Fudge walked in with a plate heaped full of food. I didn't need to see it. I smelled all of my favorites: eggs, sausage, and, of course, the King of Breakfast, bacon.

I pushed back the covers and met her halfway across the room. "Fudge, what are you doing? You have too much to do in the mornings. You didn't need to bring me a plate. I'm fine."

"You had a rough day. It won't kill you to stay in bed."

I looked at the plate she was carrying, trying to think back and remember ever getting served in bed before. Not that I'd wanted her to, but I'd been in a lot worse shape than I was now. I'd been pulled out of a dirt pit and had a broken arm, and still gotten up and went downstairs to breakfast. Come to think of it, I'd never seen Fudge bring anyone breakfast.

I was fine. Fudge knew I was fine. She'd checked in on me last night. This place wasn't like the Cement Giant, where you could get a gratuitous kick in the teeth just for looking at a guard the wrong way, but it was pretty far from holding your hand and babying you, too. Something funny was going on here.

Fudge smelled suspicion on me like I smelled the offering of bacon on her. She smiled, knowing I was onto her. I smiled back, holding my tongue as I took the plate.

She left looking satisfied, but as soon as the door shut, I shoved a piece of bacon in my mouth and grabbed my clothes. I shoveled in a couple bites of eggs in between pulling up my pants and throwing on a shirt. I might have left her alone for the cost of bacon, but I hadn't made any silent agreements to not harass someone else.

The bedroom door opened and closed, and I knew I'd find Tiffy standing there. The kid didn't believe in knocking. She said it was a waste of the noise. That knocking on wood should be saved for more important reasons other than to announce oneself.

"Something funny is going on," she said.

"I agree. Any ideas?"

"No, but there's more people than normal lingering around outside, and Fudge is trying to buy me off with brownies in bed." She looked around, her mouth in a small moue, brownie crumbs still clinging to the corners as evidence that it had worked to some degree.

She walked over to my breakfast plate. "I see she's gotten to you as well."

I pulled on my boots quickly and tucked in the

knife. "Don't look at me like that when you have chocolate breath. I'm on it."

"Okay, I'll go back to handling my business," she said, and I guessed there must be some brownies left.

"Tiffy, did you talk to your friends for me?" I asked before she walked out the door.

I'd never seen a kid make the *uh oh* face like she just did. "I might need some time. When they extended the invitation to you and you didn't meet them, well, let's say it didn't make them happy."

I kneeled down to tie my boots and realized that I probably couldn't meet them because they didn't exist. The magic had come back when I needed it most. It was still in there. There weren't any mystery creatures blocking me. Whatever was wrong was something I must have been doing.

I watched her leave, telling myself she was just a lonely kid with invisible friends, and that was all.

* * *

There was a crowd formed around the back porch by the time I stepped outside a few minutes later. Even if I hadn't known by the numbers, I scanned the faces and realized it wasn't just the people who lived here on the compound mulling around but the people from the surrounding areas. What was going on?

I spotted Bookie standing along the back of the

crowd. Our eyes met and I saw the same question on his face. He didn't know what this was about either.

I weaved through people, most of which I saw every day, some of them still giving me a wide berth, even though no one had dropped dead from the Bloody Death since I'd been there. In instances like this, though, it came in handy. I let loose a few coughs to clear my way where it was tight, and then walked along the perimeter until I was standing beside Bookie.

"You don't know either?" I asked, confirming what I thought his expression had said.

"Nope. I'd heard the chatter this morning that Dax had some sort of announcement he was making, but no one seems to have any idea what it's about. What took you so long to get out here?"

I shrugged. "No one told me." Whatever this was, it probably had nothing to do with me. Or nothing dire. Dax probably wanted to let everyone know they should be on high alert for strangers or something.

Even with the events of yesterday, it couldn't possibly be anything about my situation. Dax had been agitated the last time I'd seen him, but if he'd come to some sort of decision on the next step, he would've talked to me. No. Dax wouldn't just spring something on me, out here with everyone else, without even giving me so much as a heads-up. We were past that point.

Weren't we? But then why would Fudge try and buy me off with a plate of bacon?

"You feeling okay?" Bookie asked.

I shoved my hands in my pockets to stop them from clenching. "Yeah, right as rain."

"Okay, because you really seem off. Is it because of the…"

I knew he meant the Dark Walkers showing up but didn't want to utter the name here. "No, not at all."

I wasn't lying. I was off, but for other reasons.

I didn't know how much Bookie was aware of magic, but I wasn't ready to give a course on it and then explain that mine had gone belly up, except for occasional life-threatening event. I couldn't explain it myself, let alone to him.

Plus, it was probably only a temporary problem. I wouldn't let it be a permanent issue, even if I had to set my chest on fire to fix it. Still, this was not the day for Dax to spring anything new on me.

The devil himself stepped out onto the porch just in time to head off the next question I saw forming in Bookie's mind.

Dax scanned the crowd. He always scanned his immediate area for threats, even here. It wasn't obvious unless you were watching for it. He might shut down his emotions handily, but he was always looking for the fight. That never turned off.

When his gaze passed over mine, there was something in it that sent a shiver through me. A coldness, like he was already gearing up for a fight and this one was with me.

Oh no. He wouldn't. Not like this.

He cleared his throat, and the few people who were whispering to themselves ceased. "I'll be leaving for a while with a select few others. While I'm gone, Lucy is in charge."

That was it. Two sentences in front of everyone to tell me we were leaving. Two sentences that sent my temper to boiling. Two fucking sentences he couldn't have told me before this, in private?

He didn't scan the crowd any longer, but let his gaze stop on me again. I knew this look well. It was his *I'm in charge and I've made a decision. Live with it.* I waited for details to follow, but he turned abruptly and walked back in the house, the squeaky door rebelling as well.

I certainly wasn't going to just live with it.

Bookie immediately turned and hit me with a stare of his own, so condemning I felt it before I turned.

"You weren't going to tell me?" His words were riddled with raw, open pain, as if I'd leave here and not say something to him.

"I would've told you if I knew." Dax couldn't be including me in the "few" without so much as a word to me privately. I had to be wrong.

"Good, because that would've been fucked up."

I patted Bookie's shoulder, using Tiffy's standby consolation because I was too dumbfounded to think of what else to do. I was starting to see the merit of the move.

"I'll be back. I'm going to go find out exactly what he's talking about."

Bookie reached out and grabbed my arm as I moved to leave. "You want me to come?"

"No. This is a conversation I need to have mano a mano."

I could tell Bookie didn't like that answer, but he'd respect me enough to not try and impose his wishes on me, unlike some others.

I made my way through the crowd that was breaking into smaller groups, all speculating on the news. They were whispering and shooting glances in my direction, surely accusing me of being the reason as they worked up their conspiracy theories.

Yeah, it was *me*. *I* was the problem. I wanted to question the whole lot of them and ask how long they'd lived there and for how many of those years had Dax looked like he was thirty? Oh no, *that* nobody talked about. That didn't raise any suspicions. Me, my secrets all laid bare for the world to see, I had to be the one hiding things. Not that I wasn't, but the hypocrisy of the situation was galling right now. I didn't care who looked at me or how. I was near shaking with anger, and it focused every ounce of my attention toward one man.

I skirted one group who were already circling Lucy

and buttering her up pathetically. The dirty looks Tank had been shooting at Lucy the other night now made sense. He'd been planning this for a while. Tank surely felt like he'd been passed over for a promotion. My guess was that Tank was getting dragged along with us.

It was a bit of a shock the whole place hadn't known this was coming as soon as Lucy did. Lucy couldn't keep two beans in her mouth. And I was the one who'd been avoiding her in the mornings, or she surely would've blabbed about it. That was what a peaceful breakfast had cost me.

I barely managed to keep my comments to myself as I passed another group, all staring at me, and walked in the house. Fudge was in the kitchen arguing with Tiffy, who had probably been listening from the upstairs bedroom.

"I'm staying," Tiffy said like she was digging in firmly, and that kid could dig like a groundhog in the garden.

"It's not optional for you," Fudge said, in her best authoritative tone.

"Why?" Tiffy asked, undaunted.

"Because I said so."

I narrowed my eyes at Fudge as I passed them in the kitchen.

Fudge narrowed her eyes back. "I saw you ate all your breakfast."

I kept walking, leaving the two of them. I knew

when I was outclassed. That woman could win an argument with the devil, and I had another battle to win.

CHAPTER 13

Dax was at the bottom of the stairs talking to the guy I knew was in charge of the perimeter guards. "Just remember, if they come, let them search for whatever they want." He paused for a second, and I knew it was because I'd stopped and was waiting at his back, like he could feel my angry stare nailing him. "They'll leave once they don't find it."

He turned and started walking up the stairs as if he didn't know I was there, as if it weren't glaringly obvious I wanted to talk to him. He was probably heading to his room or some other private place where he could avoid me. Like I'd make it that easy for him. My fingers wrapped around his arm just as he hit the top landing and locked on for the duration. He could either stop and listen to me or drag me along with him, but this talk was happening.

He stopped easy enough, and I dropped my hand, becoming overly aware of the heat his body threw off.

He looked at me as if he hadn't a clue as to what I wanted, nor did he have the time.

"Who's leaving?" I asked, spelling it out for him.

"We are."

"Why?"

He let out a long sigh and gave a condescending glare. "You know why."

Score one, Dax. I couldn't argue the whys of it. I wasn't ready for a fight with the Dark Walkers. If what he'd told the guard was accurate and they would leave this place alone without me, then it had to happen.

"When?"

"Tomorrow night," he said, and turned to finish the walk to his room. I followed on his heels but didn't reach for him. The door to his room was already starting to shut, but I shoved it roughly open and then closed it behind me for good measure.

I watched as he walked over to a chest of drawers and started pulling out items and laying them on his bed.

"Why? That's too soon. It's not good timing. I'm already running shoddily with my magic coming and going in spurts. Can't we give it another couple of weeks until I sort myself out?" He went back to the drawer, and I thought I saw him pause, as if I was getting through to him, but he didn't say anything. I needed to be here, in this house. Didn't he get that? How could I get better anywhere but here? "I can't leave here. Not yet."

"You don't have a choice. You aren't safe here, and I can't afford to let them take you." There was no give in his voice, and he was moving about the room again.

I was wrong. There was no budging him.

"And what if I won't go? I don't remember relinquishing control of my life to you."

He stopped moving and finally gave me his attention again. "You did the second you decided to stay. If you don't like the way I do things—"

"I know. I can leave," I said before he could. He didn't realize how many times I'd thought of doing that very thing recently before I'd reminded myself that I needed him. Damn, though, sometimes I wanted to just kick the shit out of him. Again, another reason I was stuck. He was the only one that might be able to teach me how to do that.

"Do you think they are the only ones out there?" His voice dropped into something just above a whisper. "There's more coming, and soon."

"So we run?"

"We fight on our terms, not theirs. That's how you win."

My knuckles landed on my hips as I watched him casually go about his business.

"I do have a choice."

"Really? And what would that be? You can't stay here."

So there it was. It was go with him or nothing.

"Go pack," he said, before I was forced into making a choice I didn't want.

I walked out of his room, slamming the door. It was petty, but I needed whatever I could get right now. It was either that or strangle him. He was stupid, arrogant, and to top it off, he grew fur. He had no redeeming qualities whatsoever, but I still needed him.

Not to mention that it seemed like whenever he turned into the beast around me, the next time I'd see him he had another layer of ice packed on his glacier.

Fudge was stirring a huge bowl of chocolaty goodness when I found her downstairs, and Tiffy was long gone. It was Fudge's second batch in under a month. I guessed I wasn't the only one unhappy with the plans.

I walked past the stool and hopped up onto the counter beside the bowl.

"Why's he such a dick?" I didn't expand on who the dick was. She was smart enough to know exactly who I meant. After all, she'd tried to stall me from witnessing his dick move this morning.

She'd been right. If I hadn't been there, he would've been forced to tell me one on one. I should've stayed in the bedroom. Would that have been so friggin' difficult? Fudge was right about almost everything. I should probably start listening to her hints. I wouldn't be nearly as annoyed right now.

She stopped stirring to grab a spoon and load it up for me. "Here," she said, handing over the chocolate.

I took it without argument. After all, I wasn't mad

at her, and it must be a sin somewhere to turn down Fudge's fudge.

She went back to stirring. "It has to happen."

"I'm not mad about the leaving part. I understand that. It's everything else he does that's irritating me. Why can't he sit us down and discuss this? Why blurt out his orders?"

"You would've been fine with it then? Is that what you're telling me? You were going to be mad no matter how you found out," she said, waving a spoon covered in fudge at me. "Whether you realize it or not, you are the main reason he's doing this."

"You're making excuses for his jackass behavior."

She rested her spoon on the side of her bowl to give me her full attention. "Then why did you ask me?"

"Because you've known this particular jackass longer. Your guess is better than mine. I didn't ask him to do this."

"That has no bearing in his mind. You knew this was coming. You knew when he said there'd been strangers spotted around the area, and you knew when you visited the Rock. Did you really need it spelled out?"

I hated when someone besides me was right.

"I don't want to go." I looked down at my finished spoon.

Fudge handed me another loaded one. "It's a nice place and it won't be forever."

136

A nice place for normal people to be with other normal people. If I was a normal person, then she might be right.

"It'll be okay. We'll come back."

Hearing her say *we* came as a surprise. Dax was making her leave, too? And how could she be so sure we'd come back? I wasn't so naive to think we would. I was more inclined to believe I'd never see this place again. I wouldn't tell Fudge that. What if she really did think we'd come back? If it was painful for me to leave here, I couldn't imagine what it would be like for her.

"So, you're going too?" I asked.

"I'm an old lady, Dal. I'm too tired for these adventures, but yes, I'll be going. He wants Tiffy to go, and I can't let her go alone."

"Why does he want Tiffy to go?"

"I think he's afraid that if those things show up here, they might consider her interesting if there's no one else to distract them. That's my understanding, anyway. You'd have to ask him to be sure."

I guessed it was going to be a while until I got my answers, because I wouldn't be asking him anything right now.

"Do you know who else is going?"

"I think Tank as well, so the five of us."

"Maybe six," I said. I couldn't exclude Bookie. It would kill him, and he was my bestie. I had to tell him.

"Now you aren't planning on dragging Bookie into

all this mess, are you?" Fudge asked, looking like she wished she could take back the new spoon of fudge.

"He's my friend. If I don't include him, he'll feel hurt." I shoved what was left of the fudge in my mouth to make sure she couldn't take it back.

"But is it for the best to bring him?"

"Unlike some dictators, I believe in letting people make their own choices in this world. One of the worst things you can do to someone is steal control of their life," I said, and hopped down from the counter.

"Things aren't always so black and white, Dal."

"I'm not living in a grey world and I'm not compromising my beliefs, no matter what." I stole another scoop of fudge before I darted out.

I headed straight for the barn. If Bookie was bothered by anything, that was always my starting point when looking for him.

"You're okay, girl," I heard him saying to the horse as I let myself in and leaned against the stall wall.

"Well? What's the deal?" he asked as he looked over at me.

"You have any interest in going for a trip?"

He straightened, giving me his full attention. "Where we going?"

"I think the Rock, but I'm not a hundred percent."

He nodded like he was putting the pieces together. "Dax know I'm coming?"

"Not yet," I said, followed by a little laugh.

"Sounds good. Count me in," he said, enjoying the coming surprise as well.

Everything about Bookie was easy, so easy I wondered sometimes if maybe I was supposed to be with him. If he could just make my heart race that way Dax did, it would be a piece of cake to forget all my worries and be with him. I'd pretend I was a normal girl and he was my normal guy.

Until the impending doom came, that was. That damn impending doom was a real downer.

But it did make me think about what Fudge said.

"Bookie, you know why we have to leave?"

"Yes."

"Being around me…it's not safe." I felt like half of my friendship with Bookie had been spent putting him in harm's way, and the other half was warning him that harm was coming.

"Are we going to have the whole 'I could die' discussion again?" He groaned and flopped himself against the stall door like he was already exhausted from the mention.

"We were until you said it like that."

"So I thwarted it? Good. Total waste of time anyway." He straightened back up, all perk. "When do we leave?"

"Late tomorrow night."

"I'll be there."

CHAPTER 14

The canvas bag I'd gotten from Fudge was barely
filled. I was glad I didn't have much to pack. I didn't
want to leave, and everything I put in it made my soul
hurt. But those were the orders Dax had handed down,
the delivery still grating raw on the nerves.

My hand ran across the soft coverlet on the bed,
and I no longer had any delusions of finding a place
better than this. There was nothing more perfect than
perfection.

This might be the last few minutes I had here, ever.
Dax had left a while ago with no explanation but said
he'd be back in a few hours, which meant we'd be
leaving soon and traveling at night.

It made sense if Dark Walkers were on our trail.
No one liked to travel at night because of the beasts,
which tended to be more active after dark. I didn't
know if that included the Dark Walkers, but it was
worth the extra precaution.

The dark wasn't a problem for us. Fudge and Tiffy
had said nothing about our night travel plans. Tank
would go along with whatever Dax told him. Bookie
had expressed a concern to me, but I'd shrugged off the

question. It wasn't my secret to tell.

When I heard people stirring downstairs, I knew I was running out of time. I threw the bag on my shoulder and took a last look around the room, telling myself I'd be back.

Fudge, Tiffy, and Bookie were all waiting in the living room when I got downstairs. Bookie was resting an arm on the mantel and Tiffy was sitting next to Fudge on the couch calmly. I dropped my bag by the door with the others and walked over to the two of them.

"What's wrong with this picture?" I asked. If Tiffy was a cooperative type of girl then this would've been normal, but she wasn't, and this screamed all wrong.

Fudge immediately shot me the big-eyed owl look.

"Me saying something isn't going to set her off," I said. Tiffy either blew her stack or didn't. Went or not. No one controlled that kid. I was almost frightened of what she'd be like as an adult.

"My friends will be meeting me at the new location," Tiffy explained. "They know how to get everywhere."

I knew where this new location was, but how did she know? Fudge must have told her.

I was about to ask her and then I reminded myself that these friends didn't exist. They. Did. Not. Exist. If I kept repeating that, maybe I would believe it like everyone else. I sat quietly down beside her on the couch and didn't say anything. I didn't ask if she'd talked to them about me either.

"Not yet, but I'm working on it," Tiffy said beside me.

Was she talking about asking her friends to talk to me? It didn't matter. They had nothing to do with my problems. I wasn't going to look at her. I wasn't going to ask.

I looked, damn it.

She smiled and nodded. I sighed, feeling like I was friggin' crazy.

Tank came up from his basement dwelling, threw his bag next to the door, and realized that there was one too many piled up there. He took in Bookie's presence and let out a low groan, but didn't say anything. Although I thought I might have seen the words *fucking kids* mouthed, I wasn't a proficient enough lip reader to swear to it.

The front door opened and Dax sucked up all the space immediately. His eyes shot to Bookie and then the additional bag, then they landed on me.

He didn't say anything, but he didn't need to. He pointed to the kitchen and then left the living room. I got up and followed him, knowing an argument was on its way. I'd expected it since the moment Bookie had said he'd come.

I found I wasn't averse to arguing. It was freeing, in a way. I'd never been allowed to argue before, and that was way worse.

Bookie started walking toward the kitchen behind me, and I had to stop him. Arguing was one thing, but I wasn't in the mood to referee. I shook my head, giving him the signal I didn't need him to back me up. He nodded and took a step to follow.

"If I need you, I'll holler," I whispered to Bookie, and made eyes toward the fireplace, indicating that was where he should stay.

Bookie sighed and took another step. Dax, who was almost in the kitchen already and, I'd hoped, unaware, said, "She *said* she'd holler."

How had he heard that? Damn beast ears, was how. Didn't that stuff go away? Shift back or something? Were they still beast ears buried in his head even when they looked human?

I laid a hand on Bookie's arm. "I've got this."

"I don't like anyone fighting my battles."

"You don't get it. This isn't your battle."

I remained where I was until he finally dropped his head and went back to the fireplace so that I could go on into the kitchen.

Dax was waiting just inside the entrance looking like he was carved from stone. I didn't care. Rock climbing had always sounded like fun.

"Why can't you ever act normal?" he said the second I stepped in the room.

"What do you mean? I act normal all the time."

143

"No, you don't."

The light bulb took a second, but once it clicked on it really lit the place up. "Oh, wait, I know what you're trying to say now. You mean obey your every command 'act normal,' like all the other snoozers around here."

"Exactly."

I propped a hip against the counter. "Yeah, that's not my strong suit."

I could see the thought forming like I could read his mind, that I'd done it well enough in the Cement Giant.

"You did it well enough in the Cement Giant," he said.

I hated how I was only ever right about his thoughts when they were the irritating ones. So he was going to go there, to that place. I guess I'd thrown the first punch by springing Bookie on him. But Dax had sprung the trip on me. What did I do before that? It was getting hard to think back through all the jabs. "You know I hate talking about that place, but if you must know, it was different. I knew they would kill me."

"And?" he said.

"*And* you need me." Being needed had its perks.

"Why is he here with a bag packed and his bike outside?"

"He's coming with us."

"By whose invitation?"

"Mine."

"And you don't think you should clear that with me?"

"You don't think it might be a good idea to have someone medically trained with us?" I asked, figuring I'd take the road of diplomacy first. The high road, as some might call it.

He started shaking his head. "No. I don't need another person to take care of."

"That's fine, because Bookie and I will take care of each other." This didn't feel like the high road anymore. It was amazing how quickly you could detour. That high road needed bigger lanes or something.

"Why? Are you two a team or something?"

The tone was pure snideness.

"And what if we were? What's so bad about being a team player?"

"He's a kid, and I don't need another person to worry about."

"He's my age."

"Exactly."

"I'm not telling him he can't go."

"Then I will."

"He was yours first. You had him living here. Why do you have such a problem with him now?"

"I don't have a problem with him. I have a problem with you bringing him along. He's safer here."

"I don't make people's choices for them."

He stiffened, and I realized he was about to get into the valley right with me. "If you don't like the way it is here, you can leave."

"Maybe I will."

The tension had finally built until we were standing here, and I wasn't sure one of us would bend. So far, I'd done all the bending. I didn't have any give left in my spine. I wasn't sure if Dax was even capable of bending, as I'd yet to see any give.

Not bending didn't leave me with too many options, or none that I liked. I mentally tested my spine to see if I could give one more inch before it broke, but his high-handedness certainly didn't help matters.

There we stood, the two of us ramrod straight, seeing who would win.

"You know, the kid is medically trained," said Tank, who'd snuck up on us, or maybe just me, and was standing in the kitchen door. "It's not the worst idea to bring him along."

Dax looked over at Tank and somehow became human again. "You two want him? You two take care of him. This isn't on me."

"Fine," I said as Dax walked out of the kitchen.

Tank stepped over to the counter and grabbed an apple.

"Why is it that you say a few words and he agrees, when I argue and get nothing?" I asked while I watched him take a massive bite.

He chewed, seeming to give the question consideration. "You don't know how to handle him."

"I said basically the same thing you did right before you walked in."

He laughed. "Maybe it's just you, then," he said, smirking as he walked back into the living room.

I grabbed an apple to shove in my bag, and walked out of the kitchen. Fudge, Tiffy, and Bookie were waiting, all with a bit of apprehension as Dax was over by the door.

Dax looked down at the bags and finally said, "Let's go." He walked outside, leaving the door open for us to follow him.

Bookie looked at me and I gave him a nod. For better or worse, he was in it now.

Our happy little group headed out. Dax took the lead as Fudge and Tiffy rode on horseback together in the center. I was behind Bookie on his bike, and Tank took up the rear.

As the bikes revved up and one by one headed toward the gate, I turned around to get a final look at the farmhouse that had become my home. I hoped it wouldn't be the last time I saw it.

CHAPTER 15

We traveled a lot slower to the Rock this time with Fudge and Tiffy on horseback. Fudge refused to ride mechanical devices or make the horse move at more than a rolling trot, saying it made her old bones jostle too much. Then with the constant breaks to care for the horse, it was a long haul. The sun had lit the sky and set again when we stopped for the evening, and it was likely to take three times as long to get there as it took me and Dax last time.

Tiffy was sitting next to me on the log, which was close enough to catch some of the heat the fire was throwing off. Bookie was tending to the horse and Fudge was sorting through her bags.

"Ow! Damn bugs!" I slapped the back of my head, trying to thwart the tiny critter that had just attacked my scalp. I hated these strange bugs. "Am I the only one who's getting bit?" I asked as I looked around, and no one else was cursing and swatting at invisible insects.

"Nothing's biting me," Bookie offered. Fudge shook her head. Tank and Dax ignored me as they stood at the edge of the camp and talked. Tank's eyes were rolling like marbles downhill every time he looked at

Fudge's horse, and I knew he was complaining about the pace.

Tiffy laid a hand on my shoulder. "They aren't bugs," she whispered.

"What do you mean? What is it?"

"It's my friends."

Great. Tiffy's invisible friends, the ones I'd asked for a meeting with, were pulling my hair. "Could you ask them to stop?" It was a long shot and all, but I was willing to try anything.

"They probably won't listen. They like your hair."

I looked around, trying to catch sight of one flying by my head. As crazy as it all sounded, as little proof as I had, my gut was telling me there was something to her friends. I'd lived a lot of years being told the Dark Walkers didn't exist and I knew they did. Why should I listen to anyone say Tiffy's friends didn't? I looked around, debating on how crazy I might seem if I tried to speak to one now when I couldn't see a thing.

"So you've talked to them?" I asked, keeping my voice low enough that hopefully even beast ears couldn't hear, as I wasn't ready to totally blow my reputation.

"They're still debating what to do with you," she said as she dragged a stick through the dirt by her feet, making circles.

"I thought they wanted to speak to me?" I asked.

"They think you're S.P.I.T.T. now."

149

"They think I'm spit?"

"Not like saliva. Suspicious Person In Their Territory."

"Ow!" At least two hairs got ripped out just as Tiffy finished speaking. "There's nothing suspicious about me," I said, a bit louder in case one of them was listening, as I rubbed the back of my head, trying to determine if I was developing a bald spot back there.

Bookie glanced over but tried to pretend he wasn't looking. It was almost as bad as when he'd seen the book with the half-naked guy on it. I looked around; no one else was paying attention to us, and Dax was gone.

"Sorry, that last one was my fault."

"You pulled my hair?" I asked.

"No, but they get mad when I win." She pointed at her feet and I saw three circles running a diagonal. With a few Xs spread out.

I leaned back and looked around the area again.

"Hairy's throwing off some serious waves lately," Tiffy said, jumping us into the next weird subject.

I swear, someone needed to make up a decoder for this kid. "Waves?"

She leaned in closer and whispered, "Magic."

Maybe not so weird. I'd been feeling something too, and had wondered if it wasn't out of the norm.

"Only people like us will notice."

"You mean people with magic?"

"Yeah. There are some humans that are sensitive to

things, but that's not usually enough to pick up on actual levels," she explained. "I think it's you."

"Me? Why would it be me?"

"I think Hairy likes you."

That was when I knew I had to call it quits on this conversation, at least for tonight. I stood and grabbed the blanket from my bag, shook it out, and then settled the rest of my stuff into a makeshift pillow.

Dax walked into camp a couple minutes later. He hadn't announced it, but I knew he'd done a check of the perimeter. I glanced over at him, knowing the area was safe. Still, as I settled down on my hard bed, I transferred the knife at my hip to my hand and pulled the edge of the blanket over me.

Dax threw down a blanket only a couple of feet from mine on the opposite side of the fire, and I realized this was one major reason I didn't leave. Even when he was the biggest dick, when the shit hit the fan, the guy had my back.

There was a lot that could be overlooked in the name of loyalty. When someone was willing to put themselves in between you and danger, their rough edges seemed a lot smoother.

It was four in the morning when I awoke, and this time it wasn't to an imaginary truckload of cement. I looked around, wondering what had brought me awake, and I saw Dax sitting upright. He'd sensed something too. He looked at me, then Tiffy, who had somehow nestled in beside me without waking me, and he didn't have to say anything else. I nodded and scanned our group. Everyone else was still asleep. I looked back to Dax but only saw his retreat as he disappeared into the woods.

My heart thudded loudly in my chest as I realized how wrong it felt to simply lie here, waiting, but I didn't want to throw off any alarms to whoever, or whatever, Dax and I had sensed. I'd understood the signal Dax had given me. Take care of them because the beast would be off hunting tonight.

I lay back down as if everything were fine and tugged Tiffy closer to me, while my other hand clenched the knife that was under the makeshift pillow.

Tiffy stirred beside me, and I knew she was awake before she spoke. "Don't worry. He'll get them. If not, my friends will."

She didn't say anything else, and I heard her breathing even out as she fell back to sleep. She was so trusting that she'd be okay, that no harm would get to her. I lay awake, my hand clenched tightly on the knife, listening to every leaf rustle.

Dax didn't come back for almost an hour, and when he did, his skin was flushed and his hair was wet, like maybe he'd had to stop by a stream on the way back. His chest rose and fell, as if he'd just exerted himself.

My eyes met his and there was a subtle nod of his

head. The threat had been taken care of, whatever it was. I wouldn't ask for details now. If it had been someone he suspected to be from Newco, he would've gotten us all up and moving, in case there were reinforcements nearby. Probably just a band of bandits. We were safe. That was all that mattered.

I expected him to go back to his makeshift bed and if not sleep, at least feign it until the sun rose. He remained standing across the clearing, a rawness to him that I'd learned to recognize as the remnants of the beast. I wasn't sure what becoming the beast did to him exactly, but the aftereffects seemed to strip away his walls.

His eyes shot to where he'd made his bed close to mine and then back to me again. He didn't say anything, and disappeared back into the forest, probably to patrol the perimeter of our camp.

No matter how I told myself the threat was neutralized, sleep was lost to me after that. There could only be so much adrenaline pumped into the machine before the switch was turned on. I closed my eyes, and with nothing else to do, I tried to feel the burn of magic inside of myself. Like all times before, it fluttered out quickly.

I had to figure this out, and it needed to be soon. Lying here waiting for someone else to protect me wasn't going to cut it. When I'd gotten out of the Cement Giant, I'd thought I'd hit the ground running.

Turned out I was moving along at more of a crawl, but damn if I wouldn't find my stride.

I lay there beside Tiffy as the sun started rising, my thoughts wandering back to who Dax had found prowling around our camp. Would he know if they'd been Dark Walkers? There were all sorts of bandits that roamed the area, but not that many had the nerve to go out at night.

The stress of having Tiffy lying beside me, just a little girl, exposed to the threat I carried every day, made me wonder about the choices I'd made. Fudge, way past her prime, should be lying in a toasty bed in her room right now, not on the hard, cold ground. Had I made a mistake staying at the farm? Had I been selfish? When Dax had told me I could leave at any time, I'd always thought he said it to force me in line. Maybe he'd rethought his offer and really wanted to force me out?

What if I took them all down with me? Tiffy and Fudge were here because of Dax. If Bookie got hurt, that one was all on me. I should've listened to Fudge and not invited him along.

I heard Fudge, always one of the earliest risers, starting to move around, and I knew I didn't have to feign sleep anymore. I nearly jumped up, looking for any distraction.

We were all up getting ready to go soon as I watched Bookie out of the corner of my eye, my thoughts of the night before weighing on me.

Bookie wasn't like me, wasn't as resilient, but it was too late to send him back. He was on this journey, wherever it led, until I could figure out something else. The only solace I had was knowing exactly where we were going, and as long as we got there, Bookie would be even safer than at the farm. But I had to start putting some distance between us, because this had to be the end of the line for him. The road I was headed down wasn't leading toward pretty white fences and happy endings.

I wasn't the only somber one that morning. We all moved around in a different sort of state. No one spoke much as we all ate some jerky and packed up. Another day was here, and by that night, we'd be even farther from the farm than we were now.

I got on the bike with Bookie, and held on a little tighter than I normally did. I knew I'd have to let him go, but not yet.

I looked up at the sky while we took off. The sun was shining bright. It was going to be a beautiful day back at the farm.

* * *

We pulled up to the Rock just as it was getting dark. Dax had seen trouble coming from a long way off, and I knew arrangements had been made for us to come here. Maybe oil or something else had changed hands. Still, waiting there for the great metal door to creak open, taking just as long as I remembered it from the first time, I felt a lot like a pauper coming to a place I'd rather not be for a handout.

No one else seemed to have trepidations. If they did, they hid them really well. I tugged on the gloves I was wearing, the ones that covered the scar that was no longer in a P shape, but still there.

The door finally creaked open wide enough for us to pass, and Dax rode through, followed by the rest of us. Dax pointed toward the right and made his way down a small, quiet street. I caught glimpses of candles and fireplaces through the windows as we made our way. Every other house or so, I would see someone peeking out to get a glimpse of who was entering their little community.

Dax stopped his bike on a shared driveway between two small ranch houses, and Tank pulled in behind him. Bookie parked ours about five feet away. Dax got off his bike and started laying out the orders before Bookie had finished helping Fudge off her horse.

"Fudge, Bookie, and Tiffy, you're in that house. Dal, Tank, you're with me," he said, pointing to the blue one on the right. "Bookie, you know where the stalls are."

"I'll take care of her," Bookie said, stopping to pat the mare before he got Fudge's and Tiffy's bags off the horse.

Dax tossed his bag toward the door of where we'd be staying and then turned to leave, stopped suddenly, and said, "I'll be back in an hour," then walked off, taking Tank with him.

I wasn't stupid enough to think he'd all of a sudden decided he needed to let me in on his schedule. He was giving me a curfew.

I giggled a little as I stopped myself from telling him, *Good luck with that, buddy*. Why bother alerting him? It was much easier to simply do as I pleased.

"You good?" Bookie asked.

"I'm good. See you in the morning," I said, and watched him walk the horse away.

I turned around to take a really good look at the place, viewing it as someone who'd be living here indefinitely. The houses were charming, the town center as quaint and attractive as it had been the first time I'd been here, but all I could focus on were the walls that stood beyond, remember the metal door blocking the entrance. Back at the farm, there had been a fence, but the place always felt wide open. The walls here reminded me of another place. This was going to be a long stay, even if it were only a couple of days, which I doubted.

As much as I wanted to wander the neighborhood for exactly an hour and ten minutes, I grabbed my bag, deciding to cut my losses and grab some sleep before the night turned for the worse. I was too tired to bother spiting Dax, just to let him know he wasn't my boss. I had to stick to my personal improvement list of pros and cons. Do what was best for me, and that included not chopping off my nose when I wanted nothing more than to sleep.

I walked into the small ranch house that had a living room and kitchen off to the side. It wasn't a bad-looking little place to call home, if one were so inclined. Everything was nice in a useful, utilitarian type of way. I told myself it wasn't fair to compare it to the farmhouse, with its curtains, braided rugs, and vases of flowers. My biggest problem with the place was that I'd already found somewhere to call home, and it was miles away.

There were three bedrooms off a small hallway that all looked nearly identical. I grabbed one, collapsed on the bed, and decided to call it a day.

Sleep. Sometimes I liked it more than food.

CHAPTER 16

I hit the rocky part of the path that circled the Rock's lake for the third time before I came to terms with the fact that no matter how many laps I walked around, it wasn't going to rid me of my claustrophobia. All I saw in this place were the walls. The walls peeked out in between the houses, over a low roof or in between a tree. Even the outlet to the lake was walled off above where the water flowed. I'd spent too much time inside walls to willingly lock myself behind more.

This wasn't forever. I wouldn't let it be. I took some deep breaths like I'd read I should in a self-help book on meditation I'd found at the library with Bookie. I needed to train my brain to think positively. It wasn't a bad place. I needed to forget about the walls and focus on the pluses. Positive attitude and all. That was what I needed.

I pretended I didn't see the metal door in the distance and focused my eyes on the cluster of houses all nestled together. I just couldn't look up, or to the side, or too far back the other way. Or at Bookie, who was rushing to catch up to me because he didn't look so charming at the moment either.

There was a really smart person named Mehrabian who lived during the Glory Years who had declared that the majority of communication was nonverbal. Bookie was currently proving Mehrabian's theory. His brow conveyed worry and his pace was too fast for something not to be wrong. In return, I picked up my pace as my entire body came alert, mimicking his.

I scanned past him, to where the main community was again, this time looking at the people and not the structures. They were walking around leisurely; some kids on the other side of the lake were trying to skip stones—I think. It didn't look to be going so well. The gate was closed. So it wasn't a community problem, but something more personal to our core group.

The second Bookie got within earshot, he blurted it out, "Have you seen Tiffy? Fudge hasn't seen her in a while and is getting worried."

The tension that had been building in me turned into imaginary fingers and gripped my chest while my own hands felt numb. Bookie wasn't an alarmist. If there was anyone whose glass was half full, it was Bookie's.

"No, not recently." We didn't even know what was wrong yet and I was cursing myself for coming here. I'd known this place was a bad idea. Tiffy was already lost.

"When did you see her last?" he asked.

I looked up at the sun sitting low on the horizon,

160

telling me it had to be close to three in the afternoon. "This morning, when Fudge was making breakfast."

His face lost what was left of its color just as I could feel the blood drain in mine.

"Where do we look?" It wasn't so much a question for him but my own declaration of desperation. We hadn't been here long enough to establish where she'd go.

The place wasn't that big. Between the two of us, we should be able to make short work of it. "I'll take the west side. You take the east." He nodded and took off in the opposite direction.

I asked every person I came in contact with, regardless of whether they wanted to speak to me or not. Most looked down at my gloved hands with suspicion and took a couple of steps back as I approached. I didn't care, and took a couple of steps forward until I got my answer. I scanned their faces and realized this would've been a great time to be able to read a person.

I'd scoured the west side twice when I saw Bookie walking over.

"Nothing?" I asked.

"No," he said.

There was a holler from behind the steel gate, and both of us watched as it opened. Dax had been gone since morning, but he never would've taken Tiffy without telling Fudge. Still, my lungs ceased to work as

I hoped to see Tiffy walk through beside him, or maybe alone with some crazy story about how she was out visiting her friends.

Dax walked through beside Rocky, but no Tiffy. Bookie and I went over to them immediately, and drew a few more looks from people milling about.

"Have you seen Tiffy since this morning?" I asked Dax, not caring what anyone heard or if I sounded as frantic as I felt.

He turned and gave me his full attention for a change. "No."

"We can't find her. She's not with Fudge, either. Bookie and I can't find her."

"You sure she didn't—"

"Fudge told her she wasn't allowed outside the gates and came down on her pretty hard about it. I heard her this morning. Even if she threw caution to the wind, Tiffy wouldn't have been gone this long."

Rocky, who'd been listening this entire time, immediately turned to the two guards at the gate. "Raise the alert. Get every able body to comb through every house and corner of this place."

Within fifteen minutes, every person in the community was looking for Tiffy. After an hour, search parties had been formed and branched outside the walls and into the surrounding forest. Dax headed up one with me and a few locals. Tank led another. Bookie went with Rocky's group.

But we were running out of time. We weren't that many miles away from the walls when one in our group pointed out that we were running out of daylight. The consensus was to turn around until tomorrow. Only the toughest of Rocky's men would leave the walls of the Rock after nightfall.

I'd known we'd get limited help before we even set out, and I held back the scream of frustration. I watched them prepare to turn around. They were afraid of the beasts. I shouldn't blame them for not being willing to risk their lives. I shouldn't, but that didn't mean I didn't. Emotions rarely listened to logic, mine included.

"Head back with them," Dax said as he came to stand beside me, watching as the rest of our group prepared to return to the Rock.

The group was getting fidgety, and I knew the only reason they hadn't left yet was because of Dax.

"No. I don't want to stop looking. I know you're not going to. Tell them it's okay to leave us."

"You won't be able to keep up with me. You'll only slow me down." In other words, he was going to switch to the beast once the forest had been cleared of people.

It took me a minute to force the emotions down, but logic won out and I nodded. I wanted to keep going, but not at the cost of Tiffy.

"What are you going to tell them?" I asked, looking at the already suspicious group.

"Nothing. Let them think what they want. Try and keep Fudge calm."

"Sure," I said, but I didn't think it would actually work. I couldn't keep myself calm, not on the inside.

I walked back to the community, lagging a good ten feet behind the group and dragging my feet the whole way. I looked at every bush, tree, and boulder, hoping somehow I'd spot her on my way back.

Fudge was settled on the couch by the fireplace when I got back. Bookie had beaten me to their house and was in the kitchen making her tea or something of the sort.

I sat beside Fudge on the couch and found myself taking her hand and patting it, just like Tiffy would do. "Fudge, Tiffy is going to be okay. She's a tough girl."

Fudge only shook her head and didn't speak. I didn't have the stomach for lying. I didn't know anything. None of us did. Tiffy was six years old. How tough could she really be?

Bookie came and sat on the other side of her, handing her a cup of tea, sitting there useless with us. This was going to be a long night.

CHAPTER 17

Dax hadn't come back and Fudge was still on the couch when the morning came, although she'd finally drifted off around three or so. Tank had been in and out, charting maps of the area and trying to think of the best routes and locations for the search parties to go as soon as the sun came up.

Bookie was analyzing the list of people that should go in each group, who could track and what assets they had. I was on the floor, my back against the arm of the sofa, appearing to do nothing, while in truth I was trying to get my magic up and running so I could be more useful. I only took the occasional break to imagine the worst, becoming alarmingly close to what someone might call a pessimist.

I was on a pessimism break when Dax walked in the house. Fudge immediately sprang into a sitting position, which showed she hadn't been sleeping at all. I heard a small sound escape her lips that I knew was the unintended consequence of him walking in alone. We didn't need to ask, but he shook his head anyway. Our best hope of finding her, a man/beast with the nose of a bloodhound and eyes of a hawk, had come up empty.

Tank came in seconds later, having surely seen Dax come back.

"Any leads?" Tank asked, before he shut the door.

"No."

"Dax." It was Rocky's voice, and we all turned to see him now in the doorway, a piece of leather gripped in his hand.

Rocky looked at Dax and then around the room.

I wasn't sure if anyone else realized, but Rocky was asking Dax if it was okay to speak freely. I must have missed a signal to go ahead, because Rocky held the hide in his hand out to Dax.

"This was tied around a rock. It must have been thrown over the wall yesterday. The gate guard said he'd noticed it last night but hadn't thought anything of it. When he got off this morning, he walked past it again and stopped to check it out."

Dax nodded as he looked at the sheet. When he didn't speak quickly enough for my liking, I jumped to my feet and read it over his arm.

"'Give us the Plaguer and we'll give you back the little girl. Leave your response in the stump,'" I read aloud, knowing Bookie, Fudge, and Tank were waiting to hear.

There was no signature but a weird mark at the bottom that looked like poorly drawn crossbones.

"What is this? Who left this?" I asked, looking to

166

see if any of them recognized the symbol.

Dax spoke as the rest of them remained quiet: "Skinners."

"Skinners?"

Fudge gasped. I turned just in time to see the little hope she'd been clinging to drain from her. Her hand went over her mouth and she scrambled from the room without saying anything.

"What's a Skinner?" I asked.

"After the Bloody Death, a group of people in the Wilds went crazy. They started hunting other humans and skinning the flesh from their bodies. Somehow they got the notion that it warded off the sickness, and convinced some others of this as well," Dax explained.

"What the…" And then I remembered the first time I'd ever met Fudge, and the reason I'd hated the visions for so long. When I saw people's memories, I didn't get the bystander view; I was in their heads. It felt as if I were living through the ordeals myself sometimes.

Fudge's had been particularly terrifying, and in a world full of brutality, that really meant something. I could picture it like I'd seen it yesterday, could see out of her eyes as she sat beside a fire, watching those people painted with blood markings all over their bodies, being forced to watch her parents being skinned alive in front of her. Those people had sliced the skin off her mother and father as if trying to preserve their hides before tossing their flesh in a pile, along with the hides of the victims before them.

As if the vision hadn't been bad enough, the sounds that went along with it had made it even worse. The screams of pain that slowly devolved to guttural moans as they'd died a horrific death. The smell of blood that filled the air and mingled with the scent of urine as the overwhelming pain and fear forced their victims to lose control of their bodies.

Who knew how long it would've gone on and what would have happened to Fudge if two beasts hadn't ripped into the camp. Dax and his brother had saved Fudge from the same fate, but not soon enough to save her family from that horror.

Now these same people had Tiffy and wanted me.

The room was suddenly too small and the people too close. I moved without thought until I found myself by the table in the dining area, five or so feet away.

The thoughts spun in my head so fast that I couldn't grasp just one. I heard a muffled weeping, the likes I'd never heard before, not since my time in the Cement Giant, and I knew it came from the bedroom Fudge had gone into.

I searched out the people in the room, as if I could find some sort of answers there. Dax was silent, but still, as if he were working out all the implications in his head. Rocky was talking to Bookie and Tank in a quiet tone as the three of them took turns looking my way.

There was chair right behind me, and I was grateful for it, not that I would've crumbled to the ground. I'd been through enough bad times that I could force my body to go on autopilot in the worst of situations, but this one was testing the limits. Why was the harm done to those we cared for so much harder to cope with?

These monsters, Skinners, as they'd called them, had done this to get to me. I couldn't fall apart, but my gut tensed and I had to shove my hands underneath my legs to hide their shaking, which was splitting the lion's share of my energy with my brain, spinning with thoughts quicker than I could compute.

Rocky glanced over at me as if he was trying to decipher a puzzle and had just realized he might be missing some pieces. Instead of asking me, he turned to Dax and asked, "Any idea why the Skinners would want Dal? Newco, Dark Walkers, now the Skinners, too? Most people don't want Plaguers around. Why are they all trying to get her?"

"She can ID Dark Walkers. That's a valuable thing in this world for those who believe," Dax said.

I hoped that was all. Not even Dax knew Ms. Edith had called me the key. I hadn't told Bookie, either. No one knew but me and her, and the dead don't tell secrets.

Rocky looked at me again. "And that's all there is to it?"

"Yes." There was an edge to Dax's voice that

clearly told Rocky to back off. I never thought I'd hear that tone and like it.

Rocky heard his warning, but it took him a second before he made the decision to do as suggested. I didn't know him, but I was glad. Rocky seemed like a nice enough guy, and I'd hate to see him come to blows with Dax. I didn't care how tough you were—no mortal was going to be able to take on a beast. It would come to blows, too. Dax didn't back down. He only paused while he was figuring out a better way to annihilate you.

"How did she piss off the Skinners, too?" Tank asked, obviously having missed the warning Dax had shot Rocky. "It's a valid question," he said when he caught a stare from Dax.

"It doesn't matter. She's not going," Bookie said, dragging all the attention to him as he positioned himself next to my chair. "We'll get Tiffy back another way. Dal isn't going to them, not even for a day."

"Don't tell me what she's going to do," Dax said.

Bookie took a couple of steps toward him and away from me. This wasn't Bookie, the kid, my age, who stayed in Dax's shadow, but Bookie the man emerging.

I leaned an elbow on the table beside me and then rested my forehead on my palm. It didn't matter what Bookie or anyone else said. I wouldn't let Tiffy hang for me, even if I didn't know my crime. I just needed to get my equilibrium back before I took on the fight.

Bookie was getting his back up. He would throw himself into a volcano if he thought it was the right and noble thing to do. "Bookie, I've got to go if they—"

"You aren't going anywhere," Dax said, shutting me down before I had a chance to shut down Bookie.

From the read on the tension in the room, I was officially out of time. Luckily I had practice at not having what I wanted. I stood and walked over to the two of them and then stepped in between them. "It's my call. I say whether I go, and I say I go."

"No."

My ears hurt as they both barked at me in unison. It was a surprise from both sides. Bookie never shouted at me. He was more soft-spoken in a laid-back sort of way. Dax didn't usually raise his voice either, but it had nothing to do with being kind.

"We set up a swap. If they have her, I go. She's six! She can't handle this. I can. It's my decision and I'll make it. I'm not saying I'm going to go and not expect a rescue effort, but we can't leave Tiffy there. I go, we get her back, and then you guys figure out how to rescue me." I looked at the four of them, wondering if Rocky might be of any help.

"It's not that easy," Bookie said.

"If you could get me out of the Cement Giant, you can get me out of there."

Rocky was shaking his head and Dax wasn't

171

shaking anything. He looked completely unmovable.

"Their place is…" Rocky ran a roughened palm over his hair. Besides Dax, Rocky was one of the toughest SOBs I'd ever met. When he looked worried, I got worried.

Bookie spoke. "They're a vile people who've made a lot of enemies. They don't leave themselves vulnerable to attack. They don't have soft spots."

Did everyone know about these Skinners but me? Might have been noteworthy when I moved to the Wilds to mention that oh yeah, besides the pirates and the bounty hunters and beasts, we've also got a tribe of people that skin human beings alive. This place needed a welcome center or something.

I stood there in the borrowed living room and realized this was similar to being back in the Cement Giant. I could either let myself drown in worry and defeat or I could decide we were going to get Tiffy out and figure out how we were going to make it happen, because I was not going down as a pessimist.

"Bookie, give me a pencil," I said, knowing he'd have one stashed on him somewhere.

I grabbed the note from Dax and scribbled on the back.

Name a time and place for a meeting.

Dax grabbed the message from me and I said, "I

didn't specify swap. I left it open. Now where's this stump place?"

"It's a giant old oak stump that is used to relay messages out in the middle of an empty field," Rocky explained.

"We send the message but there won't be a swap," Dax said.

"We have to do something. Whether it happens or not is still up to us, but if they have her, we need to keep her alive until we can get her out."

Dax took the note and handed it to Rocky. "Have someone put it in the stump."

"I'll do it," Bookie said.

"I'll have one of my people go with you."

Rocky and Bookie both walked out the door, and I went to follow, having every intention of sticking that letter in the stump myself to make sure it got there, but Dax stepped in front of the door and stopped me.

"They'll have the place watched. You get caught and then we'll have neither of you."

CHAPTER 18

I'd been sitting at the kitchen table fidgeting with a broken watch Bookie had given me. Just like the Tiffy situation, I didn't have the right tools to fix this either. But it was all I could do not to go insane. I sat there and stared at a million little pieces and tried to figure out how they worked, when I couldn't even figure out how to fix the broken pieces in me. Dax had said that my aptitude was aim. If I could get my magic back, what if I could figure out how to set my aim on Tiffy?

And now of all nights, I was supposed to go to dinner? Rocky had stopped by a couple of hours after someone dropped off the note and invited us to a meal tonight. Fudge had been too tired go anywhere, and no one faulted her for it. Bookie said he'd stay behind and keep an eye on Fudge. Tank was watching this stump place with some of Rocky's guys.

When he'd come by to invite us, but mostly me, he hadn't said it, but there was a certain nuance to the invite that made it clear—the delivery might have been polite, but I needed to be there.

It didn't matter if anyone else went. That wasn't the purpose of the invitation anyway, whether anyone realized it or not. Tonight's dinner was to be a sideshow event, and I was the star. Step right up and see the freak, folks.

I was positive that the guard who'd found the note today had told everyone in camp that not only was I a Plaguer, but that I was important enough that the Skinners were sniffing around their home to get me. I had a feeling it was either go to dinner or the people here would try to put me on the spit to burn.

It wasn't that I didn't understand the issue. Rocky needed to give his people a closer look at the Plaguer, maybe steady some nerves and show them that he wasn't afraid to break bread with the diseased one and I wasn't some horrible threat. I was just some scrawny, helpless girl and no one needed to worry.

That was great for them, but I didn't want to go to dinner. I wanted to be staking out this stump place with Tank and Rocky's people. I wanted to sit here and figure out what was wrong with me. The visions were still gone, and I couldn't count on being able to nail someone in the heart if needed. I was almost like a regular human these days for what it was worth, and that was a big problem as far as I was concerned. I needed to be a badass, not a Sally Mae or some shit if I was going to save Tiffy. The things I should've been doing ran a mile long, and a dinner party was not on that list.

"You coming?" Dax asked as he walked into the

house. I hadn't expected him to come back before dinner. I'd figured I'd met him there. He'd never escorted me anywhere, so why would I imagine he'd do it now?

I nodded after the slightest delay. It was hard to be excited about the evening to come.

"You don't have to go," Dax said, and I could hear the steel behind the words. He meant it. He'd burn at the spit with me if that was what I decided to do. Or rip through the camp, which was more likely. Neither was a desirable outcome.

Sometimes Dax absolutely confounded me. Just when I expected him to throw on the dictator hat, he acted like the man again, and a loyal one that would burn with me. That was the other problem. I didn't want the whole group to be shunned or run off because I was here. If I didn't go, they'd catch the heat too, and we couldn't leave this place right now, not with Tiffy missing.

I placed the broken watch shell on the table. "Free meal. What the hell?"

"I can bring you something back," he said, almost like he wanted me to tell them to go screw.

Didn't he care about the uproar this place could break into if I didn't go? They wanted to see what kind of monster brought Skinners to their walls, and they weren't going to be happy if they didn't get a show.

"No." This had to happen, and I knew it.

176

I stood up, straightened my shoulders, and stiffened my spine. Dax's eyes shot to my bare hands. The ugly scar was on full display. I'd left the gloves lying on the dresser in the bedroom. I had my pride. It didn't matter, as people knew what I was anyway, but I wasn't hiding.

They wanted a close-up look at the Plaguer? So be it. They could see every ugly inch of me. I was learning that skinning some flesh off and getting rid of the P wasn't enough to shed the title.

I thought I saw respect there in his eyes. He walked to the door and waited for me. I wiped moist palms on legs that looked much sturdier than they felt. I shoved my hands in my pockets and then pulled them out again, ready to curse myself out before I showed these people any weakness.

Screw them if they didn't like me. It was silly to be nervous. They were just a new bunch of people. So what if they didn't want me here? When had I started caring what other people thought or wanted?

Still, my legs seemed to care, because I had a hard time making them move fast enough to keep pace with Dax, but I did just that, edging out in front of him. I wasn't looking for a shield, either. Didn't need one.

"You'd do Moobie proud," Dax said as we walked.

"Thanks," I said with as much bravado as I could drum up, and felt a little tougher.

I heard the group before I saw them. The long picnic table actually appeared to be several all butted up against each other where it sat alongside the lake, people lining the sides of it.

Fifteen strangers and one scorned Becca all looked at me in partial disgust, and occasionally not so partial. They were quick to mask it as Dax looked around, but I'd seen that look enough in my life to recognize it.

Fuck them. I didn't need these people.

"There you are, late as always," Rocky said as he walked over from the side, and he headed toward us like a jovial host and not the person who'd practically demanded my presence. He turned to the group with a palm on my shoulder, clearly making a point of touching me that didn't go unnoticed by the eyes that were now looking at his hand. "You all know Dax, but let me introduce you to Dal. She'll be staying here with us for a while."

A sea of forced smiles stared back at me.

"Dax, come talk to me for a minute?" Rocky said. I felt Dax's eyes land on me, but I refused to look at him or acknowledge any fear of being left alone. I took a step toward the table and heard Dax step away with Rocky a few seconds later.

The long makeshift table was huge, with only two seats not taken. One was sandwiched between where Rocky must have been sitting and where Becca currently sat. Rocky had probably saved that seat for Dax. The other was down toward the other end, and I moved in that direction. I might be better off on my own than next to Becca. Of all the places we'd ended up, why couldn't this have been the place Margo went?

I took my seat, as the people on either side of me tried to scoot a few more inches down the bench away from me. I placed an elbow on the table and a hand in the air. I gave them a good look at the scar and a hush fell over the table. *Ladies and gentlemen, let the show begin.*

The silence didn't last too long, as they got over the shock of a Plaguer at their table and began talking to each other. No one spoke to me. I hadn't expected them to.

A minute or so later, a few people walked out with arms laden with bowls and plates overflowing with food. The bowls were passed around as the people sitting on either side of Dax's and Rocky's empty seats filled their plates before passing the food around.

My mouth was salivating as I watched the mashed potato shrinking as it made its way to me. I'd barely eaten since Tiffy had disappeared, and my stomach was telling me it wasn't going to stand for it any longer, no matter the circumstances.

By the time the bowl was plunked in front of me, I scraped the sides but only managed to salvage a bite or two. Who was in charge of the cooking in this place? Didn't they know how to figure out how many portions they needed? The sound of another spoon clanking against a bowl got my hopes up. I barely managed to get a couple of peas as I turned the bowl upside down over my plate. I surveyed the other end of the table to watch the last of what looked like tea being emptied.

At least there was still steak to be had. Red meat could make up for a lot. I looked in the center of the table. Where was the steak? I knew that was the main course because I'd seen it on people's plates. Then I saw an empty platter sitting there. They hadn't even counted enough steaks?

How many of us got screwed out of the main course? I looked at the plates about the table, and that was when I noticed how several people didn't just have one steak, but two. That was also when I noticed the smirking and whispering to each other.

Becca was down closer to the other end. She wasn't smirking, but it didn't look like she minded what was happening either. Not a shock there. I hadn't expected much from her. I knew she'd come to the decision that I was the reason she wasn't with Dax, whether she had been the one to walk away or not.

I straightened in my chair and placed the fork I was about to use down beside my plate. I didn't need their crappy food anyway. I toyed with the idea of leaving right then, and not because I gave a shit but because I was that hungry. Except that would give the appearance that they'd run me off, so I sat and crossed my arms instead.

I caught sight of Rocky and Dax heading back.

They grabbed their spots, still talking between themselves as they settled down, fairly oblivious to me or anything amiss. I saw Becca trying to add herself into their conversation, and that didn't bother me either.

I was glad, hoping Dax would keep talking and eating until everyone's plate was as empty as mine. He got really weird about me eating because of the magic, and I didn't want a scene or him coming to my rescue over a stupid meal. I just wanted the night to be over. They'd nearly starved me in the Cement Giant. A few missed meals here and there weren't a big deal.

The talk at the table continued and I started to relax. I was a fast eater. Another few minutes and it would've been like I'd eaten anyway. I'd go back to the house or Fudge's and find something to eat after Dax went to sleep, or more likely disappeared, and call it a night.

This place and what these people thought of me didn't matter. I wasn't planning on staying anyway, and I certainly wasn't looking for a new best friend or anything. I had friends, like Bookie. They could keep their walls and their food. Stupid idiots. When was the last time any of them had ever been more than a few miles beyond their own gate? This was what they wasted their time on? Ooh, let's make the Plaguer feel unwanted? They'd have to do a lot better than eating all the food. Their meat was probably chewy anyway.

I got sick of looking at their faces and turned my

attention upward. The stars were out in force tonight, and I had a brilliant view of Orion, the Hunter. It was my favorite constellation.

I'd memorized every star by name after we had a class on them. I used to stare at them from the small view in my cell. Now I didn't have to look at small patches anymore. I could see every star in the sky all at once above my head, and I realized that it really didn't matter what anyone thought about me.

They didn't get it, how lucky they'd been. The choices they had. It made me sad for them, because it didn't really matter what you had if you were too stupid to realize it. They could have the world but they locked themselves away, expecting the few strong ones in this place to protect them. They had no idea what life had to offer, what it felt like to test yourself against someone else and come out the winner. Own your own path.

I noticed the talking at the table started to die down as I watched the stars, and I figured dinner was finally about to wrap up. I'd leave here and walk under the night stars, knowing that I was the lucky one. I knew the value of this life I was living. They obviously didn't, or they wouldn't care about such petty things.

I looked down and realized most of them weren't even half done. It had probably grown quiet because they'd run out of interesting things to talk about since they lived their lives behind these walls. I wouldn't leave, but damn I was hungry.

I was resigned to wait this out when I realized what was really causing the halt in chatter. I looked down toward where Dax and Rocky were sitting, just to gauge how much food they had left, and saw Rocky's lips were pressed into a line, an angry, mean-looking one.

That was nothing compared to Dax, who looked about to blow. What was his problem? He was shooting daggers and spreading them out liberally. He couldn't be that pissed about the food, could he? No. He wouldn't get that mad over something so stupid. I knew he liked me to eat, keep the magic strong and all, but that wouldn't piss him off that bad.

I watched him pick up his drink and plate and walk toward me, and started to wonder if he was angry with me. Did I screw something up without realizing? Nah, how could I have since we'd walked over here together? I hadn't even talked since I'd been here.

Dax paused behind the guy to my right, who'd had his back to me the entire time. "Get up and take your shit with you."

The guy didn't hesitate, and stood quickly, taking his plate and drink with him. Talk about magic—he managed to do this without looking directly at Dax once. Dax sat down in his place, his presence hitting the crowd on this end of the table like an earthquake.

"My drink tastes funny. You drink it," he said, and then placed his in front of me.

I looked at the glass and realized he had some sort

of ale. I'd really wanted tea. Even whiskey would've been better.

"Drink it," he said while I was still debating.

I wasn't a fan of ale, but if he felt that strongly about it… I grabbed the glass and took a sip.

He dug his fork into the small pile of potatoes that were on my plate. I caught the eyes around the table watching him, as if waiting for him to drop dead from the Bloody Death at any moment. But that wasn't to be the end of the show.

A young, attractive guy in his twenties was the only one who seemed to have the nerve to say anything. "Aren't you—"

Whatever was going to follow that would be a mystery, as Dax leaned forward, glacier firmly in place and freezing the hell out of anyone not on the right side of it.

"Aren't I what?"

"Nothing." The guy went back to minding his own business, but Dax didn't stop staring at him until he got up and excused himself from the meal with some lame excuse about not feeling well.

Suddenly the steak trencher had meat on it again, and my plate was being piled up higher than what I'd be able to eat, and I was no slouch.

I looked down at what I considered their food, stabbed my fork into a nice piece of red meat, and had trouble bringing it to my mouth. Did I really want to eat anything they provided? If I didn't eat it, I'd still be hungry. Being hungry sucked. Why should I let these people ruin my meal? I took a nice bite.

Turned out that the steak wasn't even a little chewy. People started eating again. No one said a word, and their eyes didn't linger too long either, or they caught such a stare-down that they didn't look again.

By the time dinner was done, I wasn't sure if Dax had eaten more off my plate or his as he reinforced his message. I didn't know if they took his meaning, or, more accurately, his warning, but I didn't care either way. I'd do my time here standing on my head. These people weren't nearly as tough as they imagined they were.

In true form, I finished the abundance of food quickly. Dax stood, his plate still partially full, as soon as I was done. We both thanked Rocky for the meal, and then I turned my back on the rest of them. Dax lingered a moment behind before catching up to me.

* * *

We were walking back to the house and the words *thank you* kept spinning around in my brain but didn't want to migrate down to my mouth. Dax deserved a thank you. I hadn't needed him to do what he'd done, hadn't even wanted him to, but it had been a decent thing to do. He'd had my back, and it had felt good

185

when he did. I should say thank you.

So why couldn't I just say the two words? Why did I feel so weird about the whole thing? Maybe I should just leave the subject alone, but then I'd be rude, and Margo said rude was a pretty bad thing to be. Even Moobie didn't like rude people. And yes, he was imaginary, but the writer of Moobie must have obviously felt that way too if he wrote it, and he was brilliant, evidenced by such fantastic stories, right? So it needed to be said, but I was about as good at thanking someone as Dax was at giving apologies.

And there was the house looming ahead and getting closer by the second. I was running out of time. If I didn't say it tonight, it would be more awkward to say it tomorrow. I had to just get it out and put it behind me.

"Thanks for... Well, you know. You didn't have to do that."

"Do what?" he asked.

Really? Questions? Weren't people supposed to just take a thank you and leave it alone? I definitely didn't want to drag this out. "You know, back there. Making it obvious you weren't afraid of catching anything from me."

"I didn't do anything much."

Was this conversation ever going to end? Was I going to have to beg him to accept my thank you? All I wanted to do was get it out and be done with the business.

"Yes, you did."

It was like the moment I convinced myself he was a complete jerk, he did something like he did at dinner. It was getting to be that I didn't know who he was anymore. There was the Dax that didn't want to come near me, called me sludge and insulted me, treated me like I was an idiot. Then there was this Dax, the one who came to my aid when it seemed like everyone wanted me gone. The one who made it clear no one could treat me like that and get away with it. The one who looked out for me and teased me. The one that didn't have a glacier built up around him.

I just wished he would make up his mind and become the other Dax for good so that my own feelings would stop yo-yoing back and forth, because I couldn't dislike this Dax, the one that had been with me tonight. I'd never be able to hate this one.

I wanted to hate him. I wanted to feel anything other than what I was feeling right now, and that was this strong urge for him to stop walking, take me in his arms, and tell me that I was the woman he wanted. That he'd look at me again like he'd done that afternoon before I'd decided to stay and told me that I could be someone special. I also wouldn't mind if he tried out a little bit of what I'd read in chapter ten of the half-naked man book, especially the page I'd dog-eared.

All of these whimsical thoughts were forgotten

with his next question.

"Why didn't you say something to me? Why did you sit there?" Dax asked. These weren't nice questions, but something closer to accusations, and I realized that his words before had had a similar tone.

"Because I had it handled."

"By not eating."

"I know you want me to eat regularly because of the magic, but one meal wasn't going to kill me." I'd thanked him. How was this turning into a fight? If I could only find that Dax manual somewhere, maybe this would make sense.

"You should've said something."

"I had it handled. I appreciate the help, but I'm not looking to have someone fight my battles for me. I can handle things on my own."

"You didn't have it handled. You sat there and didn't eat."

He sounded like they'd done it to him. "I—"

"You should've said something to me."

"We're barely friends most the time. Why would I go running to you? Why are you all bent out of whack over this? Dax, I've dealt with a lot worse," I said, and started laughing at the pettiness of the whole thing.

"I'm aware."

The logic of what I'd just said didn't seem to be hitting home with him or taking the edge off his anger. The more I said, the worse it seemed to be getting.

What was going on here? "So now you're mad at me?"

"Yes. Don't ever let someone treat you like that. Ever." He left me standing on the lawn in front of the house, utterly confused, while he walked off.

"What about when it's you who's treating me like shit? Huh? Any ideas on that?" I hollered after him, not caring that I could see curtains being pulled back by busybodies.

Dax didn't answer or acknowledge he'd heard me. Like to hear how he thought I should handle that one.

I went and sat on one of the two chairs on the front porch. The longer I lived, the more I realized I might not be the craziest person here. I might actually be the sanest one around.

CHAPTER 19

Rocky strode up to me where I was still sitting an hour later, curled up in one of the chairs that sat on the stoop.

He stopped, leaned a hip against the railing that held up the small covering over the door, and stuck his hand in his pocket. His eyes landed on me and stayed there. I didn't shift or squirm. He could stare all he wanted. No skin off my back.

"You handled yourself well tonight," he said.

It wasn't what I'd expected him to say. I wasn't sure what I'd done so well. I'd ignored everyone. That didn't usually breed compliments. "Thanks."

"I guess you're used to that kind of thing."

"I guess I am."

"You're a lot tougher than you look." He shifted, crossing his arms over his chest as he kept staring at me. "I'd heard that but I didn't quite believe it."

"I have my moments." There was something strange in the way Rocky was looking at me, like he found me interesting all of a sudden. I wasn't sure if I was flattered or annoyed that he might've been a little less than impressed before.

"I bet you do."

Okay, I was definitely missing something now. Why was he smiling at me like that? Did he want to… Nah, nobody wanted me like that. Why would this guy who had his pick of a town full of women? He was too good looking and had his shit together. I'd seen how women in the Wilds fell all over tough guys. It was an embarrassment to the sex.

Dax was walking back to the house before I could nail down Rocky's actual intent, but his posture straightened and he lost that curious look.

"Go grab your jacket," Dax said as he came to stand between the two of us.

"For what?"

"To scope out the Skinners tonight."

Hmmm, so that was what the pre-dinner chat was about. Nice how he told me these things ahead of time. What if I'd been out? I held back a laugh. Where the hell was I going?

"I'll be right back." I went inside and grabbed my jacket while I thought over the only reason Dax would include me in these plans. He thought the Dark Walkers had something to do with the Skinners.

I already had the knife in my boot, and I grabbed the one for my hip as well. Never knew when you'd lose one in an eye socket and need a spare.

By the time I walked back out, Tank was there as well, and I caught the tail end of the conversation.

"How long ago did you see them leave?" Dax

asked.

"Twenty minutes? The others are still in place watching." Tank looked over at me. "You're coming?"

Dax answered for me. "She's coming."

Yep, this was about the Dark Walkers.

As I stood among badasses of varying degrees, I knew this was the crowd I wanted to be a part of, where I wanted to fit. This was where I belonged.

I hopped on the bike behind Dax and we all headed out.

We hadn't ridden very long before we were slowing down. We got off the bikes and the three guys started covering them with branches.

"They're this close?" I asked, knowing we'd only been riding for an hour. Even at the breakneck speed we'd ridden, the proximity seemed a little too close. The idea of having a tribe of people who skinned other people on a regular basis so nearby seemed very unsettling. I guessed it was no skin off their back—not yet, anyway.

"I was here first and I don't care to move," Rocky said, and that toughness I'd sensed when I first met him was practically oozing from him now.

Dax, Rocky, Tank, and I left the bikes and approached the camp on foot, but I found out quickly that we weren't going to get as close as I thought. We made our way to some bushes that grew right before a several-hundred-foot drop.

The fortress, and that was the most apt name I could think of for the monstrosity a few miles in the distance, was walled off with metal plates. There was nothing to soften its appearance, either. It stood alone in the landscape—no trees, no large boulders, nothing that would shield us in an approach. They must have had to clear that land every day to keep on top of it. The newly discovered gardener in me couldn't help but be impressed.

The rest of me was a bit worried. Even with the small amount of tactical experience I possessed, I knew that if I ended up inside that place, a rescue was going to be tough, if not impossible.

We'd traveled specifically to look at the Skinners' compound. We had stopped our bikes and traveled on foot the last mile and now squatted, peering down at the fortress. "They" said there were no stupid questions. I was pretty sure I was about to prove "they" wrong.

"This is the Skinners' home?" I asked, hoping one of them would say no. That this wasn't it. That this plan of mine to do a swap and get saved later wouldn't land me in dire straits.

Dax looked at me and replied, "No, it's the next enormous compound five miles down the road."

I decided I liked "they" better than Dax at the moment. "*They* say there are no stupid questions."

"I think you just proved 'they' wrong."

Man, times like this it was like we were the same

friggin' person. How could that be?

"What was this place before?" I asked, seeing the remnants of the Glory Years construction underneath the facade the Skinners had built.

"It was a secret government facility," Rocky said.

I didn't say holy cow, this was going to be ugly, but I was certainly thinking it. It was actually quite quiet all around, which made me wonder if I wasn't the only one singing that tune in their brain.

Rocky dug out a pair of binoculars. "It looks just as well kept up as always. I don't know who they're doing their trading with, but they've kept it well maintained. It's hard to come by the metal they use, and some of those wall panels are definitely newer. Definitely lends credibility to the rumors."

"What rumors?" I asked, wondering if this was where I came in.

Dax took the binoculars from Rocky as he answered, "That the Skinners have worked for or with the Dark Walkers for years."

What would the Dark Walkers need with Skinners? Then again, what would they need from me? "Any reason to believe they're true?"

"No way to prove it until recently," Dax said, and all three of them looked at me.

"Guys, I can't see through metal walls."

"You won't have to. There's a party heading back from the stump," Tank said. "And one of them definitely didn't look like they belonged."

We hadn't been there long when the people we'd been waiting for approached the gate. We were positioned so that hopefully we could get a glimpse inside when the large gate opened.

It was a party of three. We'd been passing around the one set of binoculars from person to person, but as soon as they hit the clearing, Dax handed them to me. It took me a moment to find the party through the view, and Dax put his hand on the binoculars and pointed them in the correct direction.

Two of the men in the group looked rougher around the edges, both clothed in mostly leather, from their pants to their shirts. Their hair hung long and straggled. They didn't have as many marks as they'd had in Fudge's memory, but they each had a line across their forehead.

The third in the group was a woman. She looked like she didn't belong, mostly because she appeared to be cleaner, if still in rough attire. It was too dark to tell more than that as they crossed the clearing toward the entrance.

"Well?" Rocky asked.

"It's too dark and I'm too far away."

The door was opening and I was just about to hand off the binoculars back to Dax, figuring he'd be able to pick up more information on defenses on the inside than I would, when I gripped the binoculars tighter. The party walked right beneath the torches that lit the entrance. I was grateful that, even though I might have lost some of my magic, I hadn't lost it all.

"The woman with them—she's a Dark Walker." I handed off the binoculars to Dax so he could get a glimpse of her. He passed them to Tank quickly after, just before the entrance closed.

"Are you sure?" Rocky asked.

"I'm positive." Tiffy could be in there right now—not only with Skinners but Dark Walkers as well. I turned to Dax. "What did you see of the defenses?"

Dax shot me a look so intense I could almost see a little of the beast glowing through his stare. "Almost nothing."

"We're going to have to do whatever it takes," I said to him.

"We're finished for tonight."

CHAPTER 20

Sweat beaded on my forehead in the afternoon heat as I waited for Dax's next move.

He came at me, and I didn't have it in me to block anymore. If he hadn't pulled his kick, I would've been in bad shape. As it was, I ended up lying on the ground gasping.

He was relentless today, and I wondered why I'd thought some sparring would be a good idea. I didn't ask him what was wrong. I knew why he was in rare form. It wasn't because we'd put the note in the stump a day ago and not received a reply, even though we'd watched the Skinners plus one return from there. We were stuck waiting, which he definitely didn't like, but I didn't think that was the issue.

He wasn't mad because we were trying to negotiate with the Skinners. Pretending there was the possibility of handing me over made sense, and he was far superior to me in tactics and saw the logic of it. No one argued that point, not Rocky, Bookie, or Dax.

No, Dax was fuming because he knew me, better than Fudge or even Bookie. In some ways, Dax and I were as different as the night sky and high noon. Other times I wondered if we were too similar, just viewed from different vantage points at different times, both the light from stars at the heart of it. Perhaps I was just an earlier version of him, what he was like when he was my age, however long ago that might have been.

I leaned up on my elbows, and that was far up as I got. He was pacing around me, waiting for me to get back on my feet, visibly angry right now and not hiding it. I'd never seen someone who could shut their feelings down the way he could, but this morning he seemed to be in more of a *let it all hang out* kind of mood.

It was probably because of the real reason he was angry. He knew I wasn't going to stop at negotiations. If the only way to free Tiffy was to sacrifice myself, it was going to happen, even if I had to march to the Skinners' home all alone in the middle of the night.

I wasn't foolish enough to think this anger stemmed from some personal adoration for me. Yes, there was loyalty there, as he considered me part of his crew, but the real truth was he didn't want to lose the one person who could finger the Dark Walkers for him. He wouldn't allow anyone to steal his vengeance.

Rocky had sent more people to spy on the Skinners' compound, but from what I'd seen, unless you had X-ray vision, it was a lost cause. The place was locked up tighter than my fist around a piece of bacon. Or how my fist used to be. Even bacon wasn't the same these days.

Dax didn't understand, though, that I could handle whatever came, and I'd survive even the Skinners. I'd make it out the other side, magic or not, because that was what I did. I wasn't so confident about Tiffy.

That was all I could think of. Tiffy with those people. The thought of her, what they might be doing to her, was stealing every thought in my mind. Even eating was becoming a problem. I'd never lost my appetite, and I could barely eat breakfast this morning. I'd eat and all I'd think of was where was Tiffy? Were they feeding her? Was she starving, being tortured?

He paced his way over to me. Probably only stopped moving because it was more convenient to scowl down at me from a fixed position.

"Are you getting up?"

"Maybe we should call it a day. I don't have it in me right now to practice." Sparring today had been a bad idea, but I was trying to force the magic to come back. I'd hoped that if I battled it out with Dax something would click into place, light the fire in my chest again. If it didn't do that, I'd counted on it at least keeping my mind off things while we played this waiting game. But nothing was going to keep my mind off Tiffy, and the magic was still fizzling out every time I reached for it.

"Get. Up."

Dax could be as stubborn as an ox, another similarity. Was this what I'd be like in fifty, maybe a hundred years?

"Dax, I thought that this would be a good idea today, but I can't." Tiffy was gone. I couldn't sleep. I couldn't try and listen to people's memories to glean some hidden kernel of knowledge that might help. I couldn't even throw a knife that well anymore. This wasn't time to practice anything. This was a time to either knock down doors on suicide missions or lick your wounds, and I couldn't figure out which one I should be doing yet.

Dax didn't budge. I looked up at him, unable to see his expression with the bright sky behind him, but sensing the mood well enough. "Cut me a little slack. It's a bad day."

"You're not quitting."

My face wrinkled at the mention of that word in connection to myself. "Of course I'm not quitting. I don't quit. What I'm doing is taking a break." Every part of me felt sapped a thousand times worse than I'd ever felt at the compound. The idea of her out there felt like it was draining everything I had.

"Get. Up," he repeated.

"Don't you hear me?" He should, as my voice was nearing a yell. He'd defend me over a plate of food and yet he couldn't understand that maybe this was a bad day? The guy was a lunatic.

He took another step until his toes were pressed against the side of my hip. He leaned over, casting my upper half in his shadow. "Get. Up."

"Or what?" Man, could he be stubborn, but this still wasn't happening today.

"I'll kick your ass where you're sitting on it."

"Tiffy's missing. Cut me some slack." I didn't want to fight, but I didn't want to go back to the house. I didn't want to do anything other than get to Tiffy, and the frustration of not being able to do that made me feel both violent and frozen all at once.

"You want to help her? Get your head on straight and step up or you won't have anything to do with this."

The only thing my brain grabbed on to was him trying to cut me out of the loop. "What exactly are you saying to me?"

"You know what I'm saying."

"Spell it out."

"I won't have someone on my team who can't keep their emotional shit together."

That got me off my ass like the grass had been lit on fire underneath me. I got right in his face, almost nose to nose, as I went on tiptoes to look him dead in the eye, and stabbed him with a finger in the middle of his chest. "Who do you think you are? Don't lecture me. I've spent years keeping my emotional shit together." I wanted to rip his head off right then. Some of the anger might have been misplaced, but I didn't care. He deserved a healthy dose of it. He was far from one of Fudge's saints.

"Act like it. You think you're so tough, then show me. Get your shit together, because I'm not letting you go anywhere like this."

"That's bullshit. The only reason you don't want me to go anywhere is because you don't want to lose the one person who can ID Dark Walkers for you."

"Then you better get your head out of your ass and make yourself invincible if you want to be involved."

"Invincible is over. I'm a normal human being now. I don't have any magic beyond IDing monsters, but if you think that's going to stop me, you're wrong."

"No. You're wrong. You are going to get stronger even if I have to drag your skinny ass every step of the way. I'm going to make the magic come back even if I have to squeeze it from your body."

His eyes were nearly blazing, and I realized that he might really be walking the edge, one I'd only glimpsed at. "You're completely insane," I said, and right then, I believed it. That was how intense he looked.

"I'm glad you're finally catching on. Now fight or I'm going to kick your scrawny ass all the way back to the Rock."

Holy shit. He was going to beat the hell out of me just to push me. How far would he take this? Would I end up laid up in a bed recuperating for weeks? Was this the plan? Screw me up sparring so I couldn't do anything even if I wanted?

I was near burning with anger when he took a swing at me. I spun, missing his hit, and countered with a kidney shot, a burst of warmth spreading from my chest as I did.

He took another shot and I dodged it. When he turned and came at me again, I noticed he was moving slower than he was capable of. It was an act. An experiment on his part. Every ounce of magical warmth died in that instant.

He swung and I landed back on the ground, thankful that he'd pulled the punch at the last second, or I might have really ended up in bed for weeks.

He walked over and looked down at me. "What happened? You were doing good."

"Nice try, but it's gone again," I said as I got my air back. "I guess the crazy act only works once but you really do it well." Too well, I thought, and wondered how much of that was him and how much had been an act.

He took a couple steps away as I sat up, still recuperating—not that he seemed too concerned. I got myself back into a sitting position and then rested my arms on my knees.

"Whatever is wrong, adrenaline, fear of a threat, is overriding it. You've got control on some level. Tell me exactly how it feels to you now when you try and call the magic forth?"

"It sputters out. I don't know how else to describe

it."

He took a couple more steps around the area. "Did you do something weird before it happened? Eat anything unusual? Was there anything out of the ordinary?"

"No, no, and no."

"What about the night before we got to the Rock? When you woke, you seemed off."

"I'd had a bad dream."

"Tell me what it was."

"I don't remember most of it."

"Tell me what you do remember."

My palm went to my forehead before my fingers worked their way into my hair. I wanted to pull it out in frustration. "All I remember is the sensation of being covered in cement when I awoke."

"It was just a dream." Wasn't that what I'd kept telling myself?

"It was a dream, right? You don't know anything that could cause this, do you? Anything at all?" Like invisible friends, maybe? I waited, seeing if there was something he thought was capable of it.

He shook his head, but damn if I didn't think he was holding back on me.

"Dax!" We turned to see one of the teenage girls from the Rock running up to us. "Dax," she said with a smile as she got into range, and I was a bit surprised this one ever left the walls, even if it was to get close to

Dax.

"What?" he asked.

He didn't realize how curt he was being with her, but I knew why he was so distracted. The girl didn't, and I could see her heart-sized crush get a little banged up.

"Rocky said there's a message."

I jumped to my feet, shaking off the workout as I rushed back to the Rock, not waiting for either of them.

Rocky was outside the gate when I got back, Dax and the girl not far behind. Rocky handed me the piece of leather in his hands as Dax lost the message girl and then headed over toward us.

"What's it say?" Dax asked.

I handed him the hide. "They want the pirates to host a meeting between us and the Skinners tonight."

"Good," Dax said.

"It could be a setup," Rocky said.

"No. It won't be. They know better than to cross me."

Rocky looked surprised, but I wasn't. Dax had his fingers on a lot of different pulses, and sometimes a knife on the jugulars, too. Pressure could always be applied when you were the one with the control of the oil and gasoline. I guessed that pirates got their fair share of that pressure when trading with Dax.

"I'm going to go get ready," I said, putting it out there before Dax thought there was any chance of stopping me from going.

Dax didn't say anything, and then he looked at Rocky. "You got any plans tonight?"

"I guess I do now."

CHAPTER 21

The closer we got to Hell's Corner, which I'd just learned was one of the strongholds of the pirates, the more the hair on my arms stood on end. It seemed to grow darker and darker the deeper we got into the marsh, and I didn't think it had anything to do with it being night, the thick canopy of trees, or the marsh area we were entering. There was something evil that clung to this place, even though I couldn't put my finger to it.

The place was just creepy, no other way around it.

"This place is fucking creepy," Rocky said, as if he were reading my thoughts. "Remind me why we agreed to meet here?"

"Neutral ground," Dax said as we walked deeper and deeper into the area and I wished the bikes weren't a few miles away at this point.

Up ahead, there was a man standing beside a small boat that had a box hanging off the back.

"Give me a minute," Dax said to the two of us, and walked forward alone.

"How are you feeling?" Rocky asked as I watched Dax greet the pirate.

"Like I can handle whatever comes," I said, having

made up my mind that I would do whatever it took to get Tiffy back where she belonged tonight.

Rocky only smiled, and I wasn't sure what he found so amusing about my response.

Dax waved us forward and then got in the boat. I followed and Rocky squeezed in on the other side of me, while the pirate sat in the back and steered the strange box thing.

The boat moved through the swampy waters until the sky opened up a bit and a large ship sat in the near distance. The pirate pulled the small boat up to the side of it where a rope ladder hung down.

Dax climbed up first, then I went, and Rocky afterward.

Once we were on the deck, the two Skinners were easy to pick out among the crew, with the strange lines on their foreheads that may have been made with blood. There were pirates around as well, giving the Skinners a wide berth.

But there was no Tiffy. Maybe she was close by? It would be smart for them to keep her hidden. At least, that was the lie I told myself. As much as I'd disagreed with Dax when he made the decision not to tell anyone where we were going, now I was glad. I'd hate to have to go back to a hopeful Fudge without Tiffy.

A door to below deck opened and a tower of a man stepped out. All eyes shot to him, and no one needed to tell me he was in charge. He was massive, muscles bulging from his arms like I'd never seen on a human. He might've been the closest I'd seen a male come to the size of a beast. He still wouldn't be a match for one unless he could grow some claws and fangs. I'd seen what claws could do to a person.

The large man stepped in front of our group. "It's been a long while, Dax," he said.

The way the pirate was looking at him made me realize I'd finally found someone who knew something was up with Dax's age.

"Very long," Dax replied.

The pirate didn't say anything else, but nodded to Rocky before looking at me. "I'm glad I was able to offer you safe meeting grounds. If you don't mind, I'd like to speak to your companion for a moment."

What would the guy want to talk to me for?

"That's fine," Dax said as I was still trying to figure out the situation.

The man started walking toward an empty corner of the deck, but Dax grabbed my wrist before I could follow.

"It's fine. He'll be a bloody pulp before I let him hurt you," Dax said softly.

I paused for a second even after he released my wrist. The woman who finally won Dax's heart was going to be one lucky lady. The feeling of a man like him having your back was like nothing I could put into words.

The pirate was waiting, and I stepped forward, having no clue what this guy wanted from me, but knowing that we were in a delicate spot.

"I'm Jacob."

"Dal."

"I'm the Pirate King."

My manners weren't up to royal standards, even pirate royalty, so I said the first thing that sprang to mind: "I don't know how to curtsy, if that's where you're going with this."

He let out a deep laugh, and I felt a little bit better about him. He might have wanted me to be impressed with his title, but he didn't seem to take it too seriously.

"You see those two men?" Jacob asked quietly, pointing toward the Skinners. "They want me to hand you over to them tonight and then kill your companions."

My first reaction was to look over at Dax. I knew he was listening to our conversation, heard every word with those beast ears. His face, which was only in profile, turned toward me, and he winked his left eye.

"Are you going to?" I asked, still uneasy but feeling better than I would've before seeing that wink.

"No, but I want something from you in return."

"Which is?" Did this guy have any idea I had nothing?

"You're a Plaguer, are you not?" he asked, and I knew he was looking down at my hand.

"Got the scar to prove it," I said, holding it up for him.

"And you can see the Dark Walkers?"

The Pirate King believed in the Dark Walkers too. This was pretty interesting. "Yes. I can," I said, as I watched the people on the deck, all of whom were holding off their own business waiting for us to finish. If I had been looking at Jacob instead, I might have missed the slight tensing on Dax.

"I might call you from time to time to vet certain people. Do you agree to do this in return for today's favor?" Jacob asked.

Considering the circumstances, I didn't feel like I could say no, but I wasn't about to agree to an open-ended favor, either. "Perhaps we could help each other, favor for favor." *That's right, bucko.* There would be no indefinite service.

He nodded after a moment. "I can work with that."

Nodding back, I said, "You have a deal, then." I thought about sticking my hand out to shake on our agreement, but I stopped myself, not wanting the moment to become awkward.

"I want you to know that I had my man, the one who assaulted you, killed."

Whoa, now this was getting heavy. I hadn't liked the guy and all, but yikes. Didn't seem exactly fair, as I was walking around fine. *Note to self: Don't piss off the Pirate King, as he might have a tendency to overreact.*

I forced a "thank you" out, knowing it was expected.

"You're welcome. As the only known Plaguer in existence, if he had killed you, he could've cost me much."

Only known Plaguer in existence. I nodded and switched my body to autopilot while I digested his words. I was it? The last? At least until another wave of Bloody Death came through and wiped out the entire human race, that was. Then there might be none at all.

I remembered getting to the farm that first day and Fudge saying that Dax had been gone a while. How long had he searched? Was it really true? There had to be some in hiding. I couldn't be the only one.

"Be careful, Dal. Before long, I think the tides will turn, and the unwanted will be the most sought after."

I nodded, and the Pirate King left me. He briefly paused to nod to Dax, Rocky, and the Skinners before he returned to below deck. The two Skinners watched him closely him as he went, probably puzzled and wondering why he wasn't going to allow them to follow through on their double cross.

Dax took a step forward, angling himself in between me and the Skinners while Rocky came and stood beside me.

Dax, sticking his hands in his pockets as he faced the Skinners, made it clear he didn't consider them a threat.

"Why didn't you bring her?" he asked.

"We brought this instead. It's proof enough." The Skinner to the right held out Tiffy's stuffed rabbit.

I stepped around Dax and ripped the rabbit from the Skinner's hand. I wasn't sure what I would've done next, but it would've been violent if Rocky hadn't tugged me back over by him.

"We leave with the Plaguer and the girl will be returned the next day," the Skinner who had held the rabbit said.

Not tonight, tomorrow—just long enough for them to get back behind their walls. I knew then that they didn't have her. They wouldn't have killed her, not on purpose. But maybe by accident?

"Don't call another meeting without bringing the girl. We aren't talking until we see her." Dax gave them his back as he turned to Rocky and I.

"We'll kill her," the Skinner said.

"I doubt that," Dax said, and motioned to the side of the boat where the rope ladder was. He wasn't surprised. He wasn't even frustrated. He'd expected this outcome.

* * *

The trip back was the same distance but felt like it took three times as long. I wasn't sure if it was because I wanted to get Dax alone so I could nail him with

213

questions or because I felt drenched in disappointment.

We got back to the Rock, and as we paused before the gate opening, I said, "We need to talk alone before we go back."

This conversation needed to take place outside the walls, where no one could overhear us.

Dax signaled to Rocky, and we pulled off from the gate as he went inside. Dax stopped a few miles away from the Rock.

I got off the bike, needing to see more than the back of Dax's head for this conversation. He got off after me and waited. Even seeing his face, this was one of those times I had no idea what he was thinking, and nor was he giving me any idea.

I tilted my chin up, my eyes narrowing as I shot out my accusation. "You knew the Skinners didn't have her."

He didn't budge for a minute or say anything, and for once, I waited patiently.

"I didn't know anything for sure, but I had my suspicions."

"Why didn't you say anything?"

"I'd hoped I was wrong."

Hoped? It seemed such an odd thing to say considering who might've had her, unless the alternative was death. For the first time, my body refused to go on autopilot, and I had to reach a hand out and lean on the nearest tree or I would've fallen.

Why was it always the kids that slayed me? It had been the same in the Cement Giant. Seeing anyone hurt and abused was hard, but the little ones—watching them lose their innocence as their blind trust in humans was betrayed was always the worst.

It was the betrayal of trust that made everything so much more painful. By the time most of us hit our teenage years, we expected to be betrayed, and somehow it made it easier. All I could think of was Tiffy lying there with me, so sure she would be safe, and I'd let her down.

The words stuck in my throat, but I finally forced them out. "You think she's dead."

"No." A scintilla of relief came, but was quickly washed away by his next words. "I think other things might have her."

"Other *things*? What kind of *things*?" I didn't know if I felt better or worse. My legs hadn't decided either, and I kept a hand firmly on bark.

"There's certain things that aren't spoken of, even between those who have magic. Things that go on in the Wilds that people like to pretend don't exist."

He walked closer to me and I wasn't sure I wanted him to, or more accurately, I didn't want to hear what he was going to tell me. But Tiffy's life was at stake and I didn't have a choice. "What things are you talking about?"

"The things that Tiffy calls friends."

"You're saying her friends exist? They aren't make-believe?" Dax had been the only one I hadn't asked about Tiffy's friends. Even when he hadn't been avoiding me, it just hadn't occurred to me to ask him. Or maybe it had, but the lines of communication were shaky at best, and opening up with *did you see the invisible tea party last week* seemed like an awkward start.

But I'd talked to others, a lot of them. It was why I'd kept telling myself not to listen to her or my gut, and that they didn't exist. "How can that be? No one's ever seen them."

"They're real. The people who do know, they won't admit to it. Too scared. I don't know what their real name is, but they've been referred to as the Wood Mist. No one knows exactly what they are, except that a shimmering cloud has been seen after strange happenings."

"Strange happenings?"

"Crop failures or sometimes an unexpectedly abundant harvest—"

I scoffed, finding holes and knowing that this was crazy. "You're saying people believe this because they grew some vegetables?"

He walked a couple of steps away, as if he sensed I needed space, as he kept explaining. "Best crop in a decade after a three-month drought?" He waited until that sank in.

Okay, that might have some merit, but still. "I need more proof than some crops."

"Things happen. People being lured into the woods, saying they heard the sound of chimes, only to be found dead the next day."

I swallowed over the huge lump in my throat. "Hardly irrefutable proof."

"I've seen it myself, the mist. It was like a shimmering gold cloud. When you were bringing the bombs back from that place with Bookie, it led me to your stash."

I'd thought that he had spies in the woods. I knew how well Bookie and I had buried those bombs. My legs gave out and I ended up sitting in the dirt. I didn't care anymore if I looked weak. "So you saw them." My back hit the tree, and even my spine gave out. "Are they dangerous?"

"They're powerful if that's what you mean, but I don't think they'll hurt her."

My head rolled to the side as I watched him come in closer now, and I rubbed at an eye quickly before evidence could escape. "Why not?" I asked, hoping this would be one story that I couldn't punch holes in.

He sat down next to me and leaned against the trunk, his shoulder brushing mine.

"Because of how I found Tiffy. I'd gotten done with a trade in a hole about a day away. I was on my way back to the farm, heading on my usual route, but there had been massive flooding in the area, so I had to detour.

"I realized this was going to cause me to pass by a farm I hadn't been to in years, but they grew the best coffee beans of anyone. I swear, even if I hadn't remembered, I thought I actually could smell coffee as I was riding.

"I got there and found the entire family dead. Looked like it might have been a small outbreak of the Bloody Death. From the looks of it, it hadn't just happened. I went through the house looking for survivors, but all I found were bodies decomposing.

"Then I found Tiffy. She was sitting on the floor with blocks and in clean clothes, clean diaper, and was well fed. I waited the entire day for someone to come back to the house, the person who must have been caring for her. No one ever came.

"For whatever reason, her whole life they've protected her. I think the Skinners tried to get her and they took her from them."

I realized I was leaning my head on his shoulder, and I left it there. "Why didn't you tell me this?"

"Because if they have her, we might never see her again."

"They wanted to talk to me."

"Do you know why?"

"No, but Tiffy told me more than once. It was before I lost my magic. Dax, I think I have to get it back. I think if I can, they'll talk to me."

I left my head on his shoulder as I stared at the stars, wondering if Tiffy could see them too.

CHAPTER 22

I woke the next morning to Dax standing at the foot of my bed with an intent look that was reminiscent of a certain little girl who had appeared so many times in the same manner. Was this where Tiffy learned it?

But Tiffy wasn't here. It was a recent wound and it cut deep. If we didn't find her, I didn't think it was one that would ever heal. I closed my eyes, wanting to fall back to sleep and not think of Tiffy. Maybe it would have the added benefit of sending Dax the hint I didn't want to get out of bed before there was sunlight.

"Get up. I want to try something."

Dax didn't take hints so well. Lids opened against my better judgment. "Is this something that could be tried at, say, I don't know, *sunup*?"

"No. It has to happen now."

Our eyes met and I could see he wasn't going to budge. Stubborn male.

I closed my eyes again but said, "Then I guess I'll get up," with the fakest cheerful disposition ever heard. "What's this for?" The question was partially garbled on a yawn as I dragged my body upward.

"I'll tell you on the way," he said.

"Of course you will," I said, mostly to myself, since he was already leaving the room and closing my door. I wasn't foolish enough to think that he would leave me alone long enough to catch another few minutes of sleep.

I wouldn't complain about sleep, though. None of us were getting any. Every night I'd wake and see Dax's bedroom door open and the room empty. Tank was late to sleep and early to rise. I knew Fudge wasn't sleeping well, or Bookie for that matter, and neither of them even knew about the meeting with the Skinners yet. I wasn't going to accept the idea I'd never see Tiffy again, and I didn't want to crush their hopes.

It was too soon to lose another person. There should be some sort of rule in the universe that you can't lose more than one person a year. Unfortunately, the universe didn't listen very well, and I'd learned early that I definitely didn't have its ear.

I was up and dressed in five minutes, and we were out the door in another five and shortly through the gate after that. We'd been walking through the forest for a few minutes and he still hadn't told me our purpose yet, and I was waiting for my brain to wake up enough to care.

"Pay attention to where you're going so you know how to get back."

It wasn't light out yet, but we hadn't gone very far either, so I didn't think it was a problem. Plus, I was too tired to bother arguing with him. I nodded, which he probably didn't see, as he was walking ahead of me.

By the time we stopped walking, I'd woken up enough to start harassing him with some questions. "Why are we out here?" It might not have seemed like much of a question, but it was about all the heavy lifting I could handle without bacon.

"I want to try something."

"What?"

"You know your way home from here?"

"Yes, but why?"

He took a deep breath, his head tilted back, making me wonder just how much he could smell on the air. Could he sense a predator or person nearby just from a downwind?

Whatever he sensed, everything must have seemed okay, because he lowered his head and said, "You are going to wait here and I'm going to turn into the beast. My connection to magic is much stronger in beast form at dawn. I'm going to try and sense what's going on with you under the surface. After I'm done, I want you to go back to the compound. I'll be back later tonight. Understand?"

"You can do that? Maybe figure out what's wrong with me?"

"I don't know."

He walked off while I waited, wondering what he might discover. I used to want to be like everyone else.

Now I was scared to death of what he was going to sense—or not. What if there was nothing but a trickle left within me? What if I really never could be that kickass girl he'd thought I'd become?

No, it couldn't be. I could still see the Dark Walkers. I'd have bursts of magic when I needed them. That had to mean something. I knew there was some twinkle of magic left in me, but what if it was exactly that, some small amount that was slowly dying out?

He didn't return for five minutes. Five of the longest minutes I'd ever experienced, while I stood there and wondered what would happen if I was losing my magic. By the time he returned, I'd talked myself in and out of the worst-case scenario ten times.

Dax the beast entered the clearing. He was massive, easily another hundred pounds and a foot taller. Between the red eyes that seemed to glow and the fangs that were visible even when his jaws were closed, I had to consciously keep telling myself that this was the man I knew. This wasn't some wild creature that would tear me apart.

I forced myself to stand still as it—he—neared me. It came closer, and again, just like my other encounters, it started to sniff the exposed skin near my neck. A low growling noise emanated from its chest just before its tongue lapped out and licked me, and I wondered if he had to taste me to sense my magic. My breathing kicked up as he laid his hand on my chest, and I could feel the warmth of it seep into my skin, his claws not so much as nicking me.

Could I ask him what he sensed now? Could he talk as the beast? Did he understand fully in this form? I cleared my throat and figured there was only one way to find out.

"Do you..."

He was gone, taking off in the opposite direction of where we'd come from. Damn, he could move fast, almost a blur. I was still standing there clueless and a bit in awe, as I had been the first time I was standing face to face with the beast and knew it was Dax. Although at least I'd tried to ask questions, even if it hadn't worked out so hot.

The first rays of the sun hit my face with their warmth, and I knew that Fudge would be up soon. I started walking back. At least there was still bacon. And eggs. Of course, I couldn't forget the coffee either.

CHAPTER 23

I'd had breakfast, lunch, dinner, more plates of bacon than was good for me, the sun had risen and fallen, and Dax still hadn't come back. I was sitting on the couch near a lit lantern in my borrowed home with a borrowed book on my lap. It wasn't a Moobie, but some knockoff detective story by a writer who wasn't half as good. The people around here didn't seem to have very high standards, but I was desperate for anything that would keep my mind off Tiffy and the Skinners and the Wood Mists and my magic fizzling, even though I'd tried to feel it near-constantly lately.

Bookie strolled in without knocking. His eyes passed right over me as he scanned the rest of the house. "He's still not back yet?"

I shook my head, knowing he meant Dax.

"I know you know where he went."

"I really don't." Not since that morning, or I would've been stalking him myself. "Why are you so set on looking for him?"

"No reason."

That was a load of bull. He wanted to talk to Dax so they could gang up on me about not going. Even if I could tell Bookie a more definitive answer on Dax's location, something that didn't have anything to do with running through the woods and possibly eating raw meat, I wouldn't.

He looked at me, his head tilted forward and to the side, and then started shaking it slightly.

"You can give me all the condemning looks you want. I know what you want to talk to him about, and I'm not helping. I'm also not going to walk into the Skinners' camp all willy-nilly, so don't worry about it."

He switched tactics and went completely still, just staring now. It was a familiar look. He'd been taking lessons from Dax, I guessed. "Why the change in heart?"

It didn't work with Dax and it certainly wasn't going to work with Bookie. "You and Dax have been making sense, is all." As far as he and everyone else knew, the Skinners had Tiffy, and that was what I'd keep pretending until I could figure out something better to say.

His stance softened into something much more Bookie-like. "Will you let me know if he comes back?"

"Maybe."

His eyes rolled upward but he left without an argument.

When the door swung open again a few minutes later, I expected to see Bookie getting ready for a second round, but Dax had finally returned. I tossed my book on the couch and jumped up.

"What took you so long? Forget it. Just tell me? Did you sense it? What's left?" I asked as I went and locked the door behind him, not wanting to be accidentally interrupted if Bookie sniffed him out somehow.

He walked farther into the living room. He wasn't flushed like he normally was after the change, so he must have changed back a while ago. Why did he have to take so long? He knew I was waiting to find out what he'd sensed.

"It's still there, and still the strongest I've ever felt. But there's something off."

"But what? How did it feel?" I asked, wanting more information, and quicker than he was speaking.

"It feels like there's some sort of dam, like it's blocked or being held back. I've never felt anything like it. It's not gone, but it's not flowing like it should."

I dropped onto the couch.

I was sitting with Tiffy on the back porch and she said, "I think I managed to salvage some things, but I'm not sure. Time will tell."

Only a few days prior she'd said they were making a decision about me. It had to be these Wood Mist things. But why? For what reason?

Had Tiffy known that they were going to take her?

Had she gone willingly? Was it somehow my fault because they were upset with me? Did this have something to do with the Dark Walkers thinking I was the key?

And the chimes. Had the Wood Mist been trying to lure me to my death?

"What are you thinking?" Dax asked, startling me from my thoughts. His eyes narrowed, and I knew he was going to press me, because Dax didn't back off from the scent of blood.

I wanted to tell him, but what if I was really the last Plaguer, his only chance at vengeance against the Dark Walkers? If he knew the Wood Mist were the ones that took my powers, would he want to help me get them back, or would he fear what that would lead to? Right now, I could do what he needed, and it was in his best interests to help me.

If this Wood Mist didn't want me to have my powers, would he still be willing to help me get them back and possibly upset his apple cart? Would he even let me take the risk of trying to talk to these creatures that had Tiffy, or would it be the same as with the Skinners once he knew they wanted me?

"Nothing."

He opened his mouth, and I knew he wasn't going to let it go, so I took the first shot. "Why didn't you come back right away when you knew I was waiting?"

He walked over to the kitchen and took a swig

from one of the water containers. "Because I had things to handle."

I got up from the couch and took a few steps toward him, hands on my hips. "Why is it that when you turn into the beast, this vicious-looking thing with fangs out to here and eyes glowing red, you can't stand to be near me afterward?"

He stared at me with a deadened look in his eyes and flat out lied to my face. "Not true."

I thought about his answer for less than a minute before I determined it definitely was a lie. He was a better liar than I was, I'd give him that.

The first time he'd been a beast, I hadn't known it was him. When I'd seen him shortly after, he nearly lost his shit on me. He'd been all rough edges and not smooth ice. Almost every time after that, he'd kept his distance for a while afterward. Just as he had today.

Margo's voice popped into my head suddenly. We'd spent more than one afternoon with her trying to fix my inappropriate behavior. She used to tell me that sometimes people lied, and even though you knew they were lying, it was because they didn't want to discuss something with you. Polite society left the subject alone.

I used to disagree and ask her what good would come from that. So as I knew he was lying to me, the memory of Margo's words replayed over and over in my head. I should listen to them, since she wasn't here to argue her case. I'd already moved the subject of discussion from the matter I'd wanted to avoid.

Then again, the Wilds was far from polite society, and I found I really did want this answer.

"No. I think you definitely do avoid me, and I want to know why," I said.

He plunked the water container down on the counter and walked back to where I was in the living room. "Maybe I'm afraid I'll eat you. Ever think of that?" he asked, and I wasn't sure if he was kidding or trying to alarm me.

I was stunned into silence for all of half a second. "No freaking way. You're nicer to me when you're the beast. Hell, you lick me when you're Hairy."

His entire body froze; even his hair seemed to stiffen. "I avoid everybody. Not just *you*."

That answer might not have been bad if he hadn't accented the word *you* like people used to say the word *Plaguer*.

He headed toward the door, and I didn't try and stop him. Whether he would talk about it or not, I'd get my answers eventually. The best thing about this whole confrontation was it bought me some time.

I settled back on the couch with my lousy book, but I didn't read it. I kept looking at the door in between trying to mentally sift around inside myself. If they'd somehow shut my magic down, there had to be some way to break it free.

The door swung open, and I thought it was going to be Dax back to confront me. "Is he here?" Bookie asked, five minutes too late.

Tank walked in right behind him. "Dax here?"

"No. He left a few minutes ago."

Bookie scratched his head, and his sigh said he was giving up for now. "I'll see you guys later. I told them I'd go help out with Becca anyway. She's having contractions."

"What?" I asked, a rock hitting my gut as I tried to count the time that had passed. How long ago had she left? No, it couldn't be Dax's. Even if she'd been pregnant when she left the farm, she couldn't have been far along enough to be giving birth, and her stomach had been completely flat last time I'd seen her.

"I thought she was barren?" Tank asked, and my eyes shot to him.

"Not our Becca. The one from here," Bookie said, neither of them paying attention to me.

Bookie left, and Tank hesitated at the door, telling me to leave a message for Dax that he was looking for him.

I nodded as my brain did double duty.

Becca was barren? The only woman I'd been able to connect Dax to, and she was barren. No way that was a coincidence.

CHAPTER 24

Screw the book and this house. I needed wide-open air and a sky full of stars above my head. Maybe then I could recharge enough to get this magic kick-started and break through whatever they'd done to me.

I left the house, determined to get my head clear instead of sitting there and staring at the door. I headed straight to the wall and walked along to the place I'd seen an uneven surface with a few bricks missing, a spot I could use to help me scale to the top. With the way the trees were, if I positioned myself just right, I'd bet no one could see me up there. Made me wonder why they hadn't fixed it.

Had to be a soft point in defense. I'd alert them to it…just as soon as I left here for good.

I scaled the wall and found a nice, cozy place to settle in. It was a smoother seat up on top of the wall than I could've hoped for. If I had a blanket, I could've slept up here.

There was a beautiful view of the skyline, and the sound of the stream running close by drowned out any of the human noises.

I lay on my back, so all I could see were stars.

"You took my spot." Rocky's deep voice startled me, and he grabbed my arm as I jerked back toward the edge.

"Don't fall off the wall. Dax will think one of my people killed you."

He let go of me and I sat up and scooted over, making room for him as I hung my legs off the ledge.

"Sorry. I've been known to steal spots in the past."

He settled in next to me, legs hanging beside mine, completely at ease, like a guy that was used to having a lot of friends and was comfortable with people.

I did the same, except I was faking it.

"How do you like it here?" he asked.

I hated it, but even I didn't need Margo to tell me that was the wrong answer. "It's really nice."

He laughed, a husky sound that emanated from his chest.

"I don't blame you. I wouldn't like it either if I were you." He leaned forward, resting muscular forearms on his legs as he looked out over the expanse of land. "It wouldn't always be like this. If you stayed, they'd get used to you."

"Sure." I wasn't going to be here long enough. I didn't have any interest in anybody getting used to anybody else. I wanted to go home, which had turned out to be a pretty yellow farmhouse.

"When Dax said he was bringing someone by that was a little different, I knew what he meant. I was

233

nervous. It might be different where you come from in Newco, but superstition runs deep in the Wilds. I'd never met a Plaguer before. I didn't know if any of the rumors were true or if you could still get people sick. When Dax told me how long you'd been at the farm, I figured there wasn't anything to it. Like I said, they'd get used to you. You have options."

"What do you mean?" I asked, looking away from the stars and at him.

He turned his head and did the same. "I know your only concern is finding Tiffy right now, but after you do, you could stay here. It wouldn't be charity. There's a worth to what you can do and who you are." He was staring at me in a way that made me unsure whether I should be leaning in closer or jumping off the wall.

I looked back at the stars, trying to shake the uncertainty. "So you really believe in the Dark Walkers?"

"Most of us here do. I've seen some crazy shit in my life, Dal. Dark Walkers aren't that far a leap. Once the people here realized that you offered us another layer of protection from the outside, which I would make sure they did, they'd start to embrace you. You could have a good life here."

I felt his fingers push back a strand of my hair behind my ear, and I panicked as I realized Rocky might not only be offering me a job. I looked at him and wondered: was this it? Was he going to kiss me?

Did I want him to? He wouldn't be such a bad choice. He was a survivor, like me.

And he made me feel good.

"I'll definitely think about it," I said, not sure what was going to come next.

"Do that," he said, and then disappointed me because he got up. "I've got some business I still have to go handle, but I'm sure I'll see you soon," he said, smiling as he left me alone on the wall while my heart was doing laps around my chest.

* * *

I was walking back to the house to go to sleep. I really was, because I didn't want to think of men or magic or Tiffy or Becca or really just about anything else tonight.

The first thing that screwed up my plan of crawling into bed in the next ten minutes was looking over to my right at the exact right moment to see some guy backhand a girl who was nearly a foot shorter than him. My second mistake was looking around, hoping someone else was still up and over by the lake and would notice and handle the problem. I should've just kept walking and assumed there was, but of course there wasn't.

I had my own problems. I didn't need more. I should have kept walking away, but I walked toward them instead.

"Everything okay?" I asked the girl, realizing I recognized them both from the first dinner I'd had here with Rocky.

"Mind your own business," the guy said, while the girl said nothing.

I shook my head. He didn't get it. I wasn't here because I wanted to be. They'd stolen my steaks. I didn't want to help them. "If only I could. I don't particularly like either of you, but I can't allow you to strike her again."

"You need to go," he said. She still hadn't spoken.

"I told you. I can't." He had no idea how much I wanted to. It was tempting, but I'd told myself after I got out of the Cement Giant that I'd never watch someone get abused again without doing something, even if I really, *really* wanted to. "I walk away, pretend I don't see this, and it's a slippery slope. One day I wake up and realize I'm an asshole like you. Not what I'm looking to do."

"You think because you came here with Dax, I give a shit what you want?" The guy wasn't only a foot taller than the girl he'd hit, but me as well, I discovered as he got closer. The way he was eyeing me up and down, he'd noticed, too.

"No. This has nothing to do with Dax. I can handle a small problem like you on my own." I really hoped so, anyway. He didn't say anything, and then he took a step back.

"I thought so." Actually, I hadn't thought anything of the sort. But had hoped he'd think twice about laying hands, or fist, on a Plaguer.

"I think it's time to call it a night," Dax said from somewhere behind me. Damn, it hadn't been me after all.

The guy said nothing, but huffed a bit before he turned and took off before Dax reached me.

"You okay?" I asked the girl who, even after I'd come to her aid, still seemed afraid to get close to me. She nodded and mumbled something about having to get home. She took off toward the houses, the opposite direction the guy had gone.

"Come on," Dax said as we followed the girl at a distance. "You shouldn't have gotten involved."

"How am I supposed to walk away from that?" I said, waving a hand toward the girl, who was now pretending we didn't exist.

"That woman has been offered help more times than I can count, and continues to go back to him. There's nothing you can do for her."

"How come that never happens at the farm? Huh?" I knew for a fact that Dax had laid a beat-down on more than one guy who'd thought it was acceptable to hit women back at the farm. Lucy had told me during one of her morning tirades about some guy at the farm she hated who she wished would step out of line, just so he

237

would earn one of those beat-downs from Dax. "You've got all these separate rules for what I should do opposed to what you should do."

"You're absolutely right, but we're different. You've got a savior complex because of what happened to you, but you can't back it up yet. If you aren't careful, it's going to get you killed one day. I know what you went through before I got you out of that place, but you need to keep your head on straight."

It was the last thing I'd expected to hear from him. I'd thought we didn't go there with each other. We left the bad shit alone. Saving my ass didn't give him a pass, and dredging it up did nothing good. Yet here he was digging around, looking to find himself some skeletons.

We paused as the girl walked into her house. I crossed my arms in front of me as I stared at him. "That place was a lifetime ago. Leave it there."

"What if burying all your feelings about that is also burying your magic? You want me to help you, but only up to a point, only if I don't step on your toes too much."

"Because that stuff doesn't matter anymore."

"It's doesn't?" His eyebrows shot up, daring me to deny it again.

"No. It doesn't."

"You still can't sit down to a meal without looking at it like it's your last, or how you eat like someone is going to steal your food from you. What about the way you look at the walls, and the way you avoid spots that are a little too tight, like someone might shove you in and not let you out?"

What did he think I was going to do? Cry about the hole? He'd found me in it. He didn't need to know how many times I'd been there before, or for how long. It was bad enough I couldn't look at a small space without getting a chill down my spine, or talk about the laundry list of other injustices.

I was among the lucky. I'd made it out. Some hadn't. I didn't see any good in dragging out the sordid details of what had happened in my life before now.

I turned and headed toward our house, wishing he wouldn't follow me, but I wasn't that lucky.

"Don't act like it doesn't matter," he said.

I'd decided a long time ago that you were as strong as you wanted to be. I wanted to be carved from stone, so I forced away every horrible memory he was trying to pull from me, refused to let them surface. "Because it doesn't. That's not the problem with me."

"How do you know?"

Shit. Now what did I tell him? I was convinced the Wood Mist did this to me? Maybe they'd even want to kill me if I got it back. Would he choose Tiffy or his vengeance?

"Because what I went through isn't anything new, and it wasn't a problem before," I said, and walked into the house and straight into the bedroom, slamming the door for good measure.

I opened it back up and yelled, not caring who heard me, "By the way, I don't like you right now," and shut the door again.

I lay on the bed for all of a minute before I marched back out and into his room, pushing the door open.

"Why are you so intent on helping me get my magic back, anyway? What's in it for you?"

"Before you lost some of your magic, Tiffy said the Wood Mist wanted to talk to you. Maybe if you get it back, they'll try again."

I held the doorknob, but didn't feel like slamming it anymore. I thought he'd weighed vengeance at a higher price than Tiffy. I might've been wrong.

"I still don't like you right now, but I'll probably not hate you tomorrow."

"I can live with that."

CHAPTER 25

I sat on my haunches by the lake and threw a stone out toward the center, focusing on a leaf floating on the surface. It skipped once before it sank, falling way short of its mark. Nope, didn't look like the magic wanted to work today either.

I felt Dax nearing before he was standing beside me. "Come on. I've got something we need to do."

He turned and left but I remained where I was.

I heard his footsteps stop. "We need to go now."

I stood and turned around, stuck my hands in my pockets, and didn't budge any farther. "Why? Is there going to be another conversation like there was last night?"

Nothing more needed to be said. The message was clear. He'd crossed one of my lines pretty badly yesterday. I'd lain in bed for a long time last night thinking about the wounds he'd poked at. I didn't plan on letting him ruin another day. I was taking a stand on this one. Yes, I still needed him, but I had my limits.

He did a single shake of his head. It might not have seemed like a huge concession, but he got it. It was enough, for now.

I took a step toward him and then we were walking side by side.

"You do know we are equals, right? You could try *asking* me to do stuff sometimes." How was it that I ended up always doing what he wanted? He did often have some good ideas of what to do, but still. Here I was doing it again just because he shook his head, and I thought that maybe there might be a tiny hint of remorse.

I was going to have to stop this easy capitulation. It would give him a big head. I corrected myself. Bigger. I should probably ignore at least one out of every three demands if I wanted to retain any self-respect in this relationship.

"Who said we're equal?"

"What's that supposed to mean? Of course we're equals." Perfect example of what was wrong with him.

"If there was one plate of bacon left in the world and we were both starving, I'd be eating. Nothing about that is equal," he said as we walked toward the gate.

"Then how come when there isn't that much food you always share?" I asked, while I watched him signal to the guard to open the gate, and then we walked over to his bike, which he'd left here.

"Because I need you alive."

"What if you didn't? If there were only one piece of jerky and we were starving, you wouldn't give me half?"

"I'd give you half because you're one of my people."

"So what does that mean for everyone else you meet?" I looked at the people milling around the town center we'd just walked through. "Like some of the people here at the Rock?"

He shrugged. "I guess that means they're fucked." He didn't seem to care that several of them heard him as they passed by us.

"Wouldn't you feel bad?"

He tilted his head slightly closer as if he were about to tell me a secret. "No. I'd feel full." His lips turned up in the hint of a smile and we climbed onto his bike.

I had a strong feeling he wasn't teasing me, but I had enough problems right now. I'd have to save the hypothetical world from starvation another day.

I was pulling my knees and arms tight as Dax maneuvered us through the opening with barely an inch to spare. Sometimes I wondered how the bike stayed upright with the way he drove. Dax's driving was in rare form today, and I pressed my cheek against his back as he cut us too close to a tree, then a bush, before I closed my eyes.

The one thing I really hated was the lack of communication when we were on the bike. We'd whipped through the forest and I had no idea where we were going. That was what I got for wasting time on hypothetical jerky questions.

He stopped the bike about twenty minutes later, and the first thing I did when I got off was ask him, "What are we doing out here?"

He got off quickly after me and got to work stashing the bike in some shrubs. "One of the first dinners you ever had at the house, Bookie asked you if you were a hunter or a gatherer. Do you remember?"

I wasn't sure where this was coming from or how to answer. Of course I remembered everything about that night: Fudge's cooking, the conversation, the way the fireplace had crackled in the background, and the blue patterns on the plates. Every minutia of that evening had been burned into my memory.

Finally, I answered, "Sure." As if it had been no big deal.

"You said you were a hunter that night."

Yeah, I remembered that clearly too. I'd said that back when I had a much higher estimation of my abilities. I'd still be a hunter, with or without magic, but it might take a bit longer now.

He stepped in front of me. His eyes looked nearly as intense as when he was in beast form. I was starting to wonder if the glow was always there under the surface if I looked close enough.

"Are you ready to hunt?"

I knew there was only one prey he was talking about. Dark Walkers.

I'd dreamt of hunting Dark Walkers for the majority of my life. For so many years I hadn't been able to because I'd been stuck in the Cement Giant. Then I'd been stopped out of fear for my friend's lives, two of which died anyway. I'd spent a month staring at these monsters when I was taken to the holes for inventory, being held back from doing more, all because of Dax. It looked like the fetters were finally off.

Goosebumps spread across my skin. Not from fear, which would have been the rational reaction to his question, since my magic was on the fritz, but from excitement.

"When do we start?"

"Now."

He didn't wait for me to say anything else—he left and expected me to follow. This time I was right behind him.

"We go on foot from here."

My muscles were already tense, body ready for action. "Where are they?"

"I spotted a group not long ago that looked suspicious." He stopped and lifted his head to the air and then pointed up ahead.

It was a couple hundred feet farther when we came upon the group of three that were settling in and making camp.

He looked at me with the same question he'd had

in the numerous holes we'd visited.

I nodded. He was right. They were Dark Walkers.

He motioned for me to stay put while he took off. I knew he was doing a perimeter sweep to make sure there weren't any more. When he came back, there was no time to talk. He walked right into the middle of the camp.

I hurried after him, not wanting to be left out of the fun. The group of three turned toward us and Dax hooked his finger toward me and said, "She's the Plaguer you're looking for."

If I wasn't positive I was standing on the dirt, I would've sworn the ground had disappeared beneath my feet. That was how it felt to hear him say that.

I didn't have time to scream at him or ask what he was up to, as he walked to the perimeter of the clearing and leaned against the tree.

Hurt, a kind I didn't know existed, burned in me. Was Dax betraying me? The Dark Walkers looked at him, as I did. It didn't take long for us all to realize the same thing. I was on my own. One even had the nerve to laugh before they swarmed me.

I had a knife in both hands before they got in range. I'd think about his betrayal later. Right now I needed every ounce of my attention focused on not getting killed.

The first one made a grab for me, its hand tight on my wrist, but I used the knife in my free hand to cut through it. My knife didn't hesitate, slicing his flesh and bone as if it were butter. The Dark Walker stepped back, screaming as he did. If he didn't look so shocked at what I'd done, I would've thought it was a natural thing to cut through him so easily.

I glanced over at Dax quickly, thinking maybe he was going to step in as the other two came at me from different directions. He remained leaning on the tree and was looking at his nails.

I lunged in the direction of one of the Dark Walkers and landed a knife in his eye socket.

I squatted, quickly dodging a blow from the other, and with my right hand launched the other knife into the third one's chest. My knife found its home easily. That was when I thought I heard Dax yell from the side to leave one alive, but there was no stopping me. With the one knife left, I attacked the one with no hand and sliced across its throat to finish the job.

I stood, knife still steady in one hand as it dripped black blood, and the last one fell to the ground gurgling.

Surrounded by my dead foes, I turned on Dax where he was finally straightening up from his leisurely position. He walked over and clucked his tongue.

"Didn't you hear me? You weren't supposed to kill them all." He nudged one of the bodies with the toe of his boot. "Now who are we supposed to interrogate?"

"You bastard!" I screamed, not caring if there were five more Dark Walkers hiding around the bend that might hear me. "You could've gotten me killed. I thought you were supposed to have my back? What is wrong with you? What the hell do you think you're doing?"

"If I'd stepped in, that would've ruined the experiment." His calm somehow made it worse and fueled my own anger.

"Oh, well, then don't let the matter of my life interfere with your experiment." I kneeled beside the body and wiped my knife off on the Dark Walker's shirt, making sure I didn't get any additional blood on myself.

"You're fine."

I reached down and retrieved my other knife from the chest of the Dark Walker and replace it at my ankle. I wiped my palms off on my legs. "I don't know what type of people you run with, but I thought we were on the same side."

"We are, but I needed to know for sure," he said as he moved around and surveyed my kills.

"Know what?"

"If you could get past the block when it really counted."

"You could've found out a different way."

"None of the other ways were as reliable. Relax. You weren't ever in mortal danger. I knew they weren't going to kill you. Whatever their purpose for you is, they want to keep you alive. Plus, I was here. I wouldn't have let them seriously hurt you." He stood and let out an annoyed sigh. "I can't believe you didn't leave one alive for me."

"Really? Because I can't believe you left me fighting all by myself."

"Your lack of trust says more about you than me. Luckily, I'd predicted as much, and used it to my advantage."

"What is that supposed to mean?"

"It means that you don't trust anyone, and I took advantage of it."

"And you're so trusting?"

"Never said I was, but I'm not sure how many times I have to save your ass before I gain a little of it."

I wasn't sure if him telling me he'd wanted to keep me alive was draining the anger or if the adrenaline leaking out was taking the edge off. It could've been the fact that there was relief mixed in too. I might hate his tactics, but the result made me feel pretty damn good. I could take care of myself, and that was why I didn't walk over to him and punch him in the face the way I'd contemplated a few minutes ago.

As I calmed down, I saw something else in his expression. A lot of times, maybe even most of the time, Dax tended to look at me with an expression of tolerance. I got it—he was a lot older, might have seen a few more things than I had. But he wasn't looking at me like that right now. He was looking at me like maybe, just maybe…

"You were pretty amazing," he said.

Yeah, he was looking at me just like that.

I didn't want to feel my insides getting mushy. Worse, my cheeks growing all warm and flushed, like I'd just gotten told how pretty I was or something. I was acting like a silly girl. I wanted to be a warrior. I'd just killed three Dark Walkers and I was blushing over an approving look. Not acceptable. I couldn't get all soft and stupid over a compliment. I didn't need anyone's approval.

I knelt beside a Dark Walker, pretending to look over his body until my cheeks stopped burning. It was so much easier when he was insulting me. I knew how to deal with insults. That wasn't a big deal. I didn't know how to deal with this.

He walked closer, but luckily remained standing so he couldn't see my burning cheeks.

"That first Dark Walker you killed when you were a child. How did you do it?" he asked.

"Wasn't it in the report you read at the Cement Giant?" How long could a blush last? How long could my blood stay concentrated in my cheeks like this? It seemed like it was getting worse the more I thought of it.

"No. Only that you had."

I was four, but I still remembered it so clearly. I'd heard it was always like that with a first kill. I guessed being a child at the time didn't change that. "It was a teacher at my school. I took my pencil and waited for it to be distracted, looking down at some papers. I came up behind it and stabbed it in the throat."

I stood, the memory fixing the blush, and walked over to the other dead Dark Walker and gave him a kick, just to make sure I'd finished him off.

The reality of just how well I'd fought was beginning to really sink in. I'd taken all three of them on at once, all by myself. They were now dead and I only had a couple of superficial scratches. Not only that, the way it had felt still had my blood near fizzing with life. It had felt as good as it had looked to Dax.

"How did you know these three were Dark Walkers?" I asked, as I looked down at the bodies lying on the ground.

"I've had to do my fair share of killing over the years. Especially in the Wilds, it's unavoidable. Every so often, I'd come across someone different, someone not quite made the same. Tougher, the skin would look normal, but then it would be more like armor. It's how I knew they existed, even before Plaguers gave them a name."

The Plaguers had given them a name over a hundred years ago. My head jerked in his direction before I thought about how it would reveal my thoughts.

He didn't falter from my stare, surely guessing

what I was thinking and not refuting it. Really? He was that old?

"When you finally pointed one out to me and I killed it, I had my proof." He pointed to the dead bodies. "This group was an educated guess. They were out of the way of every main road that leads to anything. No one else would have a reason to be out here unless they were snooping around, possibly looking for you."

"What about drifters or the sort?"

"That's not how it works out here. This area is spoken for and everyone knows it. Rocky doesn't suffer interlopers. This area is marked clearly with Rs that are carved on a regular basis so even newcomers to the area know."

He walked over to the Dark Walker with a stump of an arm and pointed at it. "You shouldn't have been able to slash that one's arm off, not with the knives you carry. They aren't sharp enough. You shouldn't have been able to kill that Dark Walker with a pencil, not in a million years."

He squatted beside the Dark Walker and rested his forearms on his knees, looking at the stump and then at me, just like Rocky had after he'd discovered that the Skinners wanted me too. As if maybe there was more going on and I was hiding some of the pieces.

There might have been more going on, but I was as lost as everyone else.

I wiped my hands off on my shirt, making a show of how filthy I was. I lifted my head, sure I heard a stream close by. "I'll be back in a minute," I said. "Going to go clean up a bit."

He nodded then finally went back to checking out the Dark Walker corpses.

CHAPTER 26

I might have fared physically pretty well, but I was really filthy. My pants were splattered and my shirt was torn and nearly covered in their blood. A little water wouldn't do any harm. I still had to walk back into the camp later, and I scared those people enough when I was clean.

I made my way in the direction of the sound of water, catching a couple more scrapes from some nasty bushes on the way.

My pants were leather and a couple of splashes of water had them in fairly decent shape, but my shirt was probably going to have to be thrown out. One of those suckers looked like he'd exploded on me, probably when I'd sliced his neck. I pulled off the grey tank top and gave it a good rinsing just so I didn't have to walk back to the Rock with Dark Walker blood touching my skin. I wrung it out best I could, but the damp cloth was irritatingly clingy and still looked filthy.

Having done the best I could, I stood and headed back toward where Dax was, but detoured around the prickle bushes. That was when I saw it in the not-too-far distance. It hadn't rained in a couple of weeks, but there was a mud field that looked to be a mile wide, if my estimate was accurate.

"Dax?" I yelled, and then started back to find him, not sure if he'd hear me from here.

I heard nothing and then he was in front of me. It amazed me how quickly he could move, and how silently. How had I never noticed how quiet he was when I first met him?

"Do you try and make noise sometimes? Is that what it is? Because I don't remember you being this quiet before."

He wasn't paying attention to what I was saying, staring at me in a way that made my knees almost buckle. That was close to a miracle. My knees never buckled, or at least not over a look. But there he was, looking all sorts of intense, and there I was, all buckly. The energy he was throwing off felt like it was hitting me in waves. Magic, Tiffy had said, and I was inclined to agree.

I might be sexually naive, but I wasn't utterly stupid. Or not anymore. That was an *I want some sexy time* look. I'd seen enough of the men in the camp do it now to recognize it. Did he want me? No. I'd laid myself out like a free buffet for him and he hadn't even sampled.

Still, he was looking at me just like I'd seen one of those guys back at the Rock look at this one girl before I saw them all over each other beside the lake later that night.

I crossed my arms over my chest and looked at the dirt by my feet, feeling weird all of a sudden. When I looked back at Dax, he seemed normal again, even if he was still pumping out that strange magic.

"You have to see something," I said, trying to break the weird tension. I turned and headed back to the mud field, while trying to make sense of what I'd seen and felt from Dax. I knew he didn't want me, so what was that look about? Maybe I was interpreting it completely wrong. Maybe it was all the killing that made him look and feel all charged up?

I got to the field and stopped with him by my side, peeking over at him. He was looking at the field intently now, instead of me.

"What do you think? Weird, right?" I asked, and I dropped my arms from my chest, wondering if I could get him to give me the *sexy time look* again. What would've happened if I hadn't panicked back there and crossed over to him at that moment? Would he have kissed me? Would it have felt like chapter ten? Would I have "swooned in his powerful arms" just like the girl in the book?

"This isn't the first wasteland of mud I've seen," he said, his undivided attention on the field.

I looked over the expanse. It wasn't a pretty sight, but it was just mud. "Maybe an underground spring?" I asked, trying to maneuver myself in front of him, but was thwarted when he walked right up to the edge of it and then squatted down.

"It smells wrong," he said.

I followed over to where he was and his arm shot up; he still wasn't looking at me, but was blocking me from going any farther, as if I'd planned on mud wrestling. Silly man. Still, I was close enough to take a deep breath. "It smells like mud to me."

He took a deep breath, held it, and let it out slowly. "No. There's something off. Don't get any of it on you."

I leaned closer to the mud field in spite of his arm and breathed deeply, becoming more interested in the field than a look I'd probably mistaken anyway.

"I smell nothing."

"I have better senses."

"How many of these mud fields have you seen?" The thing really was a mess. There wasn't a single sprig of vegetation to be seen.

"A few, and all with the same off smell of rotting flesh."

I was glad I couldn't smell that.

He straightened up quickly and looked over toward where the trees were growing really thick.

"Wait here," he said. "I think there's another one."

"I thought *we* were hunting Dark Walkers? I can kill three alone and now I can't touch this one?"

He turned to me, and I caught his eyes shifting

down, but they shot right back up. "Yes, because you killed *all* the other ones and I wanted one alive. Stay here. I'll take him down and then you can come over while I question him."

I'd read about something like this. "You mean like good cop, bad cop?" This was straight out of Moobie.

"What the hell is that?"

"You go in like a... You go be yourself. After you're done wowing it with your charm, I'll pretend to befriend it and it'll spill all its secrets."

"You're going to befriend it? That's going to work?"

"You probably don't have experience in any other area but scaring, but yes, it should." He had no idea what he was talking about. I was getting very good at faking being nice with people.

"Wait here."

I waited, at least until he had a good lead on me, anyway.

By the time I saw the Dark Walker, it already knew Dax was about to attack. Dax moved in a blur, and it hit me how much he actually held back when he sparred with me, or I would've been one messed-up-looking chick.

Dax had the Dark Walker tackled and pinned to the ground with almost effortless ease, his heel on the Dark Walker's throat as he held an arm outstretched in his hand. "What are you doing here?"

The Dark Walker's head was immobile, but I saw his eyes shoot to my hand. The brand was no longer there, but a scar still remained.

"Yeah, that's right. I'm a Plaguer. Now what the hell are you?" I asked, deciding it was going to be two bad cops. I couldn't fake nice, not with one of them.

"Fuck you," the Dark Walker said, but it was muted somewhat by the pressure Dax applied to his throat.

His eyes kept shooting back to me, instead of on his immediate threat, which was Dax.

"You recognize her."

I'd thought it was just me, but Dax had noticed the same look. The Dark Walker looked at me like he'd seen me before.

The Dark Walker's eyes darted back and forth between us. "We've all seen her." He smiled after he said it, even as ridiculous at that might look with Dax's heel still at his throat.

"How?"

His attention focused on me alone then. "There's pictures of you everywhere. They're coming for you."

"Who?" Had to give it to the monster. He definitely had balls.

"Answer her," Dax said, and I could see his boot digging deeper into the Dark Walker's flesh.

"My people."

"Why?"

Dax applied more pressure and then released it, but the Dark Walker said nothing.

"Why?" I screamed.

The smile remained as he refused to reply.

I heard a crack before I looked to see the wrist of the Dark Walker was bent at a painful angle now. Dax must have kept a lot of the beast's strength even when he was human. No man could've snapped that bone with just his hands for leverage.

"Answer her."

"I'm dead anyway."

The words weren't bravado. I could see from the creature's face that it was useless.

Dax lifted his boot off its neck then slammed it back down on its throat, a crack sounding as he did. The thing was dead. "He wasn't going to answer," Dax said, dropping the thing's arm.

"I know," I said, squatting for a minute as I looked at the creature, and realizing the dark mist clung to him even in death.

"We're hunting them. You didn't think it was one-sided, did you?" he asked.

"No."

"They aren't going to leave you alone until they get you back," he said, squatting down beside it, and nailed me with a look. "They really must hate how you can ID them," he said, and I saw the question there, like maybe he had guessed there was more to it and was waiting to see if I'd say something.

"Yeah. Seems so."

"Come on. I'll bury these later. No one is going to find them this far out."

We'd made it all the way back when the bike died right in front of the gate. We both got off as the gate was opening, and he looked at me.

"Shit." He reached over his back and tugged off his shirt then handed it to me.

"Put this on."

"I'm fine." It was a little chilly, but we were almost inside now and I'd be in the house changing shortly.

"No, you're not."

"It's partly dry."

"Not dry enough."

"So I look like a drowned rat. Who cares? Nobody even looks at me. Mostly they try and avert their eyes."

"You can never make things easy." He threw his shirt back on as the door creaked open. Dax stepped in front of me when I would've walked forward, and I heard him say to the guard, "Don't you dare fucking look at her."

I didn't know what his problem was. It wasn't like I looked that bad. Or I hadn't thought so until I felt more than a few pairs of eyes on me as we walked toward the house.

We hadn't gotten very far before Dax was whipping his shirt off and handing it to me again. "Put it on or someone is going to get punched."

I didn't argue this time.

CHAPTER 27

I wasn't that far from the Rock, only a mile or so from the walls. I was in the safe zone, as I'd heard it described around camp. No one came that close to here, that was what they said. But here they were anyway, a group of five Dark Walkers circling me.

It was stupid, but I'd been near the gate when I heard those damn chimes. It was them, the Wood Mist. I knew it was. If I could get to them, find some way to communicate, I could make them understand Tiffy belonged with us.

Dax was all the way on the other end of the place working on his bike when I first heard them. I hadn't had time to get him or anyone else. I saw some guards walking in the open gate and I walked out.

So much for following the chimes. They'd led me right to my enemy. I'd love to see Dax walk up out of the blue, but it wasn't going to happen this time. I was on my own. Hopefully that last time hadn't been a fluke.

A knife in either hand, I prayed to any god I could: Fudge's god, the Gods of the Wilds that I'd heard some speak of—I prayed for whatever magic I had stored inside me to let loose right now.

"What do you want?" I asked.

"You."

That didn't leave much room for negotiation.

"Why?"

"It's our orders."

Two of them came at me at the same time, and I didn't even recognize my own body as it twisted and turned, evading them, and countering with my own attack. I caught one behind the knee, taking him out of commission. I heard his screech of pain as he limped and then fell. The other I nailed on the thigh.

I could see the others grow a little warier. Maybe I wasn't such easy prey after all.

"That's right. I'm not going down so easy."

The other three swarmed, while the other two were limping but still waiting to lend a hand. The heat in my chest was near to bursting, but I wasn't sure the magic was going to save me this time. There were too many.

As if adding to my feeling of impending doom, a bolt of lightning lit the sky and a downpour of rain the likes of which I'd never seen drenched us all.

They came at me, almost all at once, but two of them lost their footing while I seemed to remain steady on my feet, finding target after target. A knife in each hand, I nailed one in the chest before ducking a blow and running a knife behind another's leg and taking out its hamstrings. I was quicker than all of them, and my accuracy was insane. I only needed to see a target to know I would hit it.

The rain stopped as suddenly as it had started, and I was surrounded by dead Dark Walkers. I didn't know how long it took, as every second seemed longer during the fight, but I'd guess it had only been five or ten minutes.

I pulled the bodies under some brush, the wet ground making it easier to move them, but they were too close to the Rock to leave them here. I had to get Dax. Rocky was going to need to know as well. It was his place. I had to let him know how close the threat was getting.

I looked down at the splattered black blood all over me. If I walked back in there like this, no way I'd avoid questions, and I couldn't tell anyone else. They'd freak out for sure.

Dropping to the ground, I rolled around until you couldn't see anything but mud on me. Better than the alternative.

I looked like I'd gone mud pile diving by the time I walked back in the gates, but most of the people here thought I had cooties anyway. What was a little dirt really going to mean to them? More of them noticed than didn't as I walked to the house, but I kept on my way as if nothing was amiss.

Bookie asked when he took one look at me as I walked toward the front of the house, "What've you been doing?"

"I fell." I hated lying to Bookie, but he had enough to worry about, and there was nothing he could do about it anyway. No, I'd talk to Dax, who would be predictably calm about something like this and all would be fine. We'd bury the bodies and that would be the end of it.

Until more showed up.

"You hurt?"

"Just my wardrobe." I walked in the house and tried to step softly so I didn't knock any of the mud crusting on me onto the floor. "Dax still working on the bike?" I asked Bookie, who'd followed me inside.

"Nah, I think he finished up a while ago. Rocky was looking for you. Told me to tell you that you're invited to the dinner tonight."

Shit. Another dinner? I had dead bodies lying a mile from here piled up under a shrub. This wasn't a good time.

I paused by the bedroom door. "How did he say it?"

"Huh?"

He had no idea what I was talking about. I grabbed a change of clothes and headed into the bathroom. I'd make an appearance just in case this was another of those "calm the natives"-type deals. Hopefully, I'd find Dax there and he could help me clean up the mess before anyone tripped over a heap of legs hanging out from under a bush.

"I'm going to go clean up and change. Tell them I'm running a couple minutes behind, is all, but I'll be there soon." I shut the bathroom door before he answered, knowing I was running short on time.

"I'll hang back and wait," he yelled through the door.

"It's okay. Go ahead."

"Nah, I'll wait," he yelled.

I opened the door and saw the fakest smile I'd ever seen, and that included the ones Ms. Edith used to make. "What is it?"

"Nothing. Just figured I'd keep you company." He was shrugging so often that instead of looking like it was a relaxed posture, it appeared more like a nervous tic.

I shook my head but didn't tell Bookie he was the worst liar I'd ever met, even though he won by a long shot.

"What?"

"Nothing," he said, and launched off another flurry of shrugs.

"Tell me."

"It's probably nothing, but…"

"But what? Spit it out."

"Are you and Dax…" More shrugs. If he didn't stop shrugging soon I was going to have to pin him down to make it stop.

"Are me and Dax what?"

"Sometimes the two of you seem…close. You're always disappearing together and stuff like that."

The Dark Walkers must have knocked some of the sense out of me, because it took way longer than it should've for me to figure out where this was going.

"No. We're nothing. He needs me. I need him. That's it." It was mostly the truth, or all I'd admit to, anyway.

"Okay. I was just curious because Becca stopped by to talk to him while he was fixing the bike. I didn't know, was all." He started shrugging again.

"There's nothing between us like that," I said, and shut the door. "Give me five minutes," I yelled, thinking maybe walking to dinner with Bookie wasn't such a bad idea.

* * *

I'd been warned, but it felt a lot worse than I imagined when I saw Dax sitting there beside her. It might have just been luck that they were seated together. I could've convinced myself of that if I didn't see the way she was looking at him. He wasn't looking at her like that, but he wasn't standing up to sit beside me, either.

The bottom line was there was nothing between me and Dax, and there wouldn't be.

268

I felt Bookie's warm hand wrap around mine as we crossed the last ten feet to the table. In this messed-up world, Dax might have been my security, but Bookie was my emotional rock. I kept telling myself I needed to get some distance from Bookie, for his own safety, but then I'd lean on him anyway finding yet another excuse, like tonight.

I sat down at the table with Bookie by my side, and Dax glanced over from where he seemed deep in conversation with Becca. He nodded in greeting and then went back to talking to her, and I was glad for the support of Bookie beside me. This might end up being worse than the first dinner.

I looked down the table, but Rocky wasn't there yet, and that was when I realized something was very different this time. There were hesitant smiles, but they all looked genuine.

A pretty brunette who was sitting across from me held out her hand to shake mine. "I'm Angel. I'm in charge of the wall guards and security in this place."

I took her hand with my scarred one. "Hi."

Then a few more people did the same. I met Toby, who was in charge of the foodstuffs, Susan, the administrator, Pete, the stable guy and all-around animal expert. It went on until the majority of the people within range of me at the table had introduced themselves.

The food was served and I was among the first to

have the bowls in my hand. I noticed that Dax was paying attention as well, and it bugged me. I didn't need him to watch out for me while he sat there with Becca, and I made a point of not looking down at that end of the table after that.

I wasn't sure what was going on until ten minutes into dinner, Angel said, "Rocky said there was a chance you might be willing to stay here? He mentioned you have some unique talents?"

Holy shit, all of these people believed in Dark Walkers? Was that what this was about? Did I care that that was why they were being nice to me? Nah, not really. It was just nice to be included, especially on a night like tonight while Dax was doing his own thing.

Try as I might, I still snuck glances down at Dax's end of the table. I only saw the back of his head, but I could see the way Becca stared at him. I also knew Bookie was beside me, feeling bad for me. Damn if I'd sit here and look like I cared.

I pulled out every trick I had in my bag, every skill I'd used to keep the girls going strong in the Cement Giant, and swallowed my own sadness. Every theatrical trick I'd discovered was employed, anything to hide how I was feeling. I laid out every funny story I could think of, not knowing how they'd be received. I told them about Piggy Iggy vomiting her way through the cafeteria, Patty's bad haircuts—nothing was off limits.

I'd never tried to entertain for anyone but the girls

at the Cement Giant, and I was a little stunned to see how amused the dinner group was as I retold every story with my own personal flair.

They laughed with me, and the sound was sincere. Some of them were laughing so hard they had tears in their eyes. Rocky joined the group at some point, and instead of sitting at the other end of the table, he squeezed in down by the group surrounding me and joined in the laughter.

Wine and ale was flowing liberally as others started adding their own stories, and the dinner took twice as long as it had last time, with all the laughter.

When dinner was finally coming to an end, something I'd never expected to see happened. They were sorry I was leaving them when I stood to leave. Not only did they ask me to hang out longer, their eyes showed disappointment. This group of people, ones who'd feared me when they'd seen the scar on my hand, wondering what had been there before—they didn't want me to leave.

"I want to go check on Fudge," Bookie said, and I waved him off, as the group was still trying to talk me into staying a while longer.

Rocky got up and sat beside me, taking Bookie's seat, carrying a bottle of what I guessed to be whiskey and a couple of shot glasses. "Come on, Dal," Rocky said. "Hang out. Have a couple of drinks."

I saw a blur of movement in the corner of my eye

271

that appeared to be Dax's head turned toward us, and in my gut, I knew he didn't want me to sit here and drink with Rocky.

Rocky knew I could spot Dark Walkers. Dax was afraid he'd lose his Dark Walker IDer or something. Maybe I should let him think he could. I hated the walls, but Rocky seemed like a decent guy. His people liked him. He was in charge of this place and I hadn't heard one bad word about him from anyone.

I smiled and placed my hand on the empty glass. "You pouring or what?"

"How old are you?" he asked as he filled the glasses, and I noticed for the first time he had a killer smile. He smelled pretty good, too.

"Why? Is there a legal drinking age at the Rock I should be aware of?" I asked.

"Nope. I was just curious. Some people think you're a bit young."

He tapped his glass with mine. We both tossed back the whiskey, and a nice warmth filled my chest.

"I have a very old soul." Old and battered, but why get into the gritty details? This was the first time I'd had a pleasant night since Tiffy had disappeared, and I didn't want it to end. I didn't want to think of the pile of dead Dark Walkers I'd left outside the walls. I didn't want to think of anything. I wanted to have a good time.

"I bet you do."

The smile deepened and a single dimple dipped

into his left cheek. This guy wasn't just looking for someone to watch out for Dark Walkers; this guy wanted *me*. Like, as a woman. This was a seasoned and hardened man, not a boy, and I was the one he wanted.

The question was, did I want him? Not that I wanted a fulltime mate. I had too many other things to worry about besides finding a man, but there were other aspects I was interested in learning about. But did I want to learn them from him? His wasn't the face that I'd pictured seeing when I had my first time, but maybe it should be?

I watched as he refilled our glasses. He had nice hands, big but gentle looking. His hair was thick and his body was filled out in a way that seemed perfect. More importantly for a person in the Wilds, he was tough.

I leaned an elbow on the table and flipped my hair to the side, liking the fact that I was this man's object of desire. I'd bet this was a man that could pull off chapter ten with flair.

The only thing screwing up the moment was I felt Dax's stare land on me. I could've been wrong, though, because my radar was getting a little fuzzy as the whiskey kicked in. How had I forgotten how great this stuff was?

I caught sight of someone walking toward the still mostly full table, and saw it was Tank making his way over to Dax. Then I saw the two of them staring at me. That was when I knew the good times were coming to an end. He got up and started walking over to me, and I stood, knowing what was to come. Killjoy.

"Dal, you need to come with me," Dax said as he stood over me.

"Can't it wait? We're having a drink," Rocky said.

I looked at the two men and realized this could get ugly really quickly. I couldn't handle any more ugly. A pile of corpses were about my max for one night.

"It's all good. I've got something to handle with Dax." I patted Rocky on the shoulder, realizing I'd just touched him without thinking about it. I never did that with people. I pulled my hand back and Rocky grabbed it.

"Anything I can help you handle?" he said.

"No," Dax said, cutting that conversation off.

"I'm good," I mouthed, and walked off, hoping Rocky would stay and Dax would follow. It worked after a second of delay and a slightly hostile look between the two men.

CHAPTER 28

Dax didn't say anything on the way back, but his magic was cranking. It wasn't until we were in the house alone and the door closed that he finally spoke. "What were you doing back there?" he asked.

Even with my whiskey buzz, I heard the underlying anger. "I don't know," I said, walking in and plopping down on the couch, feeling kind of limber myself.

It was the truth. Rocky was the first man I'd ever flirted with. I wasn't sure what I'd been doing exactly. I wasn't going to tell him I was flirting and risk sounding like a total fool. Maybe he was talking about something else.

"Don't do it again."

"Don't do what? Take a shot of whiskey or talk to Rocky? What's my orders now?" I asked, kicking my ankles up onto the arm of the couch.

"Rocky isn't the man for you."

Okay, we *were* talking about the same thing, so I must've been doing it right. That was a very useful thing to know for the future, because there was a high likelihood I'd be doing that exact thing again. Why shouldn't I? I was a single woman and that was a part of life, and I was going to live it. Seemed logical to me.

"Did you hear me?" he asked, and I was thinking I could've used one more shot of whiskey right now. One more would've been useful to quiet down that last little part of me that was warning me to tread softly right now, because Dax was very agitated for some reason.

"Why? Who's right for me? You don't think Bookie should be with me. I heard you tell Becca that before she left the farm. You didn't—"

I stopped short. Even with whiskey, I didn't want to discuss that.

"Now Rocky shouldn't be with me. Who am I allowed to be with, Dax?"

I stopped looking at the ceiling and turned my head toward him when I didn't hear anything.

"Well? What am I supposed to do? Should I wait for your approval?" I mocked.

He walked farther into the house and came to stand by the couch. "Yes. Especially since you seem to be clueless about it. Rocky wants you for one reason, and that's to use you to spot Dark Walkers."

Anger had me sitting up. "He likes me."

"Because he can use you."

That comment got me to my feet. "And what about how you're using me?"

"You get something back from our arrangement. I'm not trying to get in your head and twist you up so that you do what I want."

For someone who wasn't trying, he'd done a fairly good job at it anyway.

"What about Becca? What's she get?"

"What are you talking about? There is no me and Becca."

"You use Becca because she's sterile. That's why it's okay to be with her, isn't it? It's not a guess for you, is it? You can smell it on her or something. You and Becca keep your secrets and I'll do my own thing."

"Don't do it."

"I can do whatever I want, and kiss whoever I want."

He grabbed my arm when I would've turned and walked away from him.

"Get off me."

"He kissed you?" he asked, a little too softly.

Now I was sure he was angry. I wanted to lie, but what if he said something to Rocky and then I looked like a fool? "No. But I'm saying I could."

His eyes shot to my arm and then he was pulling it closer to the lantern on the table. "Why do you have a bruise forming?"

Huh? I looked down and confirmed that there was nothing there. "I don't have a bruise."

"You will by tomorrow. Tank said you were covered in mud when you came in. What happened?"

I was gearing up for the second leg of the fight, letting my temper get the best of me before I realized this was the exact thing I'd wanted to do all night. Tell him what had happened. Then I'd found him sitting there with Becca giving him moon eyes and I'd changed my mind.

At some point in the future I'd have the liberty of choosing who had my back, but right now I needed Dax. I had to shove all the other things to the side. I'd let him keep the illusion of control if that was what I needed to do. I was good at that game. I'd been playing it for years.

"I was attacked by Dark Walkers."

"Where?"

"A little bit from here. Down to the east and around the bend by where the stream drops off. I dragged the bodies under a bush. I could use some help getting rid of them."

"Stay here," he said, and walked out of the house.

I waited ten minutes and walked out too.

* * *

"What's wrong?" Bookie asked as he caught up with me on my way toward the part of the wall I could climb.

"Nothing," I said, altering my path, since I didn't want to share that place with anyone else.

"I thought we were friends?"

"We are. That's why you're not going to press me

278

to talk about it."

Bookie was looking at where I'd just run from. "I don't know why you let him get to you so much. I know you were putting up a front at dinner, but you were amazing. You don't have any idea how fantastic you really are."

"Bookie, I'm fine. Let's just drop it." I didn't need my ego inflated to feel better. Even if I had seemed that great for one night, I was a Plaguer first, and that tainted everything about me.

"No. I won't. Back there tonight at dinner, instead of being the Dal that hangs back from strangers because you expect them to hate you, you let them see what I get to see all the time. They were blown away by you."

"I think you're laying it on a little thick now." I knew I'd entertained them, but that was a far cry from liking me. Like Dax said, I had a use. And according to him, that was all that Rocky wanted from me.

"No. I'm not. You're special. I see it, and tonight they did too. Dax knows it but he acts like an ass. I swear, I don't know what his problem is. He doesn't want anyone else near you but then does nothing."

"Bookie, Dax doesn't want me." I stared at him, hoping he'd understand and let the subject drop, because I wasn't sure I had it in me to explain it any further or argue the point. It sucked enough that he didn't want me. I wasn't in the mood to have to convince anyone else of that fact.

"Yes he does." Bookie was digging in, and I knew from previous experience that he could shovel as well as Tiffy used to. I started a lap around the lake with Bookie beside me.

"Really? Because you haven't heard him tell me that I could leave at any time. That's not something people say a lot when they want to keep you around. Sometimes I've felt like I've practically had his boot on my ass."

"He's full of shit. I don't know what he's doing or waiting for, but he's not letting you go anywhere."

I stopped walking halfway around the lake and said, "The only thing he wants me around for is to spot Dark Walkers. That's it." I turned and headed back to the house, thinking my bedroom might have been the smarter bet.

"You don't get it. You aren't the type of girl you let get away."

I shook my head but stopped arguing. Bookie didn't understand. He hadn't seen him let Becca walk away and she'd been perfect for him. She'd be perfect for any man. Even now I could see how he regretted it. If he could walk away from her, he certainly wasn't going to be stuck on me.

CHAPTER 29

Dax was predictably gone by the time I woke up. I was becoming more and more convinced that he didn't need as much sleep as a normal human, if he needed any at all. After last night, I was glad. The sting of what had been said was still smarting.

I dragged a brush through my hair, cleaned up a bit, and headed next door for breakfast. Fudge was the only one there when I walked in, and even she wasn't really there anymore. She might've looked older, but she'd never acted it, until now. She'd never looked so depleted of the life that glowed within. The fierce woman I'd known was gone.

I grabbed a piece of bacon from a mound that I knew was fried for me and folded myself into the kitchen chair opposite her.

"This is the best bacon I've ever had," I said.

"I'm fine, Dal."

She looked anything but. "Do you want to go look for herbs in the forest today?"

"I'm okay, really. Or I will be once I know something one way or another."

She was looking down at her plate and I didn't

know what to do. Did I tell her we might never see Tiffy again? Should Dax? Was it better to let her think she was dead? What if Tiffy was? We didn't really know, not for sure.

I smiled and ate a few more pieces of bacon and some eggs as quickly as I could choke them down, literally. Watching Fudge like this was the final nail in my appetite suppressant. If it wasn't for the fact that I knew the magic needed fuel if it was going to ever make a return, I might start willingly forgoing meals for the first time in my life.

By the time I left her, I might not have the burning fire of magic in my chest, but I had one burning urge in my gut.

I poked in the house but didn't find Dax there, or at the town hall. Luckily, he wasn't hard to find. I was making my way out of the gate as he was heading back. We stopped a good fifty feet from the Rock.

"I took care of the bodies," he said.

"Thanks." The conversation was stiffer than it had ever been between us, even after all the fights we'd had in the past. I'd stepped over a line last night, questioning him about Becca's fertility, and I knew it. He'd crossed a few of mine, insinuating Rocky would only want to use me. We were standing in the middle of the emotional fallout, but there were things that had to be dealt with.

"Fudge is…" I didn't like any of the words that

would fit. They all hurt my heart too much, so I left them unsaid. There wasn't anything about how Fudge was doing that Dax didn't already know anyway.

I didn't fault him for not having said anything to her. I hadn't been banging down her door to tell her either. Tell her what? A mysterious Wood Mist took the child you've cared for since she'd been a baby? She may never come back or she might?

"We need to do something. We can't wait anymore, not even a few days. She deserves answers, one way or another, even if they aren't the ones she wants to hear. This situation is eating away at her."

"I know," he said, and I could feel the mood shift between us, a weird truce of sorts for the sake of Fudge. I wouldn't rail at him for saying those things about Rocky. He wasn't going to say anything about Becca.

"I'm going to tell her. She might not believe it, but she deserves to know what we know." I pushed my hair behind my ears, waiting to see if he'd fight me for the job. He could have it if he wanted it.

He crossed his arms and his brow furrowed. "The Skinners might not have Tiffy, but they know something. They have to. They had her rabbit."

I nodded. "What if we kidnap one of their people in exchange for information?" We were both grasping, and I knew it was because neither of us wanted to give up. Telling Fudge that Tiffy might be gone forever felt a lot like quitting to me.

He shook his head. "Others have tried kidnapping their people for exchanges. It doesn't work. The Skinners don't care. They feel that if you're weak enough to get caught, you're better off dead."

"So we've got nothing."

He stared at me, and there was a long pause before he said, "I think we march right up to the gates and demand answers."

"How many people do you think we can get to help us?" I'd had a better reception at last night's dinner than the first time, but I wasn't sure if it was good enough to get anyone to accept a suicide invitation. But damn, I liked the way Dax rolled sometimes. Only a true badass would have the balls to do something like that.

"We aren't asking anyone else to come. Just me and you."

Or…maybe I'd overestimated his sanity. "That's a death wish."

"When has the threat of death ever stopped either of us?" he asked.

The man did have a point. Was I losing my edge? Was I becoming—the word was even worse than "quit" and "pity"—boring?

He turned his back on me and walked a few paces away while he said, "Do you trust me?"

Maybe? Sometimes, depending on the day and whether our goals were running parallel? Did that count? I settled on: "I trust information."

"It's a yes or no."

"Trust isn't my strong suit."

He turned, pulled out his gun in plain view of me, and lifted it in my direction.

"Dax, I don't know what you're doing, but I'm not in the mood for your crazy *maybe I'm gonna try and kill you* shit today. Fudge is in bad shape and that stuff only works once or twice, tops."

Then a bullet whizzed by my head.

My hands went to my hips. This guy was pissing me off now. "What the hell is wrong with you? I told you, not today."

He holstered the gun. "I needed to know if you trusted me before we did this. You didn't flinch. You didn't even budge," he said, seeming pleased with himself.

"Believing you are a murdering maniac and trust are two different things. Big difference," I said, holding my hands way apart and not liking the way he'd forced me to reveal that.

"Nope. Too late. You trust me and it's been proven," he said.

"Nothing of the sort has been proven," I said, and started back toward the gate, and he followed.

"Be ready after dinner tonight. Pack a bag with whatever you'll need for a few days—jerky, water, everything. I want to be gone before anyone else notices. I'll leave a note that we went to go check on my oil rigs."

"Why? What are we doing? Going to march up to the Skinners' fortress and demand answers? Just the two of us?"

"Not exactly. I've got a plan."

"You going to share it?" I asked as we squeezed in the gate that was still partially open.

"Not yet."

"Why?"

"Because I don't want you to smell of fear on the way, and it doesn't matter, because you trust me anyway."

"Shooting at me is much different than me telling you I trust you. You have to realize that," I said, wanting to somehow take back the silent admission of trust he'd tricked from me.

"Nope. Too late."

"No. It's not."

"Can't take it back."

"Yes I can. It's my trust and I can. Try and shoot at me again and I'm going to flinch big time. I'm going to be all over this place dodging."

"Sorry, got stuff to do," he said, walking off in the opposite direction of the house.

I went to go pack, trying to figure out why I was so annoyed by this.

CHAPTER 30

Dax had left a note about some nonsense I knew Tank wouldn't believe but would hopefully swear to Bookie and Fudge was true. We'd only gone a few miles at most when Dax was stopping the bike and motioning for me to get off.

"Why are we leaving the bike here? And I'm not great with directions, but aren't the Skinners that way?" I said as I pointed in the opposite direction. "And one more question, why did I need a bag for a place only a couple hours away?"

"This is where the trust is going to come into play." He was rolling the bike into some bushes. He handed me my bag off the back and started to pile branches on top of the bike.

"You're going to have to fill me in," I said as I slung my bag on my shoulder.

He dropped the final branch and wiped his hands on his legs. "I'm going to see if I can pick up some company on our way."

"Company?"

"Yes."

There was only one company you could be sure of

finding after dark in the Wilds, and it mostly had fur and claws.

"You can do that?" I asked, drawing only one conclusion: he was going to round up other beasts.

"You want answers from the Skinners or you want safe?" he asked, and I got the sense he was giving me a final chance to back out.

I notched my chin up and repositioned the weight of my bag. No one was going to call me a scaredy cat, and I was not going down as boring, either. "Go gather your little friends."

He'd never looked so proud, and I focused on not blushing. I hated when he looked at me like that. "Northwest it is," I said, and walked to the edge of the trees, ready to get this show going.

"Don't stop until dawn. We're going to have to travel at night. I'll be with you, but I won't always be in sight."

I nodded and marched off into the night. It was hard to traverse the land in the dark, but at least we had a full moon. I fell every now and then, but I got used to it pretty quickly.

Once in a while, Dax would show up in beast form and signal me to walk a different way. He never got too close or stayed in sight for very long. Each time I saw him, my heart skipped a beat as it took me a minute to look in the dark and make sure it wasn't some unknown beast.

I didn't stop to eat, but chewed on jerky as I made my way. The only breaks I took were when nature called or to chug some water from my canteen. I was the walking dead by the time the sun started coming up.

Dax appeared soon after and pointed to a clearing in the forest. I immediately took his meaning. I stopped, tucked my bag under my head, and trusted Dax would cover me while I caught a few hours of sleep.

When I woke up sometime in the late afternoon, my canteen was refilled beside me and there was a rabbit cooking over a fire. Dax wasn't anywhere to be found. I ate alone, listening to the forest, wondering about every noise I heard.

It was just starting to get dark for the evening when I saw him standing on the outskirts, still in beast form. I nodded, kicked dirt onto the fire, and packed up my stuff.

I'd been walking for about five hours and it was close to midnight, judging by the moon, when I started noticing the presence of other beasts. I'd hear noises simultaneously from all directions as I walked. I'd catch sight of fur in browns, tans, and black, unlike Dax's grey. I didn't know how many he'd gathered, but we weren't alone anymore. Whatever Dax was doing, it was working.

It was an hour or so later when Dax appeared, this time as a man. His skin was flushed the way it always was when he'd been the beast, and I tried to not look at all of the skin on display and focus on his face as he walked over to my bag. He grabbed a pair of pants out of it that I hadn't realized were in there with my things.

The amount of magic still pouring off him right now made the air fizzle even feet away. I realized it must be stronger when he was in beast form for a long time, like maybe the duration he was a beast made it harder to tone it back down.

He stepped toward me but didn't get too close. "We'll be at the Skinners' fortress soon. You're going to need to speak for us." His voice was deeper, rougher right now.

"Why?" I had no problem being a spokesperson. In fact, I preferred it, but so did Dax.

"Because I won't be capable of speech."

Whoa. Did this mean... "You're going to be in beast form?"

"Yes. It's the way this has to go," he said.

I'd be approaching the Skinners as the only human in the group. Whether or not we got any information would weigh heavily upon my shoulders. I should've been panicking, but I wasn't. "I got this."

"When we get there, demand to speak to their leader. Don't speak to anyone else. You are to tell them we want to know everything to do with Tiffy or you'll order the horde of beasts with you to rip through their home."

"You think that will work?" I asked, not wanting to

be skeptical, but I'd seen the fortress.

"They'll do it. I have to remain with the horde to keep control. Promise me you won't go within the fortress."

"How can we be sure, then?"

"Because when we march upon them, they're going to be willing to give us whatever we want to get rid of us. Remember, you need to appear in control. I won't let you get hurt."

I nodded, and he got up and disappeared again.

* * *

I stepped onto the cleared land that surrounded the Skinners' fortress twenty minutes later and I knew I wasn't alone. Dax was close by, but the nerves were the worst I'd ever experienced. It wasn't because of the Skinners, either. They were tucked behind a wall of metal. It was what I knew was with me. I could feel them, and the more that came, the stronger the feeling. I slowly walked until there were no trees or shrubs to hide in, onto land that surrounded the fortress.

I could see movement in the periphery and I briefly glanced over and saw the grey of Dax's fur. I forced my eyes forward and continued to walk, as I heard the other ones join us.

How was Dax doing this? Controlling them? There had to be twenty or thirty of them, and I could hear more coming, growling behind me.

By the time I was halfway to the Skinners' fortress, I knew I had to look. There had to be close to a hundred beasts behind me. I was stunned. There were a hell of a lot more beasts than I realized—maybe more than anyone realized existed.

I'd found the max capacity of my nerves. I was still on my feet and exuding as much confidence that I could on the outside, but I wasn't quite as steady on the inside. It was hard when I could practically feel the horde behind me. I might have fared better mentally if I could've kept an eye on them, but I had to turn and face the fortress. I couldn't ruin the mirage we were trying to display that I had them under control if I was watching my back.

By the final steps, I'd almost psyched myself up into believing I had some control of the situation.

"Open the door," I yelled as I stopped in front of their door, knowing the Skinners had to be watching us. We weren't guests that you could miss.

"Why are you here?" a voice called out.

"Send out the person in charge."

"Leave our home or we'll make you." I could hear them on the other side, whispering and moving about.

"No."

The word had barely left my lips before I was pulled roughly into the middle of a pack of beasts right before small windows were opened and a spray of bullets started whizzing through the air. Surrounded by fur on every side and being shot at, I felt pretty proud that I was still breathing at all, even if it was rough. Maybe I had a little more nerve than I thought. Or maybe I'd passed over to the place where you think you've got no shot at making it out alive and accepted death? Both were plausible.

The bullets slowed down and then finally became a trickle before halting completely. The beasts, including Dax, who was right beside me, widened their positions, and I was afraid of what I was going to see.

None of them were on the ground. There was blood but no gaping wounds. The bullets couldn't penetrate the beasts' hides. These things were tough. This might actually work.

"Send out your leader or we will rip this place to the ground," I yelled, a little louder this time, because I was still partially blocked as we all waited for more bullets.

It took a few minutes, but the door slowly opened. A single man stepped out with greasy hair pulled back from his face, not one but two lines that I was now positive were blood upon his forehead.

I approached him, but not alone. I could feel Dax's fur brushing my arm. "Are you the leader?"

"Yes," he said, and even though he was standing tall and proud, there was a slight quiver to his voice that was the only thing that told me was this man wasn't insane.

The beasts were near growling in unison, and I hoped Dax could keep control of them long enough to let me get some answers. Then they could eat him up if they wanted.

"Where's the girl?" I demanded.

"She's not here. She disappeared the first night."

"You're saying she escaped? That small girl? You and your people couldn't keep one small girl? I'm supposed to believe that?" That was exactly what I believed, but I needed this guy on the defensive. "You had her toy."

"We don't have her."

"Don't lie to me."

"I'm not. We took her but we didn't have her for more than a few minutes before she was taken from us."

I looked over to Dax, and his head tilted upward just enough to let me know he believed what he was saying.

"Why did you try and take her?"

"We didn't want her. We only took her to get to you."

"Why?"

"Because we're out of the medicine."

"What medicine?"

"We give the Dark Walkers skin and they give us medicine to ward off the Bloody Death, but they said they wouldn't give us any more until we got them the Plaguer."

"Do you know why they want me?"

"No."

My gut told me he was telling the truth. He was too scared of the horde of beasts growing restless behind me. The growling was growing, and I was afraid it was because Dax's leash on them was tentative and they saw a snack waiting in front of them.

I could feel Dax, even in beast form, growing tense. If I didn't get the rest of my answers soon, the Skinners would have to send a new person out to talk to me, because this one might be dead.

"Who took the girl from you?"

"I know nothing...but the Dark Walkers believe one of their enemies now have her."

"Which enemy would that be?"

"The Wood Mist. That's all I know."

"Not good enough. Where can we find these Wood Mist?" So the Dark Walkers knew about the Wood Mist, too.

"I don't know."

I could feel the beasts edging in closer, see them starting to circle around me, taunted by the man they weren't supposed to have.

I should let them eat him, but I didn't know what would happen if these beasts really lost it.

"Go. Now."

Their leader didn't stop to ask if we would disperse, but ran back through the gate, to the safety of his metal walls. Dax edged in closer to me, and with loud howls, the horde of beasts seemed to be breaking off from the leash Dax had them on.

With growls of frustration at having been denied their prey, they broke off, disappearing into the woods as we made our way across the fields.

CHAPTER 31

I didn't know how long I'd walked or when the last beast left, but I finally stopped because I didn't have anything left in me.

I sat down on a dead log and felt frozen.

It must have been a half-hour later that Dax, the man, walked into the clearing.

The thought I'd been dreading kept rising up and slamming into me. The thing I hated to voice but could no longer deny or pretend wasn't real. There was nothing left to try. "How do we tell Fudge that's she's really gone?"

I wished I could become the beast, like he did, and let all of this reality slip from my shoulders. I didn't want to be here, in this moment. I didn't want to live this life of hurt and heartache anymore. I understood more fully than ever how the beasts could leave their human lives behind. How easy it would be to let their humanity slip away as if it had never been.

He didn't say anything, but stared intently at me, and I wondered if he was even fully himself right now. I stood and walked over to a tree farther away from him. For the first time, I really felt like I was on the verge of being broken, and I didn't want any version of Dax to see it.

There was no sound of him approaching me. I felt the heat from Dax's body first and then his arms wrap around me. He'd never done this before, offered comfort like this. I wanted to pull away, pretend I wasn't weak, but I leaned into his body instead, drawing on the strength that was him, that never seemed to falter, and wished I could leech some of it for myself.

I turned in his arms, wanting more.

My body shook against him, restrained terror for Tiffy finding its way out no matter how hard I wanted to keep it locked inside.

Dax's hand pressed against my lower back, and I circled my hands around him as I pressed my cheek against his chest. His other hand moved up and down my back as he tried to soothe the shuddering of my body.

He didn't say anything, and I tilted my head back to look up at his face. In his eyes, I could still see the remnants of the beast. As if some of its light and essence was still glowing through him.

His wall was down almost completely, and I needed him. The man, the one who was raw and present.

I gripped his shoulders, and all I could think of was how much I needed this connection to him.

I pressed forward, lifting my face to his, and something seemed to change in him. It was like I saw the beast come awake. One hand shifted to my hair, gripping a hank of it at the base of my skull, urging my head back.

His head lowered and his lips brushed against mine. I didn't know if he kissed me from attraction or trying to offer me comfort in the only way he knew how, but I took it. I'd wanted this for so long, and right now I needed it desperately.

If being near him was akin to feeling a charge in the air, our bodies pressed together with his mouth closed over mine felt like I'd just entered the storm. My body answered his every touch as if it had been waiting for this very thing since the day I was born.

It was everything I'd imagined a kiss should be and so much more. Every nerve in me was screaming to get closer, and I was all of a sudden overwhelmed by how intense this connection was. There was no control, only need between us, and it shocked me. I pushed on his chest and gasped for air, overwhelmed by the sensation of him.

He didn't fight me, and stepped back. I didn't know if that was better or worse, but I already missed the warmth of him as he pulled away from me, trying to get some distance. I stretched my arms out, which made me awkwardly aware that my hands were still gripping him.

His face said it all. He regretted kissing me. My hands dropped to my sides and he was gone.

* * *

We didn't get back to the Rock until late next evening. We didn't speak on our way back to the house, and the settlement was quiet, everyone asleep. I was grateful we had a few more hours so I could come to terms with what we had to tell Fudge.

I walked into the house, finding it empty of even Tank.

Dax walked into his room, and when he came back out, he headed for the door.

"Shouldn't you stay?" I asked.

"I've got to—"

"Shouldn't we talk about Fudge and what we're going to tell her?" I said, trying to let him know I wasn't looking for anything more. "I don't want you to…" My hands were fidgeting, and I shoved them in my pockets as I tried to come up with why it was better for him to stay right now, when my only true reason was I didn't want to be alone. "I won't—"

"That's not the reason I'm leaving," he said. "I've spent a lot of time as the beast. It's better if I…"

I nodded and settled into the corner of the couch. "I understand. Go." As much as I'd like for him to stay, I did understand. He was always raw after the beast, and

I knew he avoided me afterward. This wasn't anything out of the ordinary for him. At least it was a relief he didn't think I was going to throw myself at him. I needed to stop being so emotional. I couldn't lean on people like this. It was becoming a bad habit.

I grabbed the lousy book I'd been trying to get through and opened it to a place I'd already tried to read. It didn't matter. I wasn't going to read it now either, but I could feel Dax still staring at me.

I heard him walk over to the couch, and then he was sitting beside me, his side brushing against mine. His strange magic was still pouring off him in waves and, as I sat there next to him, somehow creating a warmth in me as well.

"You can stop pretending to read the book," he said.

"How did you know I was pretending?"

"You've never carried the same book around with you for more than a day or so. You've been looking at that one for a week."

"Oh." I plopped the book down on the table. "You don't have to stay." Even though this was the first time he'd ever admitted it, I knew it was hard for him to be around people after the change, especially me for some reason. Maybe it was just people with magic? I didn't know.

"I'm a little raw, but not the worst."

I knew he was lying, but I didn't argue with him.

"Thanks."

He nodded.

CHAPTER 32

It was the middle of the night when I bolted upright in my bed. Last thing I remembered was sitting on the couch. Dax must have carried me here at some point. I looked around trying to figure out what had woken me this time, but when I looked around, no one was there. My back hit the bed again, lids shuttered closed, but my heartbeat was chugging along at a nice pace. That was when I realized my chest felt hot—burning, almost. I bolted back up. My magic was back. I remembered feeling warm next to Dax as he sat next to me. Had his own magic jump-started mine somehow?

The sound of chimes tinkling in the distance drifted to me. It was them, the Wood Mist. They were calling me, perhaps to my death, but that was a chance I'd have to take. I grabbed my shoes. Nearly tripping, I hopped on one leg while trying to pull them on and walk out of my room at the same time.

Not only was the door to Dax's empty room open, so was Tank's. I didn't have time to waste looking for anyone else. I needed to follow the chimes until I found their source and hopefully found Tiffy. I was on my own.

I ran out of the house, only hesitating for a few seconds to nail down the direction the noise was coming from.

It was the same direction where I'd sat on the wall. I hightailed it toward the back of the community and scaled the wall. I climbed over the edge until my feet were dangling and then dropped and rolled the last fifteen feet to the ground. My knees felt a little bruised by the drop, but I ignored it as I took off at a run in the chimes' direction.

I didn't hear footsteps behind me until I stopped to reassess the direction. I turned quickly to see Rocky running to catch up to me.

"What are you doing out here at night? It's not safe."

"I'm fine. Go back," I said, knowing it was highly unlikely he would.

"I'm not leaving you out here alone."

How did I tell him that I didn't think the beasts would bother me, but might take a nice chunk out of his thigh muscle if they needed a snack? "I'm fine, really."

I had to stop talking to him and follow the chimes. The sounds were already dying off. Where did they go? I spun, trying to listen in every direction at once.

"Dal, what are you doing?"

"Rocky, I don't have time for this talk." I must've appeared crazy, but I couldn't worry about that. I had to find the chimes. I took off running again in the last direction I thought I'd heard them, knowing Rocky was following me, but he'd have to fend for himself. *Sorry, Rocky. You're an adult and I have Tiffy to worry about.*

I ran until I couldn't hear the chimes over my own breathing, and stopped.

They were gone.

"What are you doing?" Rocky asked again as he stopped next to me, not huffing nearly as badly as I was.

"I thought I heard something."

"What?"

It was a hunch, but I thought Rocky would believe me if I told him. Maybe he'd even know something. "Have you ever heard of—"

"What are you doing out here?" Dax asked as he stepped into the small clearing Rocky and I stood in.

"I heard chimes. It's them, just like the stories you told me about. I know it's them. It's going to lead me to Tiffy. I'm positive."

"Heard what, and who are you talking about?" Rocky asked.

Dax spared a brief moment to look at Rocky before saying to me, "We'll talk about it at the house." Dax's skin was still flushed, and I could see telltale signs that he was still dealing with the aftermath of being in beast form for so long.

"I can't right—"

"Why do you think you can order her about?"

Rocky said.

Why, of all times, did Rocky have to do this now? "He's not ordering me around," I said, even though he was. This was not the time to get into it with Dax, though, or for the two of them to start. I needed to figure out where the chimes were coming from.

"He acts like he owns you," Rocky continued, but I wasn't so naïve to think this was all on the up and up and Rocky was simply trying to be a good guy. I hadn't liked what Dax had said, but there was some truth to it. Rocky wanted me pissed off at Dax and was trying to provide me with some reasons, like I didn't already have some.

Rocky got in Dax's face in a way I'd never imagined anyone would have the nerve to do. Dax's expression alone should've been enough to make Rocky back up.

And then Rocky continued, either missing the signs of imminent danger or overestimating himself. "You aren't allowed to put her on ice until you decide whether you want her or not."

Wow, Rocky did not just say that. I was ready to crawl into the first hole I could find. So this was what he was all out of sorts about? Oh geez. I didn't know if I should run for that hole, or throw myself in between the two of them, before Dax killed him where he stood.

"She's not ready for what you want," Dax said.

"It's not your call."

"Yes. It is." The words were calm, but if Rocky still didn't hear the warning in them, he was deaf. I wasn't even looking at Dax. I was too busy covering the ten shades of red my face had probably turned, but I heard it clearly.

"Rocky, it's not like that between us," I said, realizing I was going to have to forgo my hole and stop hiding, or my face wouldn't just be red from embarrassment but also with splattered blood. The beast was just beneath the surface, and I wasn't sure how much control Dax had of it.

"Bullshit," Rocky said. "He feeds you just enough to keep you emotionally hooked until he decides whether he wants to do something about it."

"If you aren't man enough to win her, that's your problem. You can't protect her and you'd never be able to handle her."

"And you think you're doing right by her?"

"You can't even get near her unless I let you. Remember that."

"When you leave, she's staying."

My head jerked to Rocky. I didn't know where that had come from. I'd told him I'd think about staying. I'd never agreed to anything. I felt Dax's eyes on me and didn't want to admit that I'd said that either, not right now.

"She's not staying anywhere with you," Dax finally said when I didn't say it. "She needs me and she knows it. She could've gone her own way a million times already."

"That's bullshit. Admit it," Rocky said.

"Admit what?"

"You say she can do whatever she wants, but you wouldn't let her go even if she wanted to. But when she's ready, and she will be, I'll be the one to help her leave you."

I expected Dax to shut him down, tell Rocky he was being ridiculous. Everything Dax said was true. He'd told me time and again if I didn't like the situation I could leave. I was with him by choice.

I centered my attention on Rocky. "You're wrong, and I can do whatever I want," I said to him. It was the truth, but I would've said anything right now to defuse the situation. The last thing we all needed on top of Tiffy missing was these two fighting.

When I didn't hear anything, my gaze went from Rocky to Dax and my blood chilled. I'd seen Dax's wall down, but I'd never seen his eyes glow like he was looking out of the beast's red ones while he was still human.

My breath caught and froze in my chest as I tried to figure out what to do first. Who to target my efforts on.

"You. Won't. Keep. Her. Anywhere." The words weren't as scary as the gravelly pitch they were said in. It was as if they were partially growled, and I swore I thought I saw a hint of fangs dropping just below his upper lip.

Rocky, a bit belatedly, realized the nature of the threat he was facing. He didn't look like he was breathing, either. I'd just gotten an answer to one of my questions. He'd had no idea Dax was a beast, but he was figuring out something was off, and quick.

I made a knee-jerk decision that Rocky was the best bet. I was afraid if I did the wrong thing with Dax, he might turn into the beast right then and there. I went to Rocky and grabbed his arm. "Let's go. I think you should talk about this at another time." It was lame, but I couldn't think of any gems under the current conditions.

Then I heard the growling, and there was no doubt where it was coming from. I grabbed Rocky's arm with both hands, tugging him in earnest now, but the growling only grew louder.

My hands dropped immediately from Rocky as I realized that was making Dax even worse for some reason. Maybe Dax thought I was siding with Rocky?

I didn't have time to ponder the whys when I heard the chimes start. They were here. They were back. Tiffy!

I stepped away from Rocky, the decision easy. If it was trying to save Rocky or finding Tiffy, there was no choice to be made.

"They're here," I said, looking up and around. I was going to figure out where those chimes were coming from.

I spun, trying to pinpoint the noise, and saw both Dax and Rocky looking up and around, the new presence, perhaps threat, defusing their own fight.

CHAPTER 33

The chimes grew louder as we all circled the area, the fight between Dax and Rocky pushed to the back burner as we all tried to figure out where the sound was coming from. It seemed to be coming from everywhere, almost on top of us, but I couldn't see the source.

One second we were alone and then we weren't.

They were everywhere, whatever they were, forming a circle around us. A quick count put them at twenty. They had no faces. Their heads and bodies were draped in robes that glittered like liquid gold, and thin hands, bordering on skeletal, peeked out of their draped sleeves.

"She must come with us." I spun, not knowing who had spoken. They had no mouths, no faces at all, and the voice had sounded like it came from all of them somehow speaking as one.

They all lifted their fingers and pointed in my direction.

"She's not going anywhere," Dax said.

Rocky and Dax took up defensive positions with their backs to each other, and me standing between them.

"What are you?"

"We are as old as time. We have been here since the first sapling tree, and we don't answer to you."

"Do you have Tiffy?" I asked as Rocky yelled to me not speak to them directly.

"Yes." I couldn't tell how many voices spoke or if they were male or female. "You must be judged."

"Judged for what?" I asked.

"Judged to be worthy."

"Will you give us Tiffy if I pass?" I asked.

"You're not judging anyone," Dax said, grabbing my arm with a death grip.

"Yes."

"Then I'll be judged," I said.

Dax's hand was on my arm and then it was gone. I didn't know if Rocky and Dax had moved or if the faceless people had moved us, but I now stood within the ring of them alone. I turned and could see Dax and Rocky screaming as they tried to get to me, even though I couldn't hear them. There was some sort of invisible barricade holding them back that they were pounding on.

I could still see Dax screaming *no* right before he turned into the beast, Rocky looking stunned beside him.

But there was no noise. All sounds in the background ceased to exist. I could see the birds chirping and flying overhead but couldn't hear them.

Within the invisible circle surrounded by these faceless creatures, it was only us.

"Will you accept our judgment?" the faceless creatures asked.

"Then I get Tiffy back?"

"Only if you pass."

"What happens if I fail?"

"You die."

"Try it," I said. I didn't know what these things were, but I wasn't going down easy.

They closed in on me, bony hands all reaching for me at once. It was no longer night—a blazing light, bright as the sun, shone on us.

"Why are you doing this?" I asked as their hands all landed upon me and I felt the rise of panic.

"Because for one to wield so much power, you must be worthy," they answered, and now it seemed like I heard the voices in my head.

"We have been blocking you, but we cannot do it for much longer. You must be worthy of this power or you must die."

"What is this power you are talking about?"

"There is a well of power that feeds all. When there were many humans, no one human could wield much. Now that there are fewer of you, some take up more than other beings. You take very much. There were others that tried to take as you did that weren't worthy. We didn't kill them, and now we cannot. We will not make the same mistake with you."

"Do your worst." It sounded like a dare. A smart person would grovel. I had nothing to be ashamed of, and I wouldn't have anyone tell me I wasn't worthy. I'd lived that life for enough years.

I felt their magic entering me with a gentle probe. There were whispers but nothing I understood. It started with a warm tingle in my fingertips and toes, then slowly traveled upward until it encompassed my whole body. My vision went dark and then I was a child again.

I was being left at the Cement Giant with Ms. Edith. My parents were there, my father stoic, my mother weeping. Then they were turning and walking away from me.

Anger and hurt welled within me, and I could feel the light burning its way through my mind, probing and digging in my memories. Years of hatred unfolded before me. I could feel the disapproval around me growing at the negative emotions I'd generated at that point in my young life.

Then the girls appeared, and Margo was so close. I wanted to reach out and touch them, wishing they were really here.

Every beating, all the sessions with Ms. Edith, the madness that being in the hole at the Cement Giant had created. I was laid bare, all my hurts, every scar I possessed; they scoured them, prodding and prying. There wasn't a spot left that they hadn't touched. Or I thought they hadn't. The whispers changed. I didn't know what was being said, but I could sense the conflict, strange words being exchanged in heated tones.

I felt some of the tendrils of their magic curling even deeper into me. It was like I could see everything that made me who I was through their eyes. The good and the bad, and they still weren't satisfied. It was as if my very soul was unfurling before my own eyes and they tried to dismantle it.

Then, when I thought there was nowhere else to look, I saw a light shining within me, covered in places with black-crusted patches. Even with the darkness dotting its surface, the light was so bright it was almost painful. In that instant, I knew exactly what they feared.

It was like there was a black hole of power within me that was waiting to go supernova at any second and burst from me. Where had that come from? I also knew what they had done. They had tried to smother my magic, and those patches of black were the remnants of what they had done to it, still clinging even now.

I felt tendrils pulling on me. They were trying to block me from seeing the source of my own power, and I realized I wasn't supposed to be there with them.

I could feel some of them trying to get to it now. That was why they were arguing. They wanted to destroy it. They were fighting me and among themselves. Not all of them wanted to judge me. Some

315

of them wanted to destroy me.

But it was too late. I had seen it and I knew exactly where in myself my power was centered, deep within me. I knew what I had to do. I remembered what Dax had said about a give and take of power with everything around you. I reached inward to the place they'd shown me. I breathed deeply, trying to take in as much as possible, stoking the white-hot burning inside of me. I stepped forward and grabbed one of the faceless as if mine and Tiffy's lives depended on it. I could feel the one I grabbed trying to struggle back from me and the interconnectedness of them, knowing that an attack on one would hurt the many. In one great whoosh, I forced it all out, every bit of magic within me, and directed it toward them.

The black pieces left from their curse flew off me as the magic burst free, the warmth of it flooding every inch of me again and forcing them out, surging through my hands into them until I felt them disintegrating.

My body gave out from pure exhaustion. I didn't know what I'd done, but it had drained me of everything I had.

* * *

I woke up with Rocky kneeling beside me and Dax supporting my back.

"What happened? We couldn't get to you, and then

316

there was a blast. Whatever was holding us back was gone," Dax said.

The silence gave me hope that the chimes and the faceless were gone.

"Is she going to be okay?" I heard Tiffy say before she peeked over Dax's shoulder.

I got to my knees and felt a hand cup my elbow as I managed to stand and go to Tiffy, kneeling so I could wrap my arms around her. Hugging her so tightly I was afraid she'd be hurt, but I couldn't bear to loosen my hold. "Tiffy!"

"She appeared in the forest at the same time the blast freed you," Rocky said.

"Have you been with them this whole time?" I asked her as I leaned back to look at her face, still not believing she'd come back.

"Yes. They came and got me the first night the Skinners took me."

Her little eyes looked skyward, and I heard the same chiming that had called me to this place, and held her to me, afraid to let her go as a golden cloud appeared shimmering above us.

"It's okay," Tiffy said. "They're only saying goodbye."

"They don't want to take you again?" I asked, wanting them to go away, not trusting they would leave her with us. I could feel Rocky and Dax get into position again—not that it would do us much good, judging by what we'd seen.

"I felt you pushing at them before and told them I had to go back home. They didn't want to let me, but I think you scared them when you got really mad," Tiffy told me as she smoothed back the hair from my face.

I saw Dax and Rocky both motioning for us to get out of there before they changed their minds. I gathered Tiffy in my arms as I stood and started walking. I was afraid to put her down as both men walked on either side of me back to the Rock.

We walked back through the gates, and everyone that saw us shared smiles, and a few even cheered when they saw Tiffy with us. Dax and I went straight to Fudge's, while Rocky made an excuse about going to the town hall. I knew he was still reeling from the realization of what Dax was, and didn't blame him for wanting a minute alone.

We walked into the house and Fudge was fidgeting around the kitchen, getting ready to prepare breakfast, probably. She turned to see who had come in and froze.

"Fudge!" Tiffy pushed out of my arms and ran to her as tears were already streaming down her cheeks.

I found myself crying as I watched them.

The door opened behind us and I heard Bookie say, "Is it true? Were you carrying Tiffy back?" Then he saw her for himself in Fudge's arms.

Tank came in a minute later and they were passing Tiffy around, taking turns hugging her.

"What happened back there?" Dax asked as we watched.

"They were behind the problem with my magic."

"It's fixed now. I can feel it. I felt it last night too, but it's even stronger now. Did they undo it?"

"More like they unknowingly helped me see what was wrong."

"Is this finished with them and you?"

"I'm not sure if they have a choice."

CHAPTER 34

I snuffed out the candles and lay in the bed, staring into the darkness. Tiffy was back. I should be able to sleep tonight, right? Nope.

I threw some pants and a shirt on and walked out of the house and to the gate. There was a guy sitting guard over the mechanical wheel that would spring me from this place.

"I need out."

"No one's—"

"I need out."

"I can't. Orders are—"

"I don't care what your orders are. I need out," I said, stepping a little closer to him, close enough that the memories started rolling in. Oh yeah, I was back in action. If I were to live another million years, I'd never ever wish them away again. "Look, I think you're probably a real nice guy, but that thing you did when you were thirteen… I'm not holding it against you or anything, but some people might."

After the look of shock then fear flashed across his face, he started spinning the wheel fervently. "You're not gonna repeat that, right?" he asked.

320

"No. I'll never say a word." And I wouldn't. I was back to being the secret keeper, and I was liking it.

I stepped out of the Rock as soon as the door creaked open wide enough for me to squeeze through. I walked aimlessly for a while, following the wall around the Rock's perimeter until I found a perch part of the way up it that afforded me the most spectacular view of the landscape I'd ever seen. Rocky really needed to work on this wall a bit, though.

This, the open air around me, the sky full of stars—this was worth fighting for, no matter the cost, even to the death.

When I heard the footsteps approaching, I ducked low behind some bushes, but then I recognized the sound of them as human.

They paused before walking the rest of the way to the gate.

"Are you really one of them?" Rocky asked.

"Do you really want the details?" Dax responded, and I realized he would tell Rocky the truth if he wanted to know.

"Maybe not."

There was a long pause as the two of them stood together, appearing almost like two men who were feeling each other out for the first time.

I wasn't sure who relaxed first, Rocky or Dax.

"So what's the deal? You finally stepping up and staking your claim or what?" Rocky asked him.

Staking his claim? To what? The Rock? What would Dax lay claim on? Dax was a master when it came to secrets. Even better than I was.

"No choice."

"So it's like that," Rocky said, nodding.

"Yeah. It's like that." Dax turned slightly toward my direction, and I tried to pull myself farther back into the shadows, but damn if he didn't look at me like he knew I was there.

"I won't roll over. Not in my DNA," Rocky said, drawing Dax's attention back to him.

"So this isn't strategic?"

"What, are you blind?"

"No. I'm not. I just didn't know if you saw it too."

"How could I not?" Rocky scoffed. "Even the kid gets it."

"So it's like that for you, too?" Dax asked, and I could hear disapproval in his voice.

"Yeah. It's like that." Rocky turned, and they stared at each other, almost like they had in the forest before Dax started losing control to the beast.

"Let the best man win," Rocky said, and walked off.

Dax stayed where he was. "And that's why you've already lost," he said, but I knew Rocky hadn't heard him.

Dax turned and stared at where I was until a few minutes had passed and Rocky was far from earshot.

"You coming down?"

Shit. I knew he'd seen me. Damn beast senses. I moved forward on the rocks and turned around to climb down. When I was close enough that he could reach me, he gripped my waist and lifted me the rest of the way.

"Thanks," I said, and then brushed my hands off on my thighs. Well, since he already knew I'd been listening, no point left in not asking. "So what are you laying claim to? You aren't going to try and take over this place, are you? I hate being the last to know things."

"Don't worry. You'll be the first to know when I make."

"Well, that's good, because I thought we'd grown a little—maybe we'd even started becoming friends."

"Come on. I'll walk you back."

"You know, I'm glad you were out here. We need to talk about what you said back at the clearing. You didn't really mean you'd try and stop me from staying, did you?"

"You want to stay here?" he asked as we got to the gate.

"I don't know." It wasn't heaven in the form of a beautiful yellow farmhouse surrounded by lots of land and a garden I knew like the back of my hand, but it wasn't such a bad place. The people here also seemed to be starting to like me a little. That was kind of nice.

"How can I stop you if you don't know?" he asked as we approached the gate.

"That's not the point."

"But your question is irrelevant until you know."

"I need to know that you wouldn't try and impede my actions, is the point." Why was he being so obtuse? I knew he understood me.

"Have I ever impeded your actions?"

"Can you stop answering all my questions with questions?" I asked, wanting a straight answer out of him. He was all of a sudden feeling very much like the over-scratched mosquito bite again.

"Can you ask a relevant one?"

I stopped walking once we were inside the gate. "Are you screwing with me?"

"Does it feel like I am?"

I let out a sigh, said, "Good night, Dax," and walked to the house alone.

"Good night, Dal," he called after me.

* * *

Tiffy was standing over my bed, smoking sage in hand. I shot up, almost burning myself in the process, but I didn't mind this time. She could wake me up every night if she wanted—for at least a week or two, anyway.

"See? It's much stronger now." This time, there

was no doubt that the smoke was glowing blue. It almost had a light of its own, it was so vibrant.

"Yes."

"Some of them don't like that, but I told them you were good people."

She doused the sage in a glass of water I had by my bed meant for drinking, and crawled into bed with me.

"What's wrong?" I asked her as she cuddled up next to me.

"I'm scared," she said, trying to squirm impossibly closer.

"It's okay, Tiffy. They didn't hurt you, and you're back with us now." I patted her back, using her favorite form of comforting others.

"No. Not for me. I'm scared for you. The Dark Walkers are coming for you."

"I know they want me, but it's going to be okay." I never thought I'd be one of those people who lied to kids, but here I was doing it.

I knew they were coming. What I didn't know was where I'd have to go to escape them. What was left after the Wilds?

"They'll never stop, no matter where you go. That's what my friends told me." Tiffy's voice got smaller the longer she spoke.

"Why? Did they tell you that?" Last thing I wanted to do was add to her worry, but I couldn't hide the urgency in my questions.

"No. Only that you are probably going to die trying to escape them, and if you don't escape, my friends must find a way to kill you themselves."

"It's going to be okay," I told Tiffy again, lying through my teeth, because there was nothing further from the truth. I had a bad feeling I was going to really find out exactly what I was made of, and soon.

Dal's story continues in book three, coming May 2016.

Other Books by Donna Augustine

<u>Alchemy Series</u>
The Keepers
Keepers and Killers
Shattered
Redemption

<u>Karma Series</u>
Karma
Jinxed
Fated

You can follow Donna through one of these social media accounts:

https://twitter.com/DonnAugustine

https://www.facebook.com/Donnaaugustinebooks? ref=bookmarks

www.donnaaugustine.com

30235500R00184

Made in the USA
San Bernardino, CA
08 February 2016